JUST HIS BARISTA

A SWEET ROMANTIC COMEDY

SOUTHERN ROOTS ROMANTIC COMEDY
BOOK 5

ELANA JOHNSON

CHAPTER ONE

MACIE

I jog back toward Bri, wishing I'd grabbed a jacket before we left her house. "How's that one?"

"Good." Sabrina Shadows hands me back my phone so I can see the video we've been working on for the past half-hour. She's honestly a saint for coming out here with me on this overcast, windy, late-January day.

It's her wedding I need a date to, so I think she feels bad. I've told her not to a hundred times. It's not like I've never been to a wedding before. Not hers, and we have gotten really close since she moved to Charleston.

Of course, now she's a fancy lawyer, with a super-hot boyfriend—oops, fiancé—and she's getting married in less than two months. My last boyfriend moved to Philadelphia without telling me.

I watch myself do the stupid dance, but I look like I'm

having fun. "Ugh, I messed up the end," I say, handing the phone back to her.

She frowns at me, fumbling my device with hers. She shivers. Actually shivers. "I don't see why you can't come to the wedding with Coy."

"Coy?" My voice goes straight into super-sonic atmospheric range. "Why would I go with Coy?"

Bri gives me a dry look—you can't get drier than the scathing, piercing, half-eye-roll she tosses at me before she goes back to her phone. "Please."

"Please, what?'

"Everyone knows you two have something going on."

"Yeah," I say. "We own a coffee shop together." And, I might add, it's doing amazingly well since I added my funds and brain power to the mix. Even Coy has said so several times.

I haven't told Bri—or anyone else—about The Kissing Incident between me and Coy. It was a one-night thing, and I was so upset, and he was so nice...

Trust me, he's not always that nice. And I'm not always so upset.

The idea of having to go to Bri's wedding alone, when everyone I hang out with is married or engaged—that upsets me.

"I need a date," I say, the desperation clawing its way up my throat. A particularly nasty gust of wind comes off the ocean, and Bri starts striding toward the parking lot.

"It's too cold for another take," she says. "Jason's leaving work right now, and I have to get Timber home before I meet him." She looks over her shoulder and whistles, calling the giant black-and-white Great Dane out of the water.

He bounds toward her, barking at a plastic bag flying through the air. I go with her, because she drove us here, and I don't have a choice. She has helped me a lot the past few months, but the street goes both ways between us. She's stayed with me a couple of times now.

She won't again, I think as I boost myself up into her new truck. She bought it specifically so she could put Timber in the back of it, and she pounds the tailgate behind me. The dog woofs again as he jumps into the back, and then Bri joins me in the cab.

She looks over to me, and I can't turn away fast enough. I know she sees something on my face, but I don't know what. I'm not like her, and I can't hide how I'm feeling as easily. She's always been able to box up everything, stow it away until later, and then deal with it privately.

I kiss my co-owner on the couch in the coffee shop we own together after something bad happens. Then I tell him it was a huge mistake, and we can't do that again. He agrees, and it's awkward between us for a few weeks, and now we're back to normal.

And "normal" for Coy and I is silent death glares, arguing, and eventual peace agreements. It's not walking through the park, all sunshiny and blue skies, laughing with a dog beside us.

I own too many dogs for that to be peaceful, and Coy's pets are reptiles. I think. He said something about them once, but I honestly wasn't paying attention. He'd also just said I was as stubborn as one of them, so that kind of clogged my ears.

As Bri drives, I edit the video. I can't really do anything about the end. I can't reshoot it, because the lighting and location will be different. I decide to cut it off a second too soon, and I add on text, a sticker or two, and post.

Then I tuck my phone under my leg, determined not to look at my social media until I'm home, safe and sound and alone. Hopefully, I'll have my pick of gorgeous men waiting in my inbox, all of them mad for me already and falling over themselves to take me to Bri and Jason's wedding.

I know a lot of people in Charleston. Okay, "know" is a bit of a stretch. I'm *acquaintances* with a lot of people in Charleston. The ones who come into the shop in the morning. I know their names; they know mine. I have their coffee orders memorized. I know what they do for a living.

They come in and go out. All day long. Some of them move on after a while, and I don't see them anymore. Some come in once and never come back. Everything at Legacy Brew feels fluid and full of movement, motion, and magic.

And I'm stuck.

I go nowhere.

Home. The coffee shop. Home. The coffee shop. Day in and day out. Heck, I go to the coffee shop, then home, then back again twice in the same day. I get off at two o'clock in the afternoon, but my friends have real day jobs that keep them in offices or kitchens until evening. We congregate most evenings on the couches and chairs at Legacy Brew, a real-life version of the TV show, *Friends*.

Except on the show, they were all single, and in my real life, I'm the only single one left.

My mind wanders to Coy as Bri navigates the suburbs and then goes out a little further. The live oaks thicken, and then she turns down a street where her house sits. I won't get out of the truck at all, because she'll just put Timber in the backyard and then come back.

"Be right back," she says.

"Yep." The need to look at my phone is strong, but I resist it. Even more horrifying than going to the wedding with Coy would be not having anyone respond to my desperate plea for a date in seven weeks.

As Bri jogs around the side of the house, Timber in front of her, I remember something specific: She went to Tara and Alec's wedding with Jason. They were just friends at the time, and I think that's being generous. They weren't friends at all. She could barely stand him.

But they'd been hanging out with the same people for a while, and they both needed a date...

She tells me now that she's always found him attractive. Anyone looking at Jason would say he's attractive. *Men* everywhere can admit it, straight or not.

I fiddle with the ends of my hair, something I do when I have thoughts I don't want to face. Right now, they're all about how good-looking Coy is. I've admitted it before, but I duck my head and brush my fingers along the ends of my hair, looking for dead-ends. I just got my hair cut and colored, so I don't have many.

My stomach growls, and man, what I wouldn't give for a dinner date tonight. As it is, after Bri drops me off at my house, I'll probably heat up a frozen pizza or call for take-out. The oh-so-glamorous life of a single small-business owner.

I sigh and sag into the passenger window as I wait. The thing is, I was perfectly happy in my life until everyone started getting married. With Callie, I cheered the loudest, because she's the nicest person on the planet.

She and Dawson should be having their baby any day now, and I close my eyes and try to find the happiness center inside myself. My mama always taught me that it's good to be happy for other people. Even if you don't think there's anything to be happy about. Even if you're so miserable and want what they have so much.

I miss my mama sometimes. In times like these, I would've called her and talked her ear off, going over and over and over everything in my head. Then she'd say, "Macie-Mae. God put you on this earth to spread sunshine, and you best figure out how to get out from underneath those storm clouds so He can use your positivity."

Macie-Mae.

No one's called me that since she died. Four years now, and I still go see Daddy, and I have two brothers who watch out for me. But none of them will tolerate an hour-long call where I whine about my lackluster love life.

Coy pops back into my head, and I can still clearly see the desire in his eyes. I can feel the tender touch of his hand as it slides down the side of my face. He kissed me good, and sweet, and long, and I sigh again just thinking about it.

He has feelings for me. No man can kiss a woman the way he kissed me and not. He didn't confess anything, and he let me put him in his place again. I'm not sure why I did it. Maybe because I'm afraid of him flying off to another city one night, and leaving me with a snake's nest of problems at Legacy Brew.

"He won't do that," I tell myself. He loves Legacy more than I do. His daddy owned it, and his granddaddy before that. The Cochrans built Legacy from the ground up, and the only reason Coy allowed me to buy in to the company was because he was about to go bankrupt.

Things are doing so much better now, and I know I'm a big part of that. But so is Coy. He swallowed his pride, and he listens to me now, and we work together...for the most part. I don't work against him, at least. He doesn't sabotage me.

When he can't sleep, I find him in the kitchen at Legacy. When I'm restless, I go there too, and he wakes me up from where I've fallen asleep on the orange couch out front. We both have extra clothes in our offices—his is twice as big as mine—and we both have keys to the shop.

He runs everything administrative, and I run the front of the house, just like I did before I bought into the shop. I also do most of the marketing thinking, and that takes a lot of time and energy. I'm the public face of the coffee shop, and he makes sure all the nuts and bolts stay oiled and operational.

Bri comes running back to the truck, and she practically leaps into it like she's swallowed something radioactive and is now superhuman. She's always been superhuman to me, as she went to college, then law school, and became a junior partner by age thirty-four. She was nominated for full partner this year, but she won't find out until April if she'll get it.

She and Jason are planning an exquisite vacation to Tahiti for their honeymoon, and I wonder what it would be like to travel like that. I grew up in Georgia, but I've either been there or here in Charleston for my whole life. I've never *wanted* to go anywhere else, and I'm not sure what type of bug bit me or how long this itch will stay.

"Did anyone comment on your video?" she asks.

"I don't know." I swing my attention to her. "I determined not to look until I get home." I give her a smile, and she returns it.

"There are some single men at the firm," she says.

"Sure," I say. "That guy who hit on you while you were dating Jason? No, thanks."

"He's actually nice," Bri says, kneading the wheel. "Just a little...eager."

"I don't mind eager."

"I know, that's why I mentioned him." She pulls out of her driveway and starts to head back toward the city.

I live in Sugar Creek, which is further west, and I love my little house. I love my job. I am a girl-boss now. I don't need a boyfriend to make my life complete.

I just need a date, so I don't have to go to a wedding by myself.

———

LATER THAT NIGHT, as I'm easing myself into the bathtub, I remember the video. I still haven't checked the comments on my post, because Daddy called me right as Bri dropped me off. He needed help with his air fryer, and that had turned into a screaming match where I finally said, "Daddy! Unplug it! Just unplug the darn thing!"

He'd been resisting that action, because he didn't want to have to reprogram it. "Reprogram it to do what?" I kept asking him, but my daddy is a little bit deaf and a little bit old, and honestly, his default should be to unplug anything with a cord, count to thirty, and try again.

The beeping had stopped, at least. I haven't heard if he got his corndog heated up to his liking or not, which means he probably did. After that, my pets meowed and whined for dinner, so I went through the motions of preparing that for them.

They're seriously so spoiled, and I barely had a warm meal in front of them before my pizza arrived. The cats—Lizzie and Emma—make do with their wet cat food, but Darcy, Susan, and Justice—the dog I got in honor of my mother after she passed—want their kibble softened with warm water, a can of green beans—with the liquid, thank you very much—and three squirts of salmon oil.

And they know if you only put in two pumps, let me tell you. Susan often looks like I'm trying to poison her if the water isn't heated to exactly eighty-two degrees or Darcy gets an extra green bean than her.

Honestly.

I make them a special breakfast and a special dinner every night, and I don't eat better than them. No pet on the planet does.

Then, I'd just wanted to wash away this day. It was my day off—I take them now instead of working seven days a week—but tomorrow, I'll have to be at the coffee shop by five-thirty to get things open by six.

Our bakers work all day so we don't have to have someone come in at three a.m. Because if I had to go over to that shop and unlock the back door for someone to make pistachio muffins that early in the morning? There'd be a cot in my office and probably a head hanging from the rafters.

I'm a morning person, but come on. Three a.m. is *not* morning. It's insane.

I've already tucked my hair into a low ponytail and then covered it with a shower cap. With the red color, I try not to wash it for several days after going to the salon. I use dry shampoo and hardly any products to keep it clean and strong, so it's fine.

I'm careful not to put my hands into the water so I can handle my device. I have a tub caddy over the water, and I've already placed my phone there. Sometimes I stream music from my tablet or put on the latest reality TV show I'm watching. The tub is my one sanctuary. The place I can shut out the world and be who I am and who I want to be.

I can be upset. I can be jealous. I can be the dark storm cloud my mama didn't want me to be.

I don't go straight to my phone, because I have a ritual for my meditation and unwinding in my evening bath. First, I light my grapefruit candle. It has a hint of vanilla and mint in it too, but it's the citrus that helps me the most. Then I crush a few petals of lavender and add them to the hot water. They drift around, though I've already filled the tub. Water is always moving too, and there's something dynamic and alive about it that I really like.

I brought in a glass of sweet tea with me, and it rests in the divot specifically for it. A few bars of my milk soaps wait too, and on the tablet stand with my tablet is a book I started last week. Bri's a fiction-reader, but I like non-fiction. This particular story is about a man who got trapped behind enemy lines in a foreign country and his journey to get home.

One more thing… I spritz my eucalyptus spray toward my feet once, twice, three times, and then replace the bottle next to the soaps.

Now I'm ready.

I pick up my phone, and I swipe, tap, and swipe some more. I'm almost afraid to go to my messages. I arrive in the app, and my eyes go straight to the envelope at the top. I see a twenty-one—praise the heavens, though about half of those will be creepers—before a text rolls down from the top of my phone.

It's Coy, and I see the beginning of his message before it pops back to the top.

Hey, Macie, I saw you left—

My heartbeat bangs against my ribs. What did I leave at Legacy Brew that he found? I pull down the notification bar and tap his text.

Hey, Macie, I saw you left off the end of that video on SnapShot. I can never get the end of that one right either. At least you posted.

I wrinkle my brow. "What?" I say to my scented candle and rising eucalyptus mist. I have no idea how to answer this. *Coy Cochran is on SnapShot?* That's the best my mind can come up with, honestly.

Another text comes in, right below his first. *I'd love to go to Bri's wedding with you. Do you still need a date?*

My eyes widen. My blood burns through my veins. My mind screams *yes! Tell him yes!*

Instead, I make a yelping sound and drop my phone right into the lavender-scented bathwater.

"Warm banana pudding," I curse, fumbling to get the sinking device.

CHAPTER TWO

COY

I STARE AT MY PHONE FOR ANOTHER MOMENT, THEN throw it onto the table in front of me. "You're so stupid," I say to myself. Across the room, Elmer and Orion bask in their blue light. I give them that right before bedtime, and I'd be embarrassed if anyone ever found my color-coded Post-it notes for their incandescent heat lamp and the full spectrum of their fluorescent bulbs.

I swear, I've kept GE in business just with two bearded dragons.

My phone doesn't buzz or chime, which means Macie hasn't answered me. She's glued to her phone, so I'm sure she's seen the messages. The first one can only be categorized as creepy—I don't have a single posted video on SnapShot—and the second?

"I'm categorically insane." I get up and run my hands through my hair. It's too long and in desperate need of a trim. I take better care of my beard, and it's sculpted and neat. I pace away from the couch where I've been watching Macie dance with the wind for the past hour.

I need a life outside of this house, those two bearded dragons, and Legacy Brew. Oh, and Macie Wilheim.

Maybe if I get on the rowing machine, I can eliminate the thoughts of the redhead who follows me into my dreams. I row for ten minutes, then twenty, then thirty. My lungs burn, and the bench actually starts to squeak.

I finally allow myself to stop, and I reach for a nearby towel. I mop the sweat off my face and forehead and get to my feet. My calves ache, but it's nothing compared to my shoulders and neck. I really can't push myself like that.

I'm not in college—or even my twenties—anymore, and there are no medals to be won. I toss the towel into the hamper on my way out of the spare bedroom where I keep my workout equipment, and I move into my bedroom, then the shower. Maybe if I stand there for long enough, my humiliation will wash down the drain.

Unfortunately, it doesn't, and I'm left with the bitter taste of it in my mouth as I get dressed and head back into the kitchen and living room. The bearded dragons haven't moved, and it's dark enough now that I step over and turn off their blue light. "Night, night, guys."

I'm eternally grateful no one's there to hear me say, "Night, night," to my freaking reptiles. I glare at my phone and leave it on the table. It's face-down, so I really have no idea if Macie or anyone else has texted or called.

"She won't call." I head into the kitchen and pick up the half-drunk can of soda I opened earlier. I don't remember drinking it, but the *snap-pop-hiss* of opening it is in my memory. Macie doesn't like to talk on the phone, and for once, that serves me well.

The night is young yet, and I can't stay here and pine after Macie. I'm not super-friends with Sabrina Shadows and Jason Finch, but Macie is. I see her hanging out with them almost every evening, and they all seem to get along really well.

There's four couples now, plus Macie. I've stepped over to say something to her a time or two, and I can see myself integrating into that group. Then there would be five couples, and I could hold Macie's hand and drive her home after we go to dinner.

I swallow and turn around, new determination flowing through my blood. She has to know how I feel about her. I kissed her like a lovesick teenager several months ago and brought her coffee the next morning.

She put a stop to that before taking the first sip, and I let her.

I'm tired of letting her.

I grab my cherry Chapstick and slide it over my lips. It's been fifty-four minutes and thirteen seconds since I called Macie. This is ridiculous. I snatch my phone from the table. There are no messages or missed calls. Anger mingles with my embarrassment, and I tap-stab to call Macie.

The line rings and rings...and rings. She doesn't answer, and I swear under my breath and hang up before her voicemail can pick up.

My phone rings a moment later, which is a good thing, or I may have thrown it through the window. It's not Macie. It's not anyone I have in my contacts, and I take a deep breath as I debate answering the call.

It's probably someone who wants to give me money for my recent car accident. It might also be my only chance at human conversation tonight, so I swipe on the call. "Hello?" I turn toward the window above the kitchen sink and look out into the quickening dusk.

"Coy," a woman says, and I frown. I do know this voice, but it's not lodging in my head right. "It's Macie. Macie Wilheim?"

Everything connects in my brain, and I say, "Oh, Macie. I thought that was you, but you're not calling from your phone."

"Yeah, I uh, dropped it."

"Oh."

"Shh," she says, and I cock my head. "I've got this." She's not talking to me, and I simply wait. Macie can do about fifteen-point-seven things at the same time, so I shouldn't be surprised she's calling me and talking to someone else.

She clears her throat and says, "I'm going to have to get a new phone, but I'm borrowing my neighbor's for tonight."

"Okay."

"I thought I'd let you know, in case you need to get in touch with me."

"So this is your new number just for tonight?"

"Yeah," she says. "It's an old phone of her son's."

"Okay," I say, and I want to know if she got my messages before she broke her phone. It took a lot of the courage I possess to send those messages, and while I had another surge that drove me to my phone to call her, all I feel now is nerves.

She says nothing, and I take a breath. "Listen, I sent you a couple of messages, maybe an hour ago? Did you get those, or did you drop your phone before that?"

"I got them," she says slowly.

"Oh." I need to eliminate that word from my vocabulary.

"I was in the...backyard, and I, uh...then panicked about my phone, and then one of my dogs threw...uh, herself a toy, and I...couldn't find my keys, so I had to walk to my neighbor's house."

I blink, trying to fill in the right words in the blanks in her sentences. I start to laugh, and she'll probably yell at me about that. She has before, but tonight, she giggles with me. "I think you're a liar, Miss Wilheim," I say, heavy on the Southern drawl. I grew up here in Charleston, and I can be a gentleman if necessary.

"Maybe some parts of that story aren't true."

"Which dog threw up?" I ask, leaning against the counter behind me.

"Guess," she says dryly.

"Darcy."

"He's a diva," she says. "He does it to punish me when he thinks I've withheld something in his dinner."

"Or he ate a rabbit earlier," I say.

She laughs again. "That too."

There's another pause, and I exhale everything out of my lungs. "So...what do you think? I own a nice suit, and I can dance."

I don't like the hesitation, and I actually roll my eyes. This woman pushes all my buttons, and I can't decide if they're the good ones or the bad ones.

"I want to say yes," Macie says. "But Coy..."

"It's okay," I say, my heart heavy but her first sentence still registering in my ears. *I want to say yes.* She wants to say yes? Why can't she say yes? I hate the word "but."

"No," she says. "Let me talk."

"All right," I say. "Talk."

"It's my best friend's wedding," she says, and I can imagine her standing up for the conversation. Macie doesn't like to sit during meetings. She says it makes her nervous. "And there will be a lot of eyes on me. My family will be there. A lot of my friends."

I say nothing, because I've learned that Macie likes to take a moment between thoughts. She'll continue, and I'm not surprised it's only a breath later.

"So...I want to go with you, but I don't want that to be the next time we go out."

My muscles twitch. "What?"

"Are you seriously going to make me say it again?"

"Are *you* seriously saying you want to go out with me *before* the wedding?"

"You know what? I'm going to hang up."

"No!" The word bursts from me before I can stop it. I smile, and I swear it's the first time I've done so in a year. A real smile. True happiness. "Have you eaten dinner?" I ask.

"I ordered pizza a while ago," she says, her tone turning flirty at the end of her sentence. I know, because I've heard her flirt with a ton of men. That sounds bad, but it's not. I've simply had a crush on her for the better part of five years, and she's had several boyfriends in that time. She's a fun, bright person, and I'm about the opposite of that.

"But there's always room for dessert," she says.

"Indeed," I say.

She laughs and mocks me when she says, "Indeed," but in a British accent.

"Do you know the best place for dessert in the city?" I ask, and maybe I'm flirting too. It's been so long since I flirted with a woman, I'm not sure.

But Macie makes me do things outside my comfort zone, and since that kiss on that orange couch... My pulse speeds just thinking about it. It's a throb I have to have again. I had a taste, and it was just as good as I'd imagined.

I want more.

I want to see if we can make a relationship work, and not the business kind. The personal kind.

"No," she says all coyly. "Do you?"

"I do," I say in all seriousness now. "Are you up for an adventure, Macie?"

"I think so."

"Great," I say. "Tell me where you live, and I'll tell you how long it'll take me to get there."

"I'm not ready to go," she says. "I didn't even drain my tub before I got out."

"I—your tub?"

"I mean—I need a few minutes to get ready," she says, but I've already started laughing. She was in the bathtub when I texted her, and she dropped her phone in the water, probably out of pure surprise.

Everything makes sense now—except she can't be that surprised that I asked her out. I laid down far too many cards when I kissed her in the coffee shop.

"An hour?" I ask.

"Yes," she says. "I can be ready in an hour."

"Great," I say. "Text me your address, and I'll see you in an hour."

CHAPTER THREE

MACIE

I swear the hour passes before I can even pick an outfit. I don't know why I'm being so anal about what I wear. It's *Coy Cochran.* I've literally never cared what I wear when around him.

"It's a date," I say to Justice, the little chihuahua who hasn't abandoned me during the past sixty minutes the way the other dogs have. I look at my reflection in the full-length mirror on the back of my bathroom door. The tub is drained and empty now, ready for tomorrow night's wind-down session.

"I can't believe I'm going out after my bath." Thankfully, I hadn't washed my hair before Coy's message had come through. My skinny jeans look just fine for a late January date in Charleston. I honestly don't know where we're going, and that probably would influence what I choose to wear.

As it is, I've chosen a purple blouse with puffed shoulders and a tapered sleeve that hugs my wrist. With my red hair, purple looks better than people might imagine, and I quickly finger-comb my curls in an attempt to tame them. That doesn't really work, and I'm still not wearing a stitch of makeup when the doorbell rings.

My first instinct is to text Coy that I'm not quite ready, and I'll be out as soon as I am. A quick glance around the bathroom counter reminds me that I don't have a working device. My neighbor will likely make me pay for all the texts and calls, and I'd rather she not even know about them. Sighing like this is going to be a really bad date and I'm nervous about it, I go to answer the door.

The six feet of male goodness on my front stoop tells me my sigh was all wrong. Another one slips from between my lips, this one saying, *Holy fried green tomatoes, look at those shoulders in that jacket.*

"Hey, Mace," Coy says, and I'm sure his voice isn't always that rumbly. Just like my stomach isn't always this tumbly. It's simply because I ate too much pizza earlier, and now I've got man-candy offering me his arm as if he's going to be the dessert.

"Hey," I say dumbly. "I..." My mind blitzes between inviting him in or simply grabbing my thread wallet and going. The clicking claws coming my way makes my decision for me. "No." I spin and hold out both hands, like I can hold back three dogs that way. "You guys stay. Stay!"

They, in fact, do not stay. And a cat has joined them,

which only adds to my embarrassment. Behind me, Coy chuckles, and it's the kind of sound I've always wanted to hear him make. I face him again, resigned to my fate. "You might as well come say hello. I need five minutes to swipe on some makeup too."

He steps up and into my house, his laughing eyes on me. "You look just great." He edges by me and closes the door, then crouches down and starts raining down love on my pets. "Tell me who is who."

I've told plenty of stories about my animals, so Coy does know their names already. "The French bulldog is Darcy. He's totally betraying me right now, because he shunned me after I had to run next door to call you."

"Figures."

Darcy keeps rubbing his gray bulldog face against Coy's palm like he can't get enough. He really is a traitor.

"The chihuahua is Justice," I say. "And that leaves the golden to be Susan."

"Do you ever call her Suzie?" He looks up at me, his dark eyes broadcasting happiness. He never looks like this at work. Coy is a bit of a contradiction inside one person. He can flip a switch when helping a customer or even talking to another employee. Me? I get glares and dark looks.

His beard is trim and neat, with perfectly crisp edges along his jaw and sideburns. But his hair hangs long, curling along his collar and around his ears. His clothes are clean and fashionable, but he doesn't tuck in his shirt or wear a belt.

That dark brown, sexy, leather jacket though... I could definitely eat him up in that for dessert.

I clear my throat to erase my thoughts, but it only sort of works. "No," I say. "I think she'd chew off one of my feet if I called her Suzie."

"Susan's just an...interesting name for a dog."

"I rehomed her," I say. "I didn't name her, and trust me, I tried Suzie and Susannah. She likes to chew things, and she goes by Susan."

Coy grins at me and then back at Susan. She's doing a golden retriever stomp-dance as she crowds her rear-end into his hand. In any other situation, I'd be embarrassed, but well. It's not like I don't know Coy. He's heard plenty of stories about Susan, including some humping ones.

"The cat is Lizzie. Emma won't come out while you're here." I look down the hall just to make sure my gray and white cat isn't going to make a liar of me. She doesn't appear, and I move past the herd of pets, adding, "I just need to put on my shoes."

My hall closet holds a rack of them, and I study my choices while Coy stands. I quickly select a white pair of runners, with pink and purple accents, and close the closet.

"Running shoes?" he asks.

"I love running shoes." I don't offer anything else, and wisely Coy doesn't comment further on my footwear.

"You were expecting something else?" As I walk down the hall to the living room, I keep my back to him, but when I turn, I raise my eyebrows.

"No," he says, tucking his hands in his jeans pockets. One shoulder lifts. "I mean, maybe. It's a date."

"I'm not one of your frilly girls," I say. "I only own one pair of heels, and I only wear them to weddings."

His tongue darts between his lips, wetting them. "So I'll get to see them."

"Maybe," I say.

His dark eyes dance with danger as he enters the living room. His gaze sweeps my kitchen, dining room, and living area, and I wonder what he sees. He doesn't comment on it, instead asking, "I won't?"

"Depends." I shove my last foot into the sneaker and stand. "The wedding is a couple of months away, and we might decide not to go together."

He swallows, and I can't help tracking the movement down his throat. A couple of steps puts me within arm's reach of him, and the scent of his cologne makes my head buzz in the best way possible. "Is that Whitewater?"

"Blue," he says. "Do you have a problem with my cologne?" He backs up a couple of steps, that dark glare I'm used to crowding into his expression.

"No." I grin at him and pat his chest as I head back to the hall closet. "Bluewater is better than white." I pluck a jacket from a hanger and start to put it on. Coy's there in the next moment, helping, his hands lightly touching my shoulders and hair.

Shivers race down my arms and tingle in my fingertips. I turn to face him as I pull my hair out of the collar and let it flow the few inches over my shoulders. "Thanks." My voice murmurs, but I swear I don't mean to make it do that.

I also don't mean to look at his mouth, but I do. I can remember the taste of it, the gentle-yet-firm pressure of his lips against mine as he kissed me, and then the way he positively claimed my mouth as the kiss lasted and deepened.

"Why would we decide not to go to the wedding together?" he asks.

I shrug, the answer obvious to me. "Because you can't stand me."

"That is so false." His eyes blaze now. "What a ridiculous thing to say."

"See? There you go."

"There I go? You literally just said I can't stand you, when I broke out the Whitewater for this date. Which *you* asked me on."

"No," I fire back at him. "*You* asked *me* for dessert."

"Because you said you didn't want to go to the wedding as our first date!"

I glare at him, but he's never cared about the sharpness in my eyes. My mind races, and what it comes up with is, "Is the Whitewater special?"

"I like to think so, yes." He clips the words from his mouth, almost like he can't stand admitting such a thing.

I reach for his collar and fiddle with it. Such a move usually relaxes a guy, or at least clues them in that I like them, that I'm not upset with them. If anything, Coy grows stiffer. "Do you use it a lot?"

"Are you asking me if I date a lot?"

Chancing my life, I look up and into his eyes. "Yes, that's what I'm asking."

"No," he says. "The bottle's almost full. Is that what you want to know?"

"Yes." I grin at him and lace my hand through his arm. "So, where are we going for dessert?"

"You still want to go?"

"I didn't get re-dressed and pull out my sparkliest pair of runners to stay home."

His attention drifts to my feet. "They are pretty sparkly."

"I'm going to take that as a compliment."

His gaze returns to mine. "You look great, Mace. Really." And that *is* a compliment, and Coy's delivered it genuinely.

Something warm glows inside my chest, and I think it might be my heart. "Thank you," I say, doing that murmuring thing again. "So...is our dessert location a secret?"

"No." He opens the door for me, waits for me to go out, and then follows, bringing the door closed behind him. "It's A Cone In One. They do tastings and tours of their facilities on Tuesdays to get people in." He checks his watch, and I swear he's the only man our age who wears one. "We better hurry if we want to make it."

Hurry we do, and I never would've pegged Coy for a bad driver. He isn't exactly bad; he's just not good. I keep telling myself he's hurried as we take the final corner on two wheels.

He's South Carolina born-and-bred, so he rushes around his SUV to get my door, and we're the last people inside the side-entrance to A Cone In One. The last tour is just starting, and Coy scribbles our names, shoves two twenties at the woman, and nods to the group in the square area where a man is already talking.

I get his drift: *Get over there so they don't leave without us.*

I do, and he joins me half a minute later, the tour guide's spiel almost done. There's a couple of families here with their kids, and then three or four other couples. They all look like they've been on at least one date before, because they're holding hands and pointing excitedly to big, silver vats of ice cream with non-sensical labels like Out of this World and Par Four.

"How do you even know what flavor it is?" I whisper to Coy, and he frowns.

"Good question," he whispers back. At least we agree on one thing.

We label our coffees and lattes with what they are.

There's no need to make the decision-making process any harder than it needs to be. People already get pretty irritated if someone steps up to the ordering register without knowing what they want.

The further along the tour we go, the more I relax. Just because I wouldn't name my ice cream things that don't give customers a hint of what they'll get doesn't mean A Cone In One is doing things wrong. They're obviously not. Their facility is huge, clean, and top-of-the-line.

We near the end of it, and the tour guide asks, "So, what was everyone's favorite flavor?"

A little boy practically jumps to the ceiling, his hand shooting up. I grin at him as he says, "The one with the chocolate."

Chuckling meets his words, Coy's included. He leans closer to me, his breath tickling the fine hairs on the side of my neck as he says, "See? This is why you name things what they are." His hand brushes mine, and I pull in a breath. He doesn't take my hand in his, and for some reason, I wish he would.

Maybe I've lost my mind. I have been thinking about him a lot lately—ever since The Kissing Incident, to be honest—and he does smell good enough to eat. I find myself leaning toward him as a woman says she liked the one "with the cherry and almonds."

"The Eagle," the tour guide says, clearly grinning maniacally for a reason I can't fathom. Probably because no one can remember any of the ice cream flavors he's had to memorize for his job. "Well, I've got three more for you to taste tonight," he says. "Then you'll be dropped off in our parlor, where all of our flavors are for sale tonight."

Grin, grin, grin as he tells us about the Arnold Palmer—which actually is iced tea and lemonade flavored sherbet—then one called Into the Woods, after Tiger Woods, and another golfer-themed flavor named Over The Phil.

I seriously don't get the nomenclature, but I'm not really into golf. I take my bite of Into the Woods, and try to get it down as quickly as possible. "Tastes like the woods," I mutter, definitely getting some grassy notes in there. The tour guide has said it's coconut and chia seeds, but he's dead wrong.

Coy's shaking his head as his tasting spoon slides out of his mouth. "This one isn't great either." He's tasting the Over The Phil, the name of which makes zero sense to me. A play on Over The Hill? What in the world does that have to do with golf or ice cream?

I scoop a tiny bit onto a tasting spoon, not wanting to be a total party pooper, and slide the white ice cream into my mouth. It's supposed to be white chocolate strawberry, but there's something very clearly off about the recipe. I swallow it quickly too, and deem the Arnold Palmer the best one of the night.

Probably because I know what flavors I'm getting, and it wasn't actually ice cream.

Out in the parlor, we join the line to get sundaes,

waffle cones or bowls, single scoops, and at least fifteen more choices from their menu board.

"Wow," I say, gazing up at it. "I guess ice cream has come as far as coffee, hasn't it?"

Beside me, Coy grins, and as a woman squeezes past us with her son going the wrong way in line, he presses into me, his hand sliding along my waist. "That it has," he says, barely putting any distance between us now that the mom is gone.

I smile to myself and let my gaze drop from the menu. "I'm just going to get chocolate," I say.

"Safe choice," Coy says.

My eyes land on a man at the register, and he turns toward his friend. I instantly know him, and my heart leaps so far up my throat, I get a metallic taste against my tongue. He laughs about something, twisting further, and I can't duck behind Coy fast enough. In fact, I don't duck anywhere. I've frozen.

Jared's seen me. And he's patting his friend's shoulder and leaning in, his eyes never leaving mine. His grin widens as he steps around the ropes keeping people in line and heads straight for me.

A horrible cackle comes out of my mouth, and I tip my head back like Coy's just told the funniest joke on the planet. One hand slides inside his jacket and around to his back while the other comes up and plays with a button near his throat.

"That might be true," I say, still giggling. His surprised

eyes meet mine, and if ever there was a time I wish I could communicate telepathically, it's now.

"Macie," Jared says, saving me from saying anything else.

I hold Coy's gaze for one second longer, then switch over to Jared. "Oh, Jared, hi." I edge further into Coy to get a little closer to him. "How are you?"

"Good," he says, not even looking at Coy. He stands probably two or three inches shorter than my business partner and the man I'm currently out with, and he doesn't have a beard. Otherwise, he's got the dark hair and eyes that I like so much. So I have a type. Sue me.

Coy turns toward him too, and I clear my throat. "Coy," I say. "This is Jared. Jared. Coy."

"Nice to meet you, man," Jared says like he's still the frat boy I went out with six years ago. He's not. He never was. The act he puts on is sickening, honestly. Does he really think women want a guy who only eats buffalo wings, only knows one restaurant for a date, and spends ninety percent of his time gelling his hair or playing basketball with his bros?

His gaze flicks to Coy's and back to me. "Did you get my message on SnapShot?"

My sparkly sneakers suddenly feel way too small, and my feet shift. "Oh, uh, yeah. I got it."

"So did you want to go to the wedding with me?"

Before I can say a single thing, Coy takes a half-step in front of me. "Actually, *man*," he says. "She posted that as a joke. Just wanted to do the dance and get the comments and likes." He doesn't look at me as he speaks, his voice cool and even. "We're dating pretty seriously and will be attending her best friend's wedding together."

I lean into him further, glad when his arm tightens around me, bringing me flush into his side. We both look at Jared, who takes a good five seconds to put two and two together. "Oh, right," he says. "Cool, man."

"Good to see you," I say in a voice that suggests otherwise. What I'm really saying is, *Please don't stand here and make small talk.*

"Yeah, it was—let me know if it doesn't work out."

I can only gape after him as he returns to his friend, who's now paid for their treats and waits off to the side.

The line shifts forward, and Coy takes the steps I can't. He tugs me along, and I go, my own mind a little numb. "We're dating pretty seriously?" I repeat some of his words as they still roll around in my brain.

"I had to tell him something," Coy says under his breath, half-turned away from me. "You posted that video a few hours ago, asking for a date." He faces me now, and I realize what he's done for me.

I reach up and touch his chest. "Thank you, Coy." My fingers slide along that perfectly neat beard to cradle his face, and the next thing I know, I'm lifting onto the toes of my sparkly sneakers and pulling Coy's face down to mine.

And before I can completely lose my mind and kiss him, someone bumps into him, and he pitches into me.

CHAPTER FOUR

COY

I'm aware of grunting and stumbling, and thankfully, I'm able to right Macie and myself before we go sprawling through this ice cream parlor.

My pulse hits my ribs violently, first from the adrenaline of nearly falling, and then from the memory of that look in Macie's eyes. She'd been about to kiss me, I'm sure of it.

My brain feels soft, then it sharpens, and the man behind me says, "Sorry. Are you two okay?"

"Yeah," I say before tucking Macie against my chest as I look in the direction of the question. "We're fine," I whisper to the father there. He gives me a small smile and focuses on his family again. I look over to where Jared and his bro-friend were standing, and they're both staring openly at us.

I smile at them too, then duck my head back to take a

deep breath of Macie's hair. She's just had it cut and colored recently, and I'm not even ashamed to admit that. It doesn't smell like chemicals tonight, but I'm getting remnants of the coffee shop, soap, and...grapefruit.

Being here with Macie is fantastic, but I'm going to text my sister and tell her how wrong she was about this place being "the best kept secret in Charleston."

"Are you..were you—going to kiss me?" I whisper.

She moves in my arms, and against my will, we separate. We're dangerously close to the ice cream counter now, where all the flavors will steal Macie from me. She searches my face and says nothing.

"What will you do if I said I was?" she finally asks.

"I'm sick of that game," I say honestly. There's obviously something between us. It might just be a fluke, or it could be that the same things that annoy her irritate me, or it could be a flash of attraction.

A flash that's lasted years for me, I think.

"We've been playing a game?" Her eyebrows go up under her bangs. "I wish I'd known."

"You know," I say as the line takes her all the way to the case with all the flavors. It extends down at least ten more feet to the cash register where A Cone In One has a single person taking orders. Such a thing would be the cause of World War Three at Legacy, and I frown down to the teenager currently explaining one of the ridiculously labeled flavors here.

"I don't know the rules to this game," she says.

"Yeah, well, join the club." I shove my hands in my jacket pockets and look at the cylinders of ice cream. "I don't want any of this."

"Oh, thank all the crayfish in the bayou," Macie says. "Me either."

I grin and take her hand in mine. "Let's get out of here?"

"Yeah," she says. "We can talk about the game on the way somewhere with real dessert." She says the last part just a little too loud, and I'm sure we're going to be jumped by some sort of Cone Police on the way out of the parlor.

We're not, and we spill into the night, the bright lights from the shop behind us splaying over the sidewalk as we laugh together. I tighten and reseat my fingers between hers, and that cuts off her voice.

I say nothing until we're back in my car, because it feels too dangerous to let my thoughts out into the open air. "If you tell me that it was a mistake to kiss me a few months ago, that you weren't about to do it again, I'm gonna call you a liar." I twist the key to start the engine and look over to her. "You don't kiss someone like that if it's a mistake."

"You might," she argues.

"And the sky was *so* blue today," I say, just to mock her.

She shakes her hair over her shoulders and fastens her seatbelt. "It actually wasn't, Coy."

"Oh my word!" I slap the steering wheel in frustration.

"I knew you'd argue with me over that. You can't even admit the freaking sky is blue!"

"There was a storm today," she says earnestly. "It actually wasn't blue."

"*Good biscuits and gravy*, you can agree with me sometimes. It won't kill you." I glare at her and jam the car in reverse. The only reason I don't fly out of the parking stall without looking is because my car beeps urgently at me and applies the brakes for me when I don't.

"Oh, good biscuits and gravy," Macie mutters. "It's Jared and his frat-friend."

Frat-friend is better than bro-friend, but I don't give her the satisfaction of knowing that. Our eyes meet, and slowly, ever-so-slowly, her lips curve upward. "The sky is blue most of the time."

"Yes, it is." I wait until the lot is clear, and then I back out of the space. I drive for a few minutes, automatically making turns without a destination, before I dare to peek over to her. "I didn't mean to make fun of your Southern swear words."

She sighs and leans her head back against the headrest before turning it to look at me. "I didn't mean to argue over the color of the sky."

"At least you're not saying that kiss was a mistake." I lift my eyebrows at her, clearly asking her what it was if not an error.

She only smiles, her eyes drifting closed in a long

blink. I spot a McDonald's up ahead and quickly get in the right lane so I can turn into it.

Macie straightens. "We're going to McDonald's?"

"I promised you dessert, and those tasting spoons of ice cream weren't even good."

"You promised me the best dessert in the city," she points out.

"Well, I'm gonna have a little talk with Anna Lee about that one," I say. "It's totally her kind of place, though, don't you think?"

"Your sister recommended that place?" Macie starts to giggle, and I join my laughter to hers even as I confirm. "Totally seems like her." She swats at my arm, but I turn my hand over and capture hers in mine. "And you listened to her? Don't you know by now that she's nothing like you?"

"I'm going to take that as a compliment," I say, still grinning as I pull behind a huge truck in the drive-through line at McDonald's.

"Good," Macie says quietly. "Because it was one."

Silence descends on us again, my voice the only one puncturing it so I can order two twist cones. Once we have our treats, some of the tension leaks away. Before I know it, I'm pulling up to Macie's house. I've never been here before, though I knew she lived in Sugar Creek. I wonder if she knows I live on the edge of Summerwood, another neighborhood surrounding Charleston, which is only a couple of miles away, actually.

"Nice house," I say as I reach the cone of my treat. It's a cute little blue house, with bright white shutters on the windows flanking the front door. From the front, it looks like what a child would draw in a rudimentary picture, with the door right in the middle, two windows on either side. A chimney even comes off the left side of the roof, which looks new.

"Thanks," she says. "I bought it a couple of years ago, with some of the money I got after my mama died."

"Macie." I look over to her, shocked. "I didn't know your mother died."

"It's been four years." She takes a monster-big bite of her cone, and I've seen her use this tactic before. She doesn't want to talk about this.

"That doesn't mean it's easy." I want to gather her into my arms and hold her close. "My daddy's been gone for over a decade, and sometimes..." I don't finish, because what am I going to say?

I'm not sobbing my eyes out at night or anything, but there are things I wish he was here for me to tell him. Like how I nearly lost Legacy Brew, but I pulled out every stop and kept it in the family. I still own over half of the company, despite bringing on Macie at forty percent ownership. That together, we've turned the ship around completely in only a handful of months, and that we're sailing really well right now.

"I know you miss him," she says. "I do too."

I look at her house again, not really seeing it. "I sometimes forget that you worked for him too." She's been at Legacy Brew for a long, long time, which was the primary reason I allowed her to buy-in to the company. I knew she wouldn't try to change what I've established there, what my father had done there, and try to make us a chain coffeehouse.

She did hire her friends, Callie and Dawson Houser, to be our marketing arm, and they've done a fantastic job getting more women with pencil skirts and men with brief-cases into our shop before and after work. It's a hangout spot in the afternoons now, and moms come with their kids. We have apple juice and chocolate milk to go with our muffins and bagels, and more often than not, Macie comes back to the shop after work to chill with her friends.

I've never joined them, and I steal a peek at her now, wondering if that's in my future. I don't dare ask, because I'm afraid she's about to lecture me about how I can never kiss her again. With my cone finished, I get out of the car and go around to her side.

She slides out of the car, her legs impossibly long in those skinny jeans. They make my mouth dry, a condition I'm sure that only another kiss with her will rectify. We walk up to her door, and she plays with her keys. "I actually had a good time tonight," she says.

"The tone of surprise doesn't comfort me," I say.

She gives a small shake of her head. "I just meant... yeah." She looks up at me. "I had a good time tonight."

I pull on every brave string inside me and slide my

hand around her waist. "Which part? My crazy driving so we didn't miss the tour? The tour that was pretty lame, with semi-gross ice cream? Or meeting some guy who, I don't know? Is one of your old boyfriends? Someone who just wants to get lucky with you?" I lean my head down, closer to hers, and take another deep breath of her skin and hair. "Or I know—the seventy-nine-cent dessert I promised you. It was that McDonald's cone, wasn't it?"

She giggles, pressing further into my arms. When she looks up at me again, she wears open vulnerability on her face. "Jared is an old boyfriend."

"Ah." I nod, unable to erase the smile from my face. "I gotta say, I'm disappointed he was the best part. I think I'm going to go with the McDonald's. I always love a good twist cone."

Macie's eyes flit between mine, soaking up what I've said. I want to kiss her again—for once, I want to be the one who initiates the union of our mouths—but instead, I step back. "I'll see you at work tomorrow."

"Yeah," she murmurs. "See you tomorrow."

It takes every speck of willpower I have to walk away from her without kissing her. But I know Macie Wilheim, and she needs some time and distance to go over everything that's happened in the last hour.

I don't, because kissing her is everything I've dreamed and fantasized about for years now. As I get behind the wheel of my car, I smile and glance back up to her front door.

She's still standing there, staring down at an empty flowerbed. I honk, and she nearly jumps up onto the roof. I burst out laughing, and Macie glares, shakes her head, and keys her way into her house without looking back.

"I think she liked it," I say to myself as I pull out of her driveway. "The date tonight...and the kissing from months ago." I can only hope and pray I'm right. I guess I'll see tomorrow, when we collide at work, if tonight has changed anything between us.

I hope so, I think. *I sure do hope so.*

CHAPTER FIVE

MACIE

I'm elbow-deep in the latte machine when a squeal fills the coffee shop. I twist to see what's happening, adrenaline shooting to the top of my head.

Amber, one of my baristas, has both hands clutched around her jowls, her eyes full of wonder and joy. I have to remove my arms from the machine and take a couple of steps to see the man down on both knees in front of her, a gemstone as big as a golf ball glittering in the sunshine pouring through the front windows.

"...love you from here to the border and back. Will you marry me?"

Amber—a cute, petite blonde who's been dating the man in front of her for over a year—bounces on the balls of her feet, getting higher and higher as another high-pitched sound escapes from behind her hands.

Smiling, I shake my head and glance over to Janice.

She's a decade older than me, and she wears a maternal look of fondness on her face. "About time," she says, but not in a mean way.

"Yes!" Amber finally shrieks, and the shop breaks out into applause. I join them, because while my insides are slowly being ripped out and then dunked in a candy-coating of bright green jealousy, I'm not a complete jerk. Amber has been dating Kenny for a while, and they're so blissfully in love—as evidenced by the deep kiss and then joyful embrace unfolding before me.

Then Amber spins and with pure light spilling from her face, she whips off her apron with a flourish. "I quit," she announces.

My hands freeze mid-clap. I open my mouth, but it simply fishes, like I'm trying to find oxygen when there is none.

She lifts her pert little nose in the air and tosses the apron on the counter in front of me. "Sorry, Mace." She doesn't sound sorry, and she squeals again as Kenny grabs her and spins her toward him.

She leaps—a literal leap—into his arms, both of them laughing, and they leave Legacy Brew in a wake of high adrenaline and girlish giggles.

I'm standing behind the counter where people pick up their reheated quiches and muffins, the scent of coffee and milk nearly drowning me, and that black apron glaring at me from the counter. I reach for it, thinking it might turn into a cobra and strike.

It doesn't, but it also hasn't been washed in a very long time, making me shiver.

The bell on the door chimes and in walks a group of businessmen and women. Our afternoon rush is about to start, and I really need all of my baristas to handle the crowd.

At Legacy Brew, we have two pretty major rushes throughout out day. The mornings are absolutely insane, and I have three people taking orders and four making them. Two bakers come in an hour before that to make sure we can handle those who are running late and need a pastry to go with their caffeine, and then two more bakers come in at noon to prep for our mid-afternoon rush, which lasts from about one to three.

We close at seven, and we get a tiny rush about five-thirty, but usually those are people who hang out at the shop until we flip the sign and turn off the lights.

My afternoon bakers make sure we're ready for the following morning too. They work through close, and while I'm technically off during our afternoon rush, I almost always stay. I come back at night to see my friends too.

In essence, Legacy Brew has become my whole life.

"Howdy, Mace," a man says, and I blink away from my scheduling problems. Amber was one of my full-time baristas, meaning I'm short-staffed instantly. Right now.

I sweep her apron off the counter and reach for an antiseptic wipe. "Hiya, Chase." I give him a grin. "How's the agency?" Chase Summers owns an insurance firm, and it looks like he's brought his entire team with him today. Everyone studies the menu board behind me, but Chase meets my eyes.

"Good enough," he says. "Can I get a dozen of your muffins, assorted flavors." He pulls out his wallet. "And I'm getting all the coffee." He scans his people before his eyes come back to me. "Can I set up here for a bit? We just need a break from the conference room."

"Someone burned popcorn in the building," a smartly dressed woman at his side says. She looks at Chase with gaga eyes, a sigh escaping that I've heard a great many times between bosses and their single female employees. It's part longing and part frustration that he doesn't see them the way they want him to.

"Sure," I say, my own sigh building in my body. Mine will be built of all irritation that I'm now going to fill in for Amber and then have to go through my stack of applications before I leave today.

"I'll have a latte," Chase says. "Light milk."

I smile and nod and move down to the register to tap in his company order, thinking, *Oh, and I need to get that latte machine cleaned and back together.*

"Shawny," I say as Chase steps to the side to let the woman order. "I need you to take this order so I can finish with the machine."

She wipes her hands on her apron, and I point to the

screen. "A dozen assorted muffins and a light-milk-latte. He's paying for everyone."

She looks down the line, visibly swallows, and nods. I know exactly how she feels, but if I don't get the latte machine back together, we'll be in even bigger trouble than we are now.

Three, four, five, six, seven—the number of times the door chimes while I finish the machine. Without the proposal, I'm sure I'd have finished it before the rush began. I press my lips into a grim line and start working on filling the orders from Chase's party while Shawny and Bella continue to take orders and money.

The shop is hopping, and I can't be mad about that. I've just finished Chase's last coffee order—a cappuccino with mint whip—and set it on the pick-up counter when a voice I know very well says, "It's *how long* for a cup of dark roast?"

Coy.

I refrain from rolling my eyes and immediately step to Shawny's side. "Thirty seconds, sir," I say. I nod to Shawny, who rings him up at the employee discount. Honestly, he and I drink and eat anything we want for free. He still pulls out his card while I turn to get his coffee.

He likes his dark and plain, but I've seen him sneak over to the flavorings bar and add a splash of coconut or a packet of cane sugar.

I meet his eye as I hand him the cup while still sliding on the cardboard heat protector.

"Why are you doing orders?" he asks.

"Amber got engaged," I respond.

He takes the coffee, one eyebrow cocked high. I'm not sure what it's saying, but I'm in no mood for a lecture.

"I'll catch up with you after the rush," I say before I turn away. Perfect Amber and her perfect boyfriend. I swallow against the bitterness and focus on getting coffee, tea, cappuccinos, lattes, and iced tea brewed, steeped, and poured as fast as possible.

I'll have to go talk to Coy at some point, where he'll tell me—again—to come into Legacy as a customer to "get the experience they do."

The wait times. How hard it is to hear when your name is called for your order. The jostling that can happen at the flavorings bar.

I've never done it, because I *know* Legacy Brew inside and out. I don't need to park out front and come in like I've never been here before. I'm not surprised he did it today. He pretends to be a customer about three times a week, coming at different times of day, sometimes with his sister to see what it's like when there's more than one coffee on an order.

He orders food sometimes, just to see if the quiche comes out cold in the middle, and a more discerning partner would appreciate the way he collects data for our business. His goal is to improve it, I know that.

At the same time, the way he operates with that cocked eyebrow and the tone of disbelief at the wait time during an obvious rush only irritates me.

Maybe that's because he honked at me last night. I'd disappeared into my house while he laughed behind his windshield and spent a good ten minutes pacing in the kitchen while I muttered curses at him.

Honking. Seriously, who does that to a woman they've just taken out? The date wasn't very good either, and even though my mind starts to argue with me that the date *was* good—it was only the ice cream that wasn't—I don't concede the point to myself.

Coy makes it so easy to be annoyed, that's for sure.

I finish the rush, and I grab Shawny as she closes out her register. "Can you come in tomorrow morning for Amber?" I ask. If I can buy myself a few days to hire and train someone, I won't have to lie awake with my panic tonight.

"Sure thing," she says with a smile.

"You did great with the orders today," I tell her.

"Really?" She wears hope and open vulnerability on her face. "Mister Cochran didn't seem happy about the wait."

"Mister Cochran is fine," I say. "Regular coffee like his can be done before the other orders." Shawny is still pretty new, and I seize the opportunity to train her a little bit.

"So next time a customer just wants a cup of coffee we can literally dispense and hand over, you do it." I smile so she knows she's not in trouble. "You take his money and go get it immediately."

"Oh, okay," she says. "Like the popcorn at the theater."

I'm not sure what she means, but I nod anyway. "Then you won't have people like him upset when they just want a quick cup."

Shawny nods and asks, "Six tomorrow morning?"

"Five-forty-five," I say. "We open at six." She'll have to get her register set up and her apron on, and I like to talk to all of my people for sixty seconds or less before we open. Then they know what quiches we have, what muffins, and what flavorings might be low and run out by the time the rush ends.

My end order-taker is supposed to man the flavorings bar during her shift, but it can be difficult when the line is out the door and down the sidewalk.

"I can come whenever you need me," Caroline says.

"Wednesday morning is yours," I say. "We'll see if we can cover for Amber until I can get someone new." I give them a smile like finding someone will be easy. I have a lot of applicants, but I hired Shawny only two weeks ago, and I feel like she was one of the last ones worth looking at.

They leave for the day, and my afternoon bakers come out of the kitchen to see what our pastry cases look like. Talia and Jean both make notes in small books, give me a smile, and chit-chat with each other until they know what the next few hours will bring to their baking schedule.

I step over to Bella, the last woman manning the registers, and start to help her get cleaned up. We wipe counters, stack all the receipts in one place, and then move onto the pastry cases, the machines and counters behind us, and the pick-up counter.

The rush is over, but Chase and his firm-mates are still here. The bell on the door rings, and I heave a sigh that speaks of how tired I am. I really shouldn't have laid awake for so long last night. My thoughts have been tangled since Coy's message, and I start when I realize it's almost four.

I should've left work two hours ago, and I need to get my phone today before the shop closes.

"Macie."

I look up into the eyes of Tara Ward. She lives down the street from me, with her new husband, Alec, her dogs, over a dozen chickens, and a Quaker parrot.

"Tara." Her name seeps out of my mouth like she's my long-lost Savior. She so is, because she's holding up a brand-new cellphone.

"My phone." I reach for the purple device, admiring it for a moment before switching my gaze back to her. "How did you know I hadn't gotten it?"

"Someone at the store answered it, and I was done for today." She smiles at me, and I lean over the counter to hug her.

"I'll come out," I say just as Alec joins her.

"We'll get coffee," Tara says.

I untie my apron and duck through the black plastic door that leads into the other half of Legacy Brew. The kitchen, which is bustling with things being mixed, kneaded, and baked.

Coy's office door stands open, but I ignore it as I head into mine. I close my door and leave the light off. I don't have a window in my office—that luxury belongs to Coy—but I have a blue-light nightlight so I can be in here without the overhead fluorescents.

I sink into my seat, sighing out the past few hours. I want to put my head down and sleep. True sleep, where I'm not irritated about the honking, wondering why Coy didn't text to set up another date, puzzling through whether I should try to get another date to Bri's wedding, and now these staffing issues.

Another sigh tells me I'm not going to solve any of the above by sitting here in the dark, so I reach to switch on my lamp. Tara got it for me for my birthday a few years ago, and it's got a thick, black base and a bright pink shade with a ribbon sewn around the edge that boasts coffee cups.

I put in a soft yellow bulb, and it makes my office light up like a cupcakery—pink and pastel and perfect.

Something softens inside me, and I'm calm enough to open my bottom desk drawer and pull out the bulging folder of applications that have come in.

We do them online now too, but I like to print them to go over them more tactilely. I like having something to hold, to scan, to point to, when I'm researching a potential employee.

I wake my computer and check the online applications. There are dozens that have been submitted in the past couple of weeks, and my heart takes flight. Hope can be a powerful thing, either for good or for worse. Right now, I'm hoping to find just one applicant that will be bubbly, personable, and capable when it comes to taking orders and running credit cards.

It sounds easy, but we have forty-two different ways a cup of coffee can be made here at Legacy Brew. Coy prides himself on having the best coffee beans from around the world, and we get a lot of customers who come to us for a specific blend.

Almost all of me wants to forget about Amber quitting and go join my friends on the couches in the front of the shop.

Instead, I open the first ten applications that have come in recently and send them to print.

The only printer here at the shop is in Coy's office, and I push myself to a stand and say, "Just grab the apps and go."

My heart pounds as I leave my office, knowing that I won't be able to just grab-and-go, but I don't want to admit that I want to linger to see if he wants to go out tonight...

I face his office and take a steeling breath. "Grab and go," I whisper, and then I close my fingers into a fist to do exactly that.

CHAPTER SIX

COY

The whirring of the printer has me lifting my head. The only person who has printer access besides me is Macie.

A thrum starts behind my tongue that has nothing to do with the late-afternoon coffee I've already consumed. I drank it black and hot today, trying to sear the sight of Macie with her hair slicked back into that sexy ponytail from my mind.

She ties her apron tightly around her waist, creating the perfect hourglass figure that I want to slide my palms up and down. I cough, the fantasy sticking in my head.

She doesn't come to get her printouts, and I refocus on the sketch pad in front of me.

"What's that?" Macie's voice above my shoulder sends my pulse into a panic, and I flip over the book as fast as I can.

In the process, I knock over my empty coffee cup, which bounces into a stack of paperclips. They fall to the floor in slow-motion, the only thing moving at light speed being my pulse.

"Chicken and waffles, Coy," Macie says, her voice full of disgust. I can't help smiling at her Southern food swear as I jump to my feet.

"You can't just barge in here whenever you want," I say.

"The door was open." Macie blinks like I've lost my mind. "Were you drawing?"

I'm still holding the pencil in my hand, and I throw it over my shoulder. "No." I lift my shoulders in a breath, practically daring her to try to see anything on my desk behind me. The pencil clatters around behind me, finally coming to rest somewhere I'll probably never find.

"Coy." She folds her arms and cocks that sexy hip. At least she's removed the apron that emphasizes her waist. That only allows me to see her skinny jeans in black.

Black swells around her hips and narrows to her ankles, where her feet disappear into an adorable pair of purple Converse. How she wears those all day long in the shop is a mystery to me, but honestly, the whole woman in front of me is as well.

"Macie," I say, a completely lame retort.

"Amber quit," she says. "I printed some applications." She tries to look behind me to the desk, where the printer rests on the left.

I lunge toward it and grab her stack of papers. "How many people are you hiring?"

She sighs, and the sound is filled with irritation. "As many as I need to, Coy. We get slammed sometimes."

"Shawny didn't know she could just get my coffee."

"I talked to her," Macie says. "She's new, if you'll remember. She took over for Chase and his whole firm, and she did great."

I hand her the papers, still blocking my desk and sketch book with my body. "Are you done for today then? Taking those home?"

She looks down at the papers, then back to me. "You know what? No." She rolls the applications into a tube, her blue-eyed gaze fierce. "I'm sick of working here for twelve hours every day and then working at home too."

I agree with her completely. I come in about ten-thirty, right when our first major morning rush ends, and I spend the first couple of hours of my shift refilling the pastry case and cleaning up after the rush.

"So you'll have time for dinner," I say, not sure where the words came from.

Macie falls back a step, her eyelashes going blink-blink-blink-blink-blink. "Dinner?"

"Yeah, it's the meal you eat in the evening," I say, keeping my lips perfectly flat.

"I know what dinner is."

"You sounded like you didn't know." I tuck my hands in my pockets. "I'm done here about eight. Maybe nine." I don't want her to think she works more than me, but she kinda does. I'm putting in eight to ten hours every day, not twelve, and Macie isn't stupid.

She narrows her eyes. "It's not good for your liver to eat so late at night."

"My liver has never complained," I say. "I know you had dumplings with Tara at almost midnight only two nights ago."

Macie scoffs, but she doesn't have a comeback. That irritates her, and she usually has something whippish to lash at me with.

I take a step toward her in the pause inside her brain. "I can call Drake's or we can go to Bun Boy. I know you like their tapas."

Macie looks up at me as I continue to close the gap between us. My office isn't decorated as if I enjoy spending time here, though I do have a couple of photographs of my family.

It's mostly filing cabinets and cork boards and computers. Macie brightens the whole space, and I let myself brush my fingers along hers.

Sparks alight through my whole body, and Macie takes in a quick breath. "I'm sorry about Amber," I say. "Are there any good applicants? Would you like me to look at them and we can go over it tonight?"

"That would make dinner a business meeting," she says, finally joining the conversation.

"Mm, yes it would." I slide my fingers between hers

completely. "Were you annoyed with me specifically earlier, or just harried because Amber had quit mid-shift?"

"Both," she says quietly.

"Why's that?"

That fire enters her eyes, and I want it to burn me with all its glorious heat. She's like this perfect storm—glorious and beautiful from afar, with layer upon layer of wind, currents, driving rain, and whipping water.

I want to be in the center of her to feel what she feels, see what she sees, and experience what she experiences. I can't do that if I don't figure out what about me bothers her so much.

"You honked at me last night," she says. "Word to the wise: Not a great way to end your first date."

I grin at her. "I didn't want you to get mugged standing on your own front step. I was being cautious."

She rolls her eyes, and I chuckle as a vein of regret tugs through me. "But noted," I say. "I will not honk at you again. I'll make sure you get indoors safe and sound first, and then I'll leave."

I haven't been on many first dates lately—none in fact in the past three years. Macie and I always start out on uneven ground, just like today when she saw my sketches.

My heartbeat thumps at the thought of showing anyone my ideas for Legacy Brew. Now that Macie is almost a half-partner, I'll have to show her eventually. But I'm not ready yet.

Something tells me Macie will push me to show her

before I'm ready, and knowing my insane attraction to her, my willingness to get ravaged by the storm inside her, I'll do it.

"Shrimp and grits," she mutters. "Fine, let's go to Drake's at eight-thirty."

"You don't have to say it like it's going to be torture." I step back and pull my hand away. "You want me to pick you up, or do you want to meet there?"

"I'll text you." She flashes a shiny new phone at me. "I got a new phone, so my old number works again."

"Great," I say, still trying to decipher the emotion in her voice when she said "Fine, let's go to Drake's." It was almost like she conceded to me when she didn't want to.

I frown as I turn to face my desk. "See you later, then."

"Coy," she says, and I twist to face her. She wars with herself, and I'm not sure what side wins, but she shakes her head, that ponytail swaying with the movement. She doesn't wear a ton of makeup, but what she does really enhances her beauty. Pretty pink gloss on that mouth, a sweep of rose on her cheekbones, and plenty of black on her eyelashes. The rest of her face is open, clear, natural, and I can look at her forever and never tire of the view.

"What?" I prompt.

"Pick me up, okay?"

"Yes, ma'am."

She ducks her head and starts to leave the office, the roll of applicants in her hand. I want to take some work from her, but she does all the hiring and training of employees, and if I do go through the applications, I won't even know what to look for.

I watch her, and she's watching me, which means she's not looking where she's going. She rams into the doorjamb with her shoulder, yelps, "oof!" and falls to her knees.

"I'm fine," she says before I can ask if she's okay. I rush to her anyway and put my hands under her elbow to help her stand.

She does, the blush in her face from embarrassment now. "Stupid door," she says. "If this building wasn't five thousand years old, it would have a normally width..widthed...widening. It would be a normal width."

I start to laugh, because I can't help it. The building is old, and the doorways are narrow and short. She's complained about it before, but I'm pretty sure she's never walked straight into one.

She reaches up and tightens her ponytail, then brushes her hands down her black shirt. "Stop laughing at me."

I start to quiet, but we both know why she walked into the doorjamb, and my own face heats as I drop my chin toward my chest.

"Coy."

"I'm trying," I say as a new round of laughter bubbles through my chest. "That was funny."

"Red beans and rice," she mutters as she clears the doorway and stalks away. I move to my office door to watch her, imagining tendrils of wind and water to be flying from her as she departs.

I'm still chuckling and smiling as Macie leaves the back of the shop and enters the front-facing part of Legacy Brew.

My sketches await, but before I return to them, I close my door. Everyone who works at Legacy Brew knows to knock if the door is closed, and it ensures I won't have anyone accidentally seeing my ideas for a new logo for the coffee shop.

My chair squeaks as I sit, and sure enough, I can't find the pencil I was using earlier. I flip over the sketch book and look at the partially finished idea.

"All of these might be stupid," I mutter to myself. Macie hired Dawson Houser's marketing firm to help the shop with marketing, and I can admit it's been amazing for us. Our profits are up over three hundred percent, and I know we could continue to increase if we modernize a few things.

Namely, our logo.

Legacy has been in my family for generations, and we've been using the same branding for at least the duration of my lifetime.

I want to take Legacy into the future, and that means new branding. Macie and I meet a couple of times each month, and we've come up with a new slogan for the shop.

We'll provide the coffee while you're making a legacy for yourself.

I do love it, though it's a little bit long. If I can get a new logo that speaks of building a legacy and sipping coffee, then I can have it painted on our front windows. We can create new marketing campaigns for the radio and local media, online social sharing and more.

I take in the sketch, and it's not bad, but it's not quite right either. I want the word *Legacy* to be the biggest. That's the name of the shop and what we're leaning into.

I've drawn modern letters with sharp angles and added drawings of families, businessmen and women, and groups of friends—all of them sipping coffee while they supposedly plan and carry out their legacies.

This one feels a little busy to me, and flip back a page to another idea I sketched out last week.

It's more like a rectangle instead of a circle, with the street Legacy Brew sits on drawn along the bottom. People move toward the shop and away from it, all of them holding cups of coffee or tea.

I've drawn LEGACY above that, like one of those big giant signs that topped businesses in the forties and fifties.

"It might be too cartoonish," I say to myself. I don't want Legacy to be a cartoon, but I do like how it establishes that we've been around for a while, and we're still serving the best coffee in Charleston.

I have probably another six-point-seven started and incomplete drawings in this book, but I close it and slide it into my bottom drawer. I have coffee beans to order and payroll to approve, and though I love drawing and sketching, I actually have to run this business sometimes.

I open my spreadsheet with the coffee orders that need

to be done today and reach for my cherry Chapstick, a new smile on my face.

All because I have a date with Macie that evening. "You're going to try to start out on even ground," I tell myself, wondering if that's actually possible for us.

Then I slather on my Chapstick, my defense against anything hard or non-wonderful, and get to work. Something with Macie will come to me as I put in orders and experiment with blends, I'm sure of it...

CHAPTER SEVEN

MACIE

My doorbell rings, sending my pulse up to the backs of my eyes. It immediately rebounds to my chest, leaving me disoriented for a couple of seconds.

"It's only seven-forty," I say above the Watchdogs who've gone into B.A.R.K mode at the sound of the doorbell. I've only done half of my makeup, and I can't answer the door with only one eye shadowed. Still holding my eyeliner brush, I quickly tap on my phone to check my security camera.

Maybe it was a package delivery or a prank kid from down the street. My doorbell rings right as I pull up the feed, and I see Jessie Byers standing there.

She's holding what looks like clothes draped over her arm, and I jump to my feet. "Hush up!" I yell to the dogs, and thankfully, they do. I tap the unlock button on my security app and then tap to talk to her through the speaker.

"Jess, I'm doing my makeup. I just unlocked the door. Come on in."

She looks like she's seen a ghost as she looks around to see where my voice is coming from. I grin and add, "I can't wait to see that skirt."

I'm wearing a pair of black leggings right now, because I haven't quite settled on a second date outfit yet.

Jessie enters my house, and I re-lock the door behind her, then turn away from the mirror to go greet her. "Back here," I call. "Do you dare to see me with only one eye done?"

"Of course," she says as she appears at the end of the hall, my dogs rushing toward her. "Why are you getting all dolled up?"

My chest pinches, but I can't come up with a reason not to tell her. "I have a date," I say, almost hoping she won't ask with who. Jessie isn't as pressing about who I date the way Tara, Bri, and Callie are.

Which reminds me... Bri had texted earlier today right when I'd gotten home to ask me if I'd gotten a date to her wedding from my video.

I definitely have, even if this thing with Coy doesn't work out. I stopped responding to the comments and private messages, and it takes me a moment to realize why.

I really want this thing with Coy to work out. None of the other men who volunteered to take me to Bri's wedding are even close to him in terms of good looks and the charm someone can portray in a video or a message.

"Oh, fun," Jess says as she enters my bedroom. "Maybe one of these skirts will get to go out with you." She lays two of them on the bed, and I'm in love already. Both of them boast loud prints that seem to clash with each other.

One is dark brown or black, with bright swirls and flourishes of flowers across it. I want to put it on right now, and I reach for it. "I love this one."

"I designed that fabric," Jessie says fondly. "It's rayon, so it'll flow like silk but be heavy enough to ditch the leggings."

She picks up the flowered skirt and hands it to me. "You can wear anything with it too. A plain blouse in any color. Or a patterned blouse with a dominate color. Something dark too." She smiles at the skirt as if they've bonded somehow, and they probably have.

Jessie loves clothes, and she's been sketching and designing them for years now. She works with her husband at a busy real estate firm in Cider Cove, but she has a sewing studio in their house.

Justice enters the bedroom and whines for me to lift her onto the bed. I do, my other two canines joining her there, the catastrophe they imagined averted.

"I made it to your measurements," Jessie says.

Susan won't stop sniffing the skirt, and I push her back. "She can probably smell Cha-Cha on it," I say.

"She doesn't go far from me while I sew," Jessie admits.

"I obviously can't do anything without a canine peep show." I step into the skirt without removing my leggings. "It's a little tight."

"Take off the leggings," Jessie says as she sits on the bed and my dogs flock to her. "It's literally made to the quarter-inch for your curves." She gives me a sunny smile and turns her attention to Susan and Darcy. They jostle for position, the golden retriever muscling the Frenchie out of the way, as if she never gets any attention.

"Sorry," I say as I strip off the skirt and my leggings. "They have personal boundary issues."

"I love them." Jessie giggles as Susan starts licking her face. "You're the best doggy ever, aren't you?"

I step into the skirt without the leggings, and Jessie is right. And a genius. The skirt feels like it's made of the finest fabric in the world, and I turn to look at myself in the full-length mirror on the wall behind me.

"Wow," I say, fingering the folds of it. "Jess, I love this. Thank you."

"Do you want to try on the other one?"

"Of course." I do that, and they're both perfect. The second skirt is another floral pattern, but this one has leopard-spotted pockets on the front and back. It's eccentric and funky, just like Jessie.

"How much do I owe you?" I ask.

"Fifty?" Jess guesses. "That'll cover the fabric and notions."

"You should get paid for your time."

"They're the same pattern," she says. "One I added pockets to, and I get to see my fabric design in action." She grins and stands next to me as we gaze into the mirror together. "Who are you going out with?"

"Coy," I say before I can censor myself.

Jessie sucks in a breath, and while it's not a sigh, I can categorize gasps too. She's stunned. Shocked. Frozen in stun and shock.

"I know," I say. "We're..." I don't want to finish that sentence, because everything that comes after it feels negative.

"He's taking me to Bri's wedding," I say. "So we thought we'd try to...go out to...see if we can figure out how to get along." I don't tell her anything about The Kissing Incident, because I'm not sure how to put the hottest kiss of my life into words.

In my mind, I see Coy standing in his office this afternoon, his fingers rooted firmly between mine. When he'd pulled away, I'd felt something of mine go with him.

Jessie takes a breath, her arm linking through mine. "I hope it goes well for you."

"I have some good examples to look to." I meet her eyes in the mirror. "How's Lance?"

"Oh, he was Grumpy Gus today." She waves her free hand. "I left early to get away from him."

I laugh, because Lance and Jessie are wild about each other, even when he's grumpy about something at work. It makes me think that maybe Coy and I can be like them too. I think of that book he had on his desk today. I wish I'd been able to tame my tongue so I could see it for longer, but I hadn't. So I'd only gotten a glimpse, and my brain hadn't been able to come up with what it was.

"Let's find you a top," Jessie says, and she goes into my closet and starts looking through the hangers holding shirts there. I hang back and watch her, marveling at the things she picks. I wouldn't choose them at all, but after several minutes, she turns toward me with five or six options.

I let her play fashion designer and model dresser, trying on everything she gives me and letting her style it for me. She eventually declares a pink paisley-printed top with bell sleeves and a scalloped hem as the winner, and she asks, "Do you have a brown belt?"

Without waiting for me to answer, she ducks into the closet again. "I have a big, wide brown one," I say. "Hanging on the back of the door."

She returns with it only a moment later, and she cinches it around my waist. The bottom scallops of the pink top peek out below the belt, yet another thing I would've never done.

"Can you breathe okay?" she asks.

"Yes." I smooth my hands over my stomach and then the belt. "Jess, you're a genius."

"Can I do a video real quick?" she asks, already

pulling her phone out of her brown corduroy pants. They're cropped above her ankle, and she's wearing a peasant top in blue and white plaid with it.

"Sure," I say. "What do I do?"

She grins at me as she taps and swipes on her phone, seemingly without looking. "You strike some poses, and then turn around. I like to put up these styling videos without editing them, and they're less than a minute."

"Do I say anything?"

"Nope." Jess lifts her phone and levels it at me. "I narrate. Move away from the mirror."

I take a breath and move to the opposite wall, which holds a giant clock above my head but nothing else.

"Ready?"

"Yep." I nod and put my hands on my waist, cocking one knee forward and pushing my hip away from the camera. I know how to use my curves to my advantage, and I grin as Jessie does.

"Tonight, we have someone going out on a second date," she says. "The skirt is rayon, with the most gorgeous floral pattern on it. It's a statement piece, ladies, and we know what that means."

She whips the camera toward her and says right into it, "Don't detract from the statement piece. *Add* to it."

She flips the camera back to me, and I settle onto both feet and fold my arms.

"She has an amazing figure, which I chose to accentuate with a belt. That really brings in her waist and flares her hips, drawing attention *down* to the skirt. The top is perfect with the scalloped hem, but if you don't have that, it's fine. Just flare your blouse a little.

"We chose a dominate color with a print, because again, we're not trying to compete with the statement piece. We're trying to accentuate it. We could've gone green or blue or purple too, but this is what she had in her closet, and you know how I feel about that. Use what you have to the best advantage you can. Let's see the whole thing full-circle." She mimes for me to turn around, and I fly into motion.

I turn slowly as Jessie says, "Use those hips, ladies. Find clothes that fit and then you'll be ready for your next date!"

I face her again and she lowers the phone. "Thanks, Mace," she says. "That was awesome."

"I sort of zoned out listening to you," I say. "I love your videos." I step into her and hug her right as my doorbell rings.

Darcy, Justice, and Susan fly into combat mode, all three of them barking like the end of the world has arrived on my doorstep.

"Hush," I yell at them as they tear out of the bedroom, ready to bite jugulars if necessary. "It's just Coy."

I follow them down the hall and then shoo them into the living room and close the gate so they can't rush my date.

"I'll slip out after you go," Jessie says from down the hall.

"Okay. Thanks so much, Jess." I grin at her and then go to open my front door. I feel perfectly pieced together, and I can't wait to see Coy's reaction to my outfit.

I come face-to-face with him at the same time I realize I never finished my makeup.

A sigh hisses out of my mouth that says, *Sausage gumbo, why does this always happen to me?*

CHAPTER EIGHT

COY

"You look absolutely incredible," I say, my voice mimicking that of a hoarse amphibian. I haven't been talking to anyone for hours, but that's not the reason why.

It's *Macie.*

Macie in that skirt. That belt around her amazing waist. Her hair flowing over her shoulders. That pink top that makes everything else pink on her body scream at me to kiss it.

She throws her hands up and covers her face. "Don't look at me," she cries. Then she turns and quite literally runs away from me.

"Mace," I call after her as she rounds the corner. Three dogs stare at me from behind a gate at the end of the hall. Macie's effectively caged them in the living room, and the littlest one—a chihuahua—jumps up onto the couch and growls at me like I've come with a net to cart them away to a life of doggy doom.

I'm not sure if I can enter the house or not, and I lift my foot hesitantly. "Mace?"

To my surprise, Jessie Byers steps out of the hallway. She gestures me in with her hand and a happy smile. "Come on in, Coy," she says. "She just has to…" She looks over her shoulder and back to me.

I go in and close the door behind me. I'm holding a bouquet of dahlias, because those are Macie's favorite flower, and I look at them like they've turned into aliens.

"Did you see her?" Jessie asked.

Oh, I'd seen her. But I'm not sure how to answer the question. "For like two-point-seven seconds," I say. "What was that about?"

"She only had makeup on half her face," Jessie says in a voice I can barely hear. "Pretend you didn't see, okay?"

"I didn't see," I say. Macie's deliciously curvy body had effectively distracted me from her makeup—or lack thereof.

Jessie gives me a quick hug, careful not to smash the flowers, pats the dogs as she says goodbye to them, and then she says, "Have fun tonight," before she exits the house.

I look down the hall in the direction Macie scampered, but I don't see anything but doors. My eyes meet the dogs' again, and since I know they're all bark and no bite, I step over to them.

"She cages you in here, huh?" I say to them, easily stepping over the baby gate she's set up between a coffee table and the edge of a loveseat.

Susan the golden retriever sniffs me furiously while the little chihuahua does the same, stretched out as far as she can from the couch cushions.

"Hey, Justice," I say to her as I sit beside her on the couch. Darcy puts his velvet paws on my knee, his cute little scrunched Frenchie face begging me to lift him up.

I do, not expecting him to be quite so solid. "Wow," I say as I put him next to me. "You need to go on a diet."

"Did you just call my dog fat?" Macie demands.

I jump to my feet, colliding with Susan, the golden retriever, as she tries to jump up onto the couch.

We basically do a chest bump, but ten times harder, and one of us is a sixty-pound canine.

I go flying backward and Susan yelps like I've chopped off one of her paws for sport. My nose stings, and I instantly reach up for it. I moan as the tinny taste of blood touches the back of my throat.

"You poor thing," Macie says, and the gate comes down. "Oh, no. Are you okay?"

My eyes water, and my humiliation doubles when Macie goes to her dog instead of me.

Irritation fires through me, and I push myself down the couch, dislodging more dogs in my haste to get away from stainable things.

"I'm just great," I say as I stand. Blood steadily drips

into my hands, cupped as they are under my nose. I hurry into her kitchen and lean over the sink. There's not a dish to be found. Nothing sits out of place whatsoever, and it reminds me of how tightly she runs the coffee shop.

When there aren't customers, she has our people clean. There's always something that needs to be refilled, replenished, shined spotless, or soaked.

Dog claws clatter on the hard floor, clearly the gait of a big dog. I look down at the golden furball, who's obviously fine. "Sorry, Suzie," I say.

"She doesn't like to be called Suzie," Macie reminds me.

I look down at *Susan*, who wears the smiling face of all golden retrievers. "Yeah, she looks irate," I gripe. "Do you have something I can use that I can throw away?" I cut a look at Macie out of the corner of my eye.

"Oh, fish and chips." She sucks in a breath. "You're bleeding."

"Glad you noticed."

She flies into action, grabbing a roll of paper towels and shoveling them at me like I need a hundred of them for a nosebleed.

"Okay," I say after I take three from her. "This will do."

Macie wears panic on her face, and she clutches the roll of paper towels to her chest. "Sorry," she murmurs.

I hold the paper towels to my face and lean my head

back. I'm sure I have blood clinging to my nostrils and probably my upper lip, so I ask, "Bathroom?"

"Down the hall, first right." She takes me by the arm and leads me that way, the tension between us turning to fireworks. She leaves me in the bathroom, and I lower the paper towel to my worst nightmare.

Okay, fine, that's dramatic, but I am bloody from nose to chin. Nothing water won't fix, so I flip on her sink and start getting cleaned up.

With that done, I wash my hands and reach for one of her pristine, robin's egg blue towels. I approach the doorway and hear her talking.

"...jump like that, you devil," she says. "You guys have to stop acting like every noise and person who comes is going to claw out your throats."

I smile at her dog lecture, my chest expanding in a satisfied way that she's standing up for me.

"He's a nice guy," she says next, and that lifts my eyebrows. "I want him to come back, so no barking. No jumping. Personal space boundaries."

Something scrapes, and I leap away from the door, rehang her towel the best I can, and exit the bathroom.

Macie has re-caged the canines in the living room, and she tugs nervously on the scalloped end of her shirt. "Hey," she says. "I'm so sorry. Susan has some..." She flicks her eyes to the dogs, all of whom look properly chastised. "Issues."

"We all do," I say, and I drink in the beauty of her face

when she turns it toward me again. I step toward her, easily sliding my hand along that wide belt that marks her waist so well.

"I'm not sure you heard me, but I said you looked amazing when you first came to the door."

She fiddles with the collar on my shirt. "Did you now?"

We sway slightly, and I swear the entire earth has been knocked off its axis. "I did. You're gorgeous, and this belt..."

Macie's eyebrows go up. "The belt?"

"All of it." I step back, sensing I've identified the wrong piece of clothing. "The skirt is absolutely stunning."

That gets her to smile, and I feel like I just dodged a landmine.

"Jessie made it," she said. "It's her fabric design too."

"It's incredible," I say, swallowing the rest of my words. I've already told her—three times—how good she looks. My mouth is practically watering.

I gesture toward the door, because being in her house feels very intimate all of a sudden. "Should we go?"

"Yes." She precedes me down the hall. "How did closing go?"

"Just fine," I tell her, though one of the dishwashers in the back had blown a gasket and started spraying water everywhere. Four batches of muffins had been soaked, but Talia and Jean had agreed to stay for another hour and remake them. I fixed the pipe and hose single-handedly, and in only minutes too.

Macie won't even know when she shows up in the morning. Her wind and rain seems semi-blown out tonight, a lot like her hair, which is even more gorgeous draping over her shoulders in those soft waves. My fingers itch to touch it, but I settle for letting her step outside and following her down to the sidewalk before I take her hand in mine.

She glances over to me, and my heart plays leapfrog with itself for three-point-two seconds and two-point-five steps before it settles back to normal.

That coincides with the fact that she slides her hand further into mine instead of pulling away. The cement in front of me is smooth and even, the normal lines in it from being poured years ago. But it feels like it might crumble and disintegrate at any moment. After all, this is such new ground for Macie and I.

"This is your car?" she asks as we approach the black sedan parked on the curb. She has a big driveway, but there had been an SUV parked there, and I hadn't recognized it. I didn't think Macie had a roommate, but I don't know everything about her yet.

"Yes." I reach to open the door for her. "It's a bit of a drop down, I'll admit."

"You have two cars." Before I can respond, she eases into the car without a problem, which only heats my blood back over the boiling point.

I close the door and take a deep breath. "Keep it together, Coy," I mutter to myself. I go around the back of the car to give myself a minute to pull at my collar and take another couple of breaths before I have to confine myself with her perfume...and her.

"It's not torture," I whisper, thinking of how she made it sound like this late dinner at Drake's would be just be okay.

It's going to be great. I called and got my car detailed while it sat in the parking lot behind Legacy, and as I sink into the leather driver's seat, I get a noseful of the vanilla and butterscotch that's left behind.

"This is a nice car," she says. Her eyes are wide and innocent as they meet mine.

"It was a gift from my mother," I say as I start the ignition.

"Wow. For my last birthday, my daddy sent me a card with thirty-two dollars in it." She adjusts her seatbelt across her chest. "One for every year I've been alive." A fond smile touches her face, the emotion of it striking me in the chest.

"What would your mama have given you?" I ask.

She whips her attention to me again, and I'm pretty sure she thinks I'm on the offensive. I do my best to smile as I say, "If my daddy were still alive, I think he'd have given me an airplane ticket to go with him to Venezuela, so we could taste-test the beans and consider bringing them back to Charleston." I ease away from the curb, both hands on the wheel.

Macie gently coaxes one of them away, and I gladly give it to her. "My mama loved to make custom items for people," she says. When she speaks of her mother, all of her bluster is gone, almost like the woman stole her thunder when she died. "So I'd probably have gotten a wreath for my front door. Or a whole set of them." She smiles. "Once, she made me a set of a dozen gnomes, one for each month of the year, for my non-existent front garden." She giggles, regaining some of her fire and fierceness. "I was living in an apartment at the time, you see."

"Mm." I reach for my cherry Chapstick, sure if I use it now, the slight taste will be gone before dinner arrives.

"You love that stuff," Macie says as I cover my top lip.

I see no reason to deny it. "Yeah," I say.

"Why?" She takes the tube from me after I cap it. For some reason, watching her hold something I smear on my mouth heats me from the inside out.

"Uh..." I glance over to her. "It's how I gear myself up for, uh, battle."

"Battle?" Her eyes hold amusement, and I look back to the road so I don't crash us into a ditch. Or another car. "We're going to dinner."

"It's just something I do to feel...more...in control."

"Like a habit or a ritual."

"Sure," I say.

"Like Callie's power panties."

I choke, because I'm not well-versed in anyone's underwear, least of all Callie's. Macie giggles and says, "I'll tell you about it later."

"Oh-kay."

Silence flows over us now, and it's not so bad. Most of the time, the silence between us is filled with angry words and tension, so this is definitely an improvement.

Macie lives in Sugar Creek, and it's a quick trip to Drake's which is on the northwest side of Charleston, barely into the city at all. I like the fringe eateries, bars, and breweries—they remind me of Legacy—but Drake's isn't an unknown dive.

The lot is full, and I'd called and gotten a reservation by pulling some strings, despite tonight being a non-weekend evening.

"It's jazz night," I say as I pull into a spot behind the restaurant. "There's a quartet here." I look over to her, and she smiles.

"I love live music," she says.

"Do you?" That's something I don't know about her. "What's another thing you love I don't know about?"

Macie immediately ducks her head, and my default is to let her recede. Rather, she usually stomps back to her office, and I slam my door, and we don't speak again until one of us *has* to in order to keep Legacy running.

But I don't want to do that with her anymore. "Hey." I touch her chin, and she lifts it. "I know this is a little weird, but we're..."

Dating is what I want to say, but I'm not sure that's one hundred percent true. She needed a date to a wedding, and I volunteered. She said we might as well not wait two months to go out. So here we are.

It's not really fake, but it might not be real either.

"We're what?" she asks.

"You tell me what," I say. Someone has squeezed glue down my throat, and I can't get more words out. I want to ask her what that kiss meant in the coffee shop, months ago. I want to ask her why she suggested we go out now when she didn't have to do that. I want to know what she thinks we are.

She looks away, her jaw tightening.

"Yeah," I say as I unbuckle my seatbelt. "That's about where I am." I open my door and add, "Stay right there. I'll come help you out of this low-rider."

I love my luxury sedan, but it does ride right on the ground. Macie wasn't wearing heels when I picked her up, but that doesn't mean it's going to be easy for her to get out of the car in that form-fitting skirt.

I open the door and offer her my hand. She takes it and rises from the matte black car like a phoenix rising from the ashes.

"Coy," she says, stepping right into my chest. She puts a hand there and looks at her own fingers. I keep my head tipped down, her sweet scent of powder, hair spray, and toothpaste clouding my senses in the best way possible.

"I'd say I think we're trying," she says, almost to herself.

"So I won't introduce you as my girlfriend," I whisper back.

She looks at me, her eyes open to the idea, but her voice absolutely silent.

"Yet," I say.

"But we're not pretending, like Callie and Dawson or Tara and Alec," she says. "Right?"

I think of that kiss on that orange couch. "I'm not pretending," I assure her.

She nods and finally inches past me and out of the way so I can close her door. Macie usually isn't quiet about things, but this dark, building storm is almost as sexy as the way she blusters.

I'm a couple of steps behind her, but I swear I hear her say, "I'm not either," in a voice that I'd label as scared.

I wish I could see down this road we're on, because if we try and fail... Things won't be pretty at Legacy Brew, and I won't jeopardize my coffee house for anything.

Not even for Macie? my mind whispers.

I obviously am, and I reason as I move to her side that we've never gotten along as well as we are right now. A break-up will just land us back where we were when I showed up in the middle of the night at the coffee shop, found her crying on the couch, and kissed her.

CHAPTER NINE

MACIE

I'm eternally glad I've laced my arm through Coy's before we enter Drake's. The first person I come face-to-face with is Ethan Boggs, and my feet grow roots and stop right where they are.

Coy twists back to me, surprise etching itself along his eyebrows. "Mace?"

"Macie!" Another man's voice drowns out any response I might've come up with. Before I can pull up the roots and regain my composure, I'm knocked backward by the beefy body of my ex-boyfriend's brother.

Yeah, Ethan has always been a little over-the-top. A little over-eager. A lot in love with me.

I can't believe he works here.

"Ethan," I say as diplomatically as I can. We're still careening backward, and I stumble under his added weight, praying someone or something will stop us before I fall. The door behind me does that, and I grunt as my back meets it.

I blink, trying to get my bearings, and my eyes meet Coy's. His are narrowed, and I must give off enough *help me* vibes for him to get it. He comes over—I've been knocked back at least five steps—and says, "Macie, sugar, are you okay?" in an ultra-sexy, twice-as-low voice than he normally speaks in.

That gets Ethan off of me, and I feel like everything I worked so hard to put together has been knocked loose. I straighten my belt, tugging the hem of my shirt into place, then pat my hair and look from Ethan to Coy.

"Coy," I say. "This is Ethan Boggs." I'm not sure if he knew Andy's last name, as nothing registers on his face. "Ethan, this is Coy Cochran."

I give neither of them identifiers or labels, and the absence of them—especially for Coy—screams into the busy, bustling restaurant. I swear everyone has stopped eating and drinking to focus on the three of us, and I clear my throat when neither one of them says anything.

"I believe we have a reservation." I step to Coy's side and take his hand in mine, praying he'll know that right now, I definitely want to be his girlfriend.

"Yes." He clears his throat. "We do. Eight-fifty."

"Ethan, I didn't know you worked here," I say as he goes back to the podium. His face bears some redness, but he's perfectly polite—not at all the bowling ball he'd been thirty seconds ago—as he faces us with two menus. "I started a few months ago," he says.

I nod, because Andy left last summer, and I'd have no reason to keep in touch with Ethan. "That's great. Do you like it better than that delivery company you were with?"

"Yes." His face brightens. "You remember that?"

My pulse flits through my body, but I nod anyway. "Yeah, sure." I look over to Coy. "Coy and I own Legacy Brew together."

Ethan's eyebrows fly up. "You do?" He looks between the two of us.

"I bought into it last year," I say, quite proud of it. I love that coffee shop with everything I have, and the shrill ring of doubt about me and Coy sounds in my head once again. I tell myself that I just need a date for Bri's wedding, and if I don't have to spend every night alone between now and then, why not spend them with Coy?

"Wow, I'm starving," Coy says, and Ethan jerks to attention.

"This way," he says, taking off at a near jog through tables and booths.

"Smooth," I mutter to Coy.

"He was standing there, staring at you," he grumbles back. "Who is that guy?"

So he can't read my mind or my mood quite yet. Well, my mood he probably can.

I don't answer as I navigate through the restaurant, with its dark woods and rich carpet, to the booth Ethan's standing beside. I slide in first, and he hands me an open menu. "Dalton will be your waiter tonight," he says. "He's assisted by a new waitress, Rosa." He hands Coy his menu, turns on his heel, and marches away.

I sigh, this one holding all kinds of past pains I don't want to bring up. I'm going to have to talk about The Kissing Incident, and I'm actually surprised Coy hasn't asked about it. He brought it up on our first date, but the conversation moved quickly, and we never really resolved things.

With a jolt of white hot fear that feels like being struck by lightning, I realize I'm on a date with him. A *date*. I used to kiss men at the end of my dates. Once that physical barrier is broken, I'll kiss before, during, and after a date. When I see my boyfriend at work, on the street, in the grocery store.

Another sigh tells me how much I miss kissing. I love the intimacy of it. The way a mouth can say so much without saying anything at all. I want to know what Coy's will say, and a needy desperation coils within me.

"Okay." I reach for my silverware, which is wrapped in a dark navy cloth. As I spread the napkin across my lap, I look down, which makes talking to Coy easier. "Remember Andy? That guy I was dating last year?"

"Yes," Coy growls out.

"That's his younger brother." I wave in the general direction that Ethan went in. "He has—*had*—a bit of a crush on me. That's all."

"He practically knocked you down." Coy settles his own napkin on his lap and looks at me again. "You and Andy must've been serious for you to have such a close relationship with his siblings."

I shift slightly in my seat, the skirt and belt suddenly too tight. "Uh, yeah." I look out at the other patrons of this restaurant. I've been here before, but only a couple of times, because this place is fancy, and I'm not really a fancy-type woman. The low, yellow lights, the way the whole place is cast in shadows, I can almost pretend Coy can't see me.

"That night you found me in the coffee shop? On the couch?" I don't dare look at him, and he says nothing. "I thought Andy was going to propose that night. Instead, he told me he'd moved to Pennsylvania to start a new job."

The anger of that situation licks through me hot enough to churn up some courage. "He broke up with me, and I slunk back to the shop. That's why I didn't want...to kiss you again."

He blinks, but otherwise, his face remains smooth, impassive. "And now?"

"Now what?"

"Do you want to kiss me again?" He folds his arms on the table in front of him, his dark eyes dancing with something dangerous and delightful.

I know how to play this game, with men like him. I actually really love playing like this. "Wouldn't you like to know?" I fire back at him.

He starts to chuckle, the sound growing and growing. I give him a satisfied smile and sit back in the booth just as our waiter arrives with his protégé.

Our flirt fest gets put on hold while we order wine and appetizers. The moment the waiter and his trainee leave, I lean forward again. "What about you?"

"What about me?"

"Come on." I grin at him, glad I've used my Berrylicious lip gloss tonight. It will make my lips look like ripe raspberries in this light, and I suddenly see why using something on my mouth makes me feel more in control. In fact, Coy drops his gaze to my mouth for a couple of beats of time before they lift back to meet my eyes.

"Who have you been out with in recent years?" I don't remember him dating anyone in at least the past five years, but I haven't really been paying attention to Coy's love life.

He laces his fingers together. "I haven't dated much, to be honest." He lifts one powerful shoulder, drawing my attention there. His phone starts to vibrate before I can figure out how to flirt with him next, and he flips it over.

"It's my mother." He looks up, an edge of fear in his eyes now. "This will take ten seconds if I answer. If I don't…"

"Go ahead," I say. "I'll keep."

Coy slides on the call at the same time he slides out of the booth. "Momma," he manages to say before a busboy is on top of him.

Men grunt. Soda slops. Silverware clinks and clanks. Plates clatter. Glasses break.

The entire black tub of dirty dishes falls to the ground right at the end of our booth, and something cold and wet splashes my bare legs.

I cry out, not sure if I should scoot further into the booth or get out. I can't really get out, because the busboy has just dropped to his knees at the end of my bench.

Coy groans, then exhales in a gust of air. A mighty sigh of frustration.

My eyes catch up to the situation as the noise disappears. The conversation has indeed stopped now, and all eyes are on me. I quickly realize that's not true.

They're on Coy, who isn't standing up any longer. They're watching the busboy and the two other waiters who rush over to help.

He says, "I'll call you back," and his hand lands on the end of the table. His body follows, and he adds, "I'm so sorry. It was my fault. I didn't even look before standing up."

He stands there helplessly as everyone who works for Drake's assures him and reassures him that he's fine.

To my horror, Ethan returns with an older gentleman, and I wonder if Coy and I will ever be able to have a decent date. One filled with delicious wine and starry skies, lots of good food and coffee and chocolate cake as the clock strikes midnight.

I can make that happen, and a plan formulates in my

head as the older gentleman says, "I'm so sorry, you two. I think we should move you to a new table. Would you come with me, please?"

The busboy moves out of the way, and I manage to get out of the booth. I look down at my legs, finding bright red liquid slowly crawling down my left calf.

I look up at Coy, whose gaze rebounds from down to up, meeting my eyes. He turns instantly to the staff there and says, "We need something to wipe down with, please."

"We can just go," I murmur to him. I hope with everything I have that my skirt isn't ruined. It's a dark background, and the flower pattern makes it hard to tell what should be red and pink and what shouldn't be.

I balance on my left toe, like I can't put weight on my leg because it has soda pop on it.

"No," Coy says, taking me under his arm and pulling me to his side. "We'll take another table, and a couple of hot cloths, and we'll be fine." He nods like he's spoken it, and therefore it will be so.

The older gentleman consults with Ethan quickly, and then looks at us with bright hope in his eyes. "Right this way."

We're led to another table, and our waiter arrives without missing a beat, setting down my red wine and Coy's Diet Coke.

"Those appetizers are on their way," he says. "Are you ready to order?"

I haven't brought my menu with me, but I know what I

want. "I'd love the chicken pot pie," I say. "With the creamy mashed potatoes, please."

"That comes with seasonal veggies or a house salad," Dalton says, looking at the woman at his side. "So we ask them which they want. If she hadn't said what potato she wanted, we'd ask that too."

The woman nods, frantically scribbling on her menu pad. "Veggies or salad."

I smile at them. "What are the seasonal veggies?"

Dalton looks at Rose, and she nearly comes out of her skin. Then she blinks and snaps back to what she knows. I've seen so many people do this while working at Legacy Brew, and I see Rose in every young woman I hire. I see myself in her.

"Tonight, the chefs have broccoli, cauliflower, and zucchini," she says. "They're prepped with a little lemon zest and a touch of chicken broth. Delicious."

I love a salad with a lot of ranch dressing, so I'm torn. I cock my head like it's a really hard decision and finally say, "I'll take the veggies."

"What else do you want?" Coy asks. "The salad?"

"I do love a good salad," I tell him with that flirty smile playing with my lips.

"She'll have a house salad too," he says, and before I can protest, he adds, "With ranch dressing, I'm guessing." His eyebrows go up, and I nod.

Warmth fills my chest as he orders a steak sandwich

with French fries and extra horseradish, and I contain my surprise until the waitstaff leaves.

"Horseradish?" I ask. "I didn't know you had a spicy tongue."

"You didn't?" He grins at me. "I know you beat me most of the time, but I've bested you a time or two in our arguments."

"A time or two?" I scoff in mock protest. He's won way more than that, you know, if I was keeping track. Which I'm not.

Holy smoked salmon. I'm *flirting* hardcore with Coy Cochran.

I slide my hands across the table, clearly inviting him to hold them. He does, the movement easy and natural. "I don't want us to be weird at work," I say, letting some of my worries come out of my mouth.

"But I also don't want to introduce you as the man I co-own the coffee shop with."

He nods, most of the sly look in his eye gone. It still rides in his lips, but he straightens those in the next moment. "Yeah, I didn't like that either."

"I also think we should stay in next time we go out."

"Stay in...when we go out?"

"Yes," I say. "I'll cook for you."

His eyebrows go up, and his hands tighten around mine. "You cook?"

"Believe it or not."

"You're not going to poison me, are you?"

"Coy." I tilt my head to the side. "You don't really mean that, do you?"

"No," he says.

"Because I haven't poisoned a boyfriend before." I wait to see if he notices the label I've given him, and boy, does he.

He inhales wrong and starts to cough and choke, releasing my hands to lift his cola to his lips. His face has gone to the color of a red, ripe tomato, and I'm not sure why. We've been skirting this topic all night.

He touches me like a boyfriend would. He dresses the way a boyfriend would. He stands up for me and orders for me the way a boyfriend would.

Are you going to kiss him the way you would a boyfriend?

That's the question of the evening, and when my eyes lock on Coy's again, I'm positive he's wondering the same thing.

CHAPTER TEN

COY

I'm back in front of Macie's house, and while our date started out pretty rocky, what with the bloody nose, and then the meeting of her ex's brother, and then me literally bringing Drake's to a halt.

But it's had a pretty fantastic couple of hours since then. Easy conversation, with plenty of flirting on both sides, and the clock is already nearing midnight.

"I'm sorry I kept you out so late," I say.

"You should be," she fires back. "I have to be up and at the shop in about six hours."

"I'll come in and help you so opening goes faster."

She leans her head back against the rest and smiles. "It's fine, Coy. I had a great time."

"So did I." My mouth is having a hard time curving upward, and I tell myself to get out of the car. Now. I do, and I help her to her feet too. "I'm not going to drive away until you're inside, safe and sound."

She laughs lightly, though I know she's tired. I look up to her front door, the porch mocking me. Can I kiss her right here? What if I lean in, and she stops me?

Then she stops you, I tell myself. It won't be the end of the world, and I won't have to end things with her. Maybe she's just not ready to kiss me again.

I'm so ready to taste her again. She teased me with that passionate union all those months ago, and I'm pretty sure I've been dying a slow death every day since.

Without her lips on mine, there's not enough air in my lungs. Without kissing her, I'm never satisfied, even after I've eaten an enormous meal.

My nerves assault me, telling me not to try, because we might crash and burn. I go up the steps, her hand in mine. She steps over to the keypad on her door and types in a six-digit code. The lock disengages.

Macie turns back to me, and I take her into my arms in one fluid movement. "I keep dreaming of the day we'll be able to go out without blood, other bodily fluids, dish catastrophes, or honking on the date."

I smile at her, my heartbeat sprinting like a thoroughbred horse rounding the last lap of the Kentucky Derby. I'm in the front, and if I can just hold on for a little bit longer, I'll win.

My arms draw her closer and closer, then I lean down. I've kissed women before, and when they tip their head back to receive me, I'm fairly certain they want to kiss me too.

Macie does that, and I close the last few inches to her, praying I don't crash and burn on this kiss. I've dreamed about it for so long, and I've lost so much sleep going over and over and over that kiss in the coffee shop.

Her lips are soft and full, matching up with mine exactly right. She tastes like the butter mint we got after our meal, with a hint of fruitiness from the wine, and the vanilla from the ice cream we had with an enormous piece of chocolate cake.

I stroke my mouth against hers again and again, not able to get enough now that I've started. She kisses me back the same way she did in the shop months ago. Like she's got so much to say and no way to say it unless our mouths are touching.

The kiss continues, both of us pouring everything we have into it, the same way we do at Legacy Brew. Nothing she does is ever small or quiet, and I'm just trying to keep up with her.

We pull apart simultaneously, and with my heartbeat prancing through every part of my body, I whisper, "So this is not pretend."

"No," she whispers back.

I touch my mouth to hers again, my eyelids fluttering at the tender, sweet way she kisses me back. There's no roaring wind this time. No race to the finish line. The sweet version of kissing Macie is almost hotter than the passionate one.

"I pull away again and slide my lips along her cheek to her jawline. She tips her head back to allow me a kiss there, and I say, "And we're not just trying."

She doesn't say anything, and I quickly add, "I mean, of course that's what we're doing. When you're dating someone, you're trying to determine if you'll be able to..." I pause, because I can't say what's on my mind.

You're trying to determine if you'll be able to fall in love. Live with that person forever.

Yeah, I was one-point-four seconds away from saying that, but no.

"We're dating," she says.

I smile as I touch my mouth to her neck. "I guess what I'm saying is, it's not temporary." I lift my head and open my eyes. Macie's take another moment to do the same, and then she meets my gaze. "We're not just trying on a dress so we can go to Bri's wedding together." I clear my throat. "So you'll have a date, I mean."

She searches my face. "Coy." She's really asking me so many questions by saying my name like that.

She brought up the kissing in the shop already tonight, and I figure I didn't crash and burn by taking her kiss tonight, so talking about it again can't be all that bad.

"I kissed you in the shop last year." I start to sway with her right there on her front porch. It's a good thing she lives in a sleepy suburb, or her neighbors would've gotten a show tonight.

"Because I've, uh, been harboring a secret crush on you for a couple of years." I lean my head to kiss her again, but her palm lands on my chest, and she pushes me back.

"A couple of years?" Her eyes widen and start storming. "You're not serious."

"Five, actually," I say. "Five-point-one years exactly."

She blinks—blinks—blinks. "Tell me that's a lie."

I swallow, my voice gone, leaving me to shake my head. *Not lying.*

"Coy." She steps out of my arms and toward the door.

"I don't like how you went from 'Coy' to 'Coy.'" The difference in the way she's said my name is noticeable, and the disdain in the last one rings in the air between us.

She reaches for the doorknob as she gives me a withering glare. She twists and pushes, her body going with the motion of the door swinging in.

Except the door doesn't swing in. She barges right into it, yelps, and immediately ducks her head and cradles her face. "My nose."

It's really not funny, and thankfully, I manage to turn my laugh into a cough. "I don't think we'll ever have a date without blood," I say. "Tip your head back. Let me see."

She reluctantly does, but she's not spewing blood the way I did earlier tonight. I can hardly believe that all happened *tonight*. I feel like Macie and I have traversed several continents in the past few hours alone.

"It hurts," she says, lowering her head.

"It's not bleeding." I offer her a small smile. "Don't be mad."

She keys in the code on her door again, and the lock untwists. She opens the door, and that causes her canine crime lords to go into full Bark Mode.

"Hush, you idiots," she calls down the hall to them. "It's just me." She steps into the house, and I follow, because I don't want her to end the date like this.

Why we can't just have a normal experience together, I don't know. "Macie," I try again.

She faces me, unrest on that pretty face.

"Don't be mad for too long, okay?"

Her jaw hardens and juts out, but she says, "Okay."

"Why are you mad anyway?" I put my palm against her door, which causes her little chihuahua to send growling my way.

"Really, Coy?" She cocks that sexy hip, and my mouth goes dry.

I slide my hand along the top of it. "Yeah," I say. "Really."

"Don't talk to me in that sexy, low voice," she scolds. "You've had a crush on me for years? *Five* years?"

I simply stuff my hands in my pockets and wait for her to go on. She will, I'm sure.

"But you've rejected my ideas for twice that long," she says, the storm really picking up speed now. "You've been barking at every man I've ever gone out with, but never been man enough to ask me out yourself." She shakes her head, that curled hair swinging with the motion. "And not only that, but you refused to let me come on as a partner at Legacy until you were literally days away from having to close the doors. It's insane. You're insane."

She steps back, and my hand falls to my side. "Not all of us have your fire," I say.

"Don't you dare," she says. "You have plenty of fire, Coy. You've shot it at me over and over in the past *five* years." She starts to close the door, but our date can't end like this.

"Macie, come on."

"I just need to think."

"You don't like to be alone while you think."

That gets her to stall the motion of closing the door. Her eyes go wide again, then narrow just as fast. I'm about to be skewered, and I'm actually craving it. Then she won't walk away mad and stuff silence between us. I'm so tired of the tense silence between us.

"We always do this," I say, gesturing between us. "We argue and spit insults at each other, and then you stomp into your office. I pace in mine. Eventually, we come together again, and I don't want you to be stormy and silent until you forgive me." It's insane that she has to *forgive me* for liking her! Insane.

Her big dog down the hall barks, and Macie jumps. "I won't be mad for very long," she says.

I try grinning at her again, and she actually softens.

"Thank you," I say. "So we can go out this weekend? I didn't talk to my mother, but I bet she wants me and Anna Lee to go out there tomorrow night. It's a weekly thing."

She nods, and a new level of exhaustion sweeps across her face. Nothing I say now will do me any good, because when Macie is tired, she doesn't hear me.

"Okay," I say. "I'm still awaiting a date where one of us doesn't fall, doesn't start bleeding, and there is no mowing down of busboys."

She returns my smile, and wow, I'm going to see that softness in her eyes, the tenderness in her entire countenance, every night before I fall asleep. She only fuels my fantasies, and I need to get off this porch before I say or do something stupid.

"I won't come in tomorrow morning," I say. "I know that'll annoy you and throw off your routine."

"I like my routines," she says with a touch of defensiveness in her voice.

I step up into her house, my feet barely fitting in front of hers. Her dogs go nuts, but both of us ignore them.

"I know you do, doll. That's why I won't disrupt them." I hold onto her waist and kiss her forehead, then her cheek, and then her chin. She makes a soft sound I can't quite categorize in the moment.

"I'll see you tomorrow." I back up, putting distance between us, and when she doesn't move, I reach to bring the door closed the rest of the way. That gets her to retreat into her own house, a somewhat dumbfounded look on her face.

She must snap out of it quickly, because the lock engages. I smile to myself and practically skip back to my car. I really want to show up at Legacy in the morning and do all the things Macie would before she arrives.

I won't, because I'm already walking on shattered ground with her, and if I can prevent a misstep, I will. It's the ones I don't know are missteps—like crushing on her for so long—that make the relationship a battlefield.

"But it's a relationship, Coy," I murmur to myself as I pull away from the curb. "It's not temporary, and it's not fake."

It could be everything I want, everything I've been dreaming about all this time, but I don't vocalize that quite yet. My bearded dragons will hear all about it when I get home, but for now, I sit with the fantasy and let it bloom into something bigger than I've allowed myself previously.

CHAPTER ELEVEN

MACIE

I know Coy is hiding something in his office, so when I show up at the shop the next morning, I get all settled in my office first. Put my purse in the slim closet behind the door. Hang my hoodie on the back of my chair. Tie on a clean Legacy Brew apron.

I'm tired, but not the bone-weary kind of tired. The keyed-up kind of tired. The kind that a cup of coffee will only enhance. The kind that speaks of the knee-melting kiss I got last night.

It took me a long time to fall asleep, partly because of the kiss, partly because of Coy's confession after the kiss, and partly because Darcy-the-Diva had found a package of fruit snacks under the couch and eaten them, plastic bag and all.

I really need a doggy door, so I don't have to get up

and let her out every hour as she has gastrointestinal issues.

Normally, I don't leave the dogs locked in the living room area, but I'd forgotten to take down the gate before I'd left last night.

"Last night." The words come out like a sigh. Without Susan body-slamming Coy, or Ethan at the restaurant, or the busboy collision, it probably was the most perfect date in the world. At least the best one I've been on in a few years.

All of these happy, sunshiny, cotton candy thoughts cease as I leave my office and face Coy's door. I glance over my shoulder like he'll be there. He's not. Even Janice and Kathleen aren't here yet. I always arrive first, and I love these first few minutes in the shop where I'm alone.

I feel the calmest in the pre-dawn moments I have here, and I push past the little voice in my head telling me to leave Coy alone. He'll tell me and show me what he was doing when he's ready.

"He may never be ready," I say to the dormant back of the house. After all, he's liked me for years and never said anything. All signs pointed to the complete opposite, in fact.

The doorknob doesn't turn, just as I suspected it wouldn't. I sigh anyway, the mighty sound of a defeated woman.

I turn away from the disappointing door and go about my opening routine. Check the front of the house. The vacuum lines in the rug around the couches and chairs make me smile.

The tables are wiped clean, and I take the refilled and ready containers of sugar and sugar substitute packets to each one, straightening the already aligned chairs as I go.

If Coy were here, he'd see how I do pause by the door and take in Legacy Brew as a whole, the way a customer would. The queue line is marked by a chest-high brick wall, the top of which is dust-free. The floor is swept and mopped. Our pastry case gets lit up with the flip of a switch, and right now, it sits empty and waiting for its delights.

Our machines are partially hidden by a counter that goes up, and on top of that, we place our hot options. Quiches, bread pudding, and ham and cheese kolaches.

Then the registers. I check to make sure there are pens in the holders, our special coffee-of-the-month mats in place, and nothing there that shouldn't be.

The pick-up counter is beyond that, and it's been sanitized already. The flavorings bar has every bottle in its holder, all the packets neat and straight and full, and I sigh once again.

This one is filled with contentment. I love this place, and I want everyone who walks through the door to love it too.

Behind the counter, Coy's made sure his night crew has cleaned and left everything ready for me this morning. For some reason, a smile comes to my face and stays as I start the first pots of coffee. No one wants to walk into a coffee shop that doesn't smell like coffee.

I always brew Coy's favored Columbian brew first thing in the morning, though it's not our customers' favorite blend. It is the strongest, and it gets people in the mood for their iced teas and coffees, their lattes, and their cappuccinos.

We sell a lot of regular cups of coffee in the morning, and I get three more pots brewing with the blend out of Indonesia—the kind I drink all day long—and one of decaf with a blend from Hawaii.

I start moving back and forth between the back of the house and the front, and I have the pastry case full before my bakers arrive. They chatter with each other, and I usually join in.

Today, I don't. Coy had been right last night that I don't like to think alone. I usually call Bri or Tara, but last night, I hadn't. It was too late, number one. Maybe not for Tara, who owns her own catering company and often works late nights.

Still. I wasn't going to call her immediately and ask her what to do about Coy. I quietly start freaking out again, and I take a deep breath to calm the rising emotion.

The machines are humming and blinking, ready to dispense hot water for tea, and warm milk for a majority of our drinks. We offer cow's milk, almond milk, and coconut milk, as well as pure cream for those who want a shot of perfection in their dark roast.

I'm craving a macchiato this morning, and I pause to make one hot before the rest of my staff gets here. I love the way the hot milk mellows the strong shots of coffee, and sometimes I go off the beaten path and add whipped cream instead of milk foam.

Today, I do neither. I could add a squirt of hazelnut from the flavorings bar, and that would be heaven. I don't, instead simply lifting the hot drink to my lips and inhaling the warm, earthy, rich scent of coffee that further soothes my soul.

It's like stepping into the warmest, calmest bath when you're freezing and feeling wildly out of control.

"We're all here, Mace," Janice says, and I turn toward her.

"Great," I say. "Staff meeting out here, please. Will you get everyone?" I glance around, realizing that Shawny and Belle have already set up their registers. The cups are stacked high beside the machines and canisters.

We're ready for another day of battle. While Janice tells the kitchen I need them for a moment, I press my palm to the line of switches in the shop. Light floods the space, and again, I can't help smiling.

Even if my nose is a little sore. Even if I need to hire someone today or I'll have to work on my days off. Even if Coy didn't own up to his feelings before I got my heart broken by Andy.

That's not his fault.

"Macie?" Janice says.

I blink out of my thoughts. "Thanks for being on time, everyone," I say. I smile around at all of them. They're clean and crisp in their black-from-head-to-toe clothes. Their Legacy aprons hang perfectly around their necks, and they're all wearing the deep purple ones we use on Tuesdays.

We use several different iterations of our brand, and Shawny wears one with the round, official logo, but Belle's apron says, "Where coffee meets destiny."

It's a slogan Coy's father came up with years and years ago, and a strong sense of nostalgia engulfs me. I miss him terribly, and all the people I've lost in the last decade seem to crowd around me in this moment.

I clear my throat. "We have bacon and spinach quiche this morning, as well as a veggie-only option. Our regular ham and cheese kolaches, of course. Our muffins this morning are the lemon-poppyseed, pistachio, and double chocolate bomb. Janice?"

"Kathleen got some amazing apples from the Cherry Tree Lane orchards, and we've got our first batch of apple fritters rising. We should have a dozen by opening, and we'll keep frying until we run out." She smiles around, and I want to wrap her in a hug.

Tears come to my eyes for reasons I can't fathom. I should be overjoyed at the way my staff comes together— and I am. I should be thrilled I have a new man in my life —and I am.

I just need some time to let it all wash over me. I smile shakily around at everyone. "Any questions?"

Shawny looks like she might throw up, but she shakes her head. She's never opened before, but we don't even have a line on the sidewalk yet. Of course, we don't open for another ten minutes, and anything can happen before I unlock that door.

"All right," I say. "Let's make today great." The meeting disperses, and I reach for Shawny. "Let's chat for a few minutes." I give her a smile, and I feel so much like my mama right now.

She always told me to make the day great before I left the house in the morning. Before she died, she'd say, "Call me and we'll talk for a few minutes," whenever I had something strangled going on in my life.

I need her right now, and I don't have her. I can't replace her, but I remind myself that I do have other women in my life I can talk to. Callie, Tara, Jessie, Bri, Kathleen, Janice, all of them would sit and listen to me and help me. Heck, Shawny probably would.

"Opening is just like the mid-day rush," I start. "It's somewhat easier, because our businesspeople in the morning generally just want coffees. Remember, if it's something you can dispense, you do it as they pay."

Shawny nods, her eyes still wide. "Got it."

"I'm here," I say. "If you get behind, just say my name. Belle is amazing, and she'll help you if you need it."

The other barista is behind the register, checking

something in the pastry case. Belle's been here for several months now, and she's a pillar I can rely on in the mornings. She works until eleven, and then she heads to her college classes for the rest of the day.

Someone knocks on the glass behind me, and I twist toward them. "I hate it when they do that. We're clearly not open."

The last time I opened the door for someone before we were open, it was my boyfriend-at-the-time. That memory flashes through my head though I don't want it, and I turn back to Shawny.

"Go check that you're ready. You've got this."

She nods and goes to do what I've said. I brush my hand over the plants that line the area in front of the registers and marks the line between where customers pay and the seating area.

I want to flop into the deep burnt orange couch and sip my macchiato while customers come and go. I can't do that, and Coy's idea that I experience Legacy Brew as a patron grows in my mind. I do that in the evenings, and a new thought niggles in my mind.

Maybe he'd join me while I sit right here on this couch and these chairs with my friends...

The idea sits there, and I don't try to shake it away as I go to unlock the door. It's time, and I smile at the Knocker as I swing in the door. "Good morning," I chirp. "Welcome to Legacy Brew."

He gives me an irritated smile and enters the shop.

Four more people follow him, and that's not bad for a pre-six-a.m. line.

I look down the street, ready to return to the shop to help wherever possible. During the slow-down this morning, I can go over the applications I ignored last night.

But I freeze, because Coy lifts his hand in greeting though he's halfway down the block still. A smile fills his face, shoots across the space between us, and infuses into my chest.

He really is a gorgeous man, with his dark brown hair swept to the side the way it is, his clean-cut beard, and those big, big hands. I feel them resting on my hips, right below where my belt sat last night, though he's still yards away.

"Hey," he says as he nears. He holds up a brown pastry bag, and surprise lifts my eyebrows and widens my eyes.

"You bought something somewhere else?"

"Only your favorite," he says.

I feel totally inadequate to be in a relationship with him. He knows so much about me, and I'm playing catch-up all the time. I thought he was my enemy, and I've never bothered to catalog the things he likes or does.

I step outside of the shop and let the door close. I move away from it as a couple of women approach from behind me. "What's my favorite?" I flirt with him shamelessly, despite the big windows that all of our employees can see through.

I pluck the bag from him with one hand, feeling the weight of it, and put my other on his chest. "I don't think we should..." I glance toward the shop's windows. "Be blatant at work."

"We should talk about that for sure," he murmurs. He keeps his hands at his sides and smiles at me. "Open the bag."

I back up a few steps and part the flaps on the top of the paper bag. The scent of lemon and lime escapes and makes my mouth water. I jerk my eyes back to his. "These are those citrus tarts from that dessert truck."

He's absolutely right. I love these, and every time I stop by Little Tartlet, they're out of the citrus ones.

I suddenly don't care who's watching. I close the flap on the bag and move into his arms in the same motion. Those hands slide along my hips, which I love, and I stretch up to kiss him.

I keep it chaste and short, and I murmur, "Thank you," against his mouth before settling back on my feet. I lace my fingers through his and turn toward the shop. "Are you coming in?"

"Yeah." He clears his throat. "I thought I'd help you with the applications. Maybe I can weed through them and give you the top three." He lifts his eyebrows, clearly asking me if that's okay with me.

My first thought is no, he can't do that. He doesn't know what I'm looking for in an applicant. Then the weight of the tartlet bag in my hand hits me, and I say, "Sure, thank you."

This man clearly knows me better than I thought he did, and if I only have to look at three applications and set up three interviews, I'd be stupid not to accept the help.

We enter the shop to a line that's at the end of the brick wall. "Wow," I say. "I didn't realize so many people had come in." I immediately look to the registers, because I promised I'd help Shawny and instead, I was standing on the street kissing my boyfriend.

We separate without saying anything, and I like how in-tune we are. Most of the time, I feel like we're dancing to two different songs, but something shifted in The Kissing Incident that we're just now capitalizing on.

—————

"CAN you come sit with us for a minute?" Bri asks as she pays for her coffee and lunch. Jason, her fiancé, stands with her, and they both look at me with hopeful eyes.

"Yeah," I say, deciding on the spot. "Let me finish this order, so save me a spot on the couch."

"We'll do our best," Jason says.

A few minutes later, I manage to grab a pistachio muffin and another macchiato. I sink into the cushion at the end of the couch, my thigh pressing into Bri's.

"Hey." She pats my leg and smiles. "You look a little harried."

"Our slow-down barely happened," I say. "It's going to be a blood-bath this afternoon during cleaning." I take a sip of my coffee, determined not to ruin lunch with thoughts of what the rest of the day might bring.

One thing at a time has become a good motto for me since beginning my career as a barista here at Legacy Brew. It's actually something I learned from Coy's dad.

"How was your trip to prison?" I ask.

"He's in the county jail," Bri says. She's an amazing friend, and I love her with my whole soul. But she's very by-the-book. Prison is not jail, and jail is not prison.

She and Jason work at a family law firm, and they're both very, very good at their jobs. So of course jail is not prison.

"And I don't like going there," Bri says. "But I think we're really close to getting what we need."

"We have to be," Jason says. "Our court date is next week." He sips his coffee like going to court is the same as taking his fiancée to a fancy dinner. I've never been to court, and the very idea terrifies me. I remind myself that Bri and Jason feel at-home there, the same way I do here in the coffee shop.

I sigh and slouch further into the couch so I can lean my head on Bri's shoulder. "How's Timber?"

"Amazing." Bri puts her hand on my leg. "What's going on with you?"

"Nothing," I say.

"Sure," Bri says in a dry voice. "Because this is such normal behavior for you."

I lift my head. "I'm acting normal." Past her, Jason's eyes widen and his eyebrows go up. "What?" I ask. "Jason?"

"You're like calm water when you're usually high energy," he says bluntly.

"Jace," Bri chastises, whipping her attention to him. She looks back to me, her hard expression softening. "He just means you seem very tired."

"I had a late. Date. Last night." I hit the T's hard, a smile coming to my face.

"You had a date?" Bri turns toward me fully now. "With whom?"

I grin at her and sit up to pinch off a piece of my pistachio muffin top. "I don't want to say right now. It's very new."

"Obviously," Bri says. "As you made a video to get a date to my wedding only a few days ago." She gasps, her dark eyes widening. "You're dating someone from the comments."

"Ew, no," I say. "But it is someone who volunteered to take me."

"Way to go, Mace." Jason holds out his fist for me to bump, which I do, both of us grinning.

"Let's order focaccias from Tara tonight," Bri says.

"You aren't going to get his name out of me with pastrami

and cheese," I say. "Unless she does the hot ones. Mm, the crispy bread." I grin at her, but I'm not going to tell her about Coy right now. If I'm not, I should probably not kiss him where our security cameras can see us. And our employees. And any random person walking down Lavender Street.

"I'm texting her right now," Bri says.

"She's doing that fifty-five-plus cupcake party," I say. "She won't have time for focaccia."

"Then Alec," Bri says. "He's an excellent chef. *Very* crispy bread."

"Hey, you guys."

We all look up at the sound of Callie Micheals' voice. She's holding a to-go cup of coffee in one hand, the other resting on her belly.

"Callie." I jump to my feet to hug her. "What are you doing here? You should be in the hospital, delivering this baby." She's absolutely huge and due any day now.

"We have a meeting with Coy," Dawson, her husband, says as he joins her. "It's her last day of work."

"Maybe." Callie shoots him a look.

He gives her a mighty glare back. "It's your last day of work, whether you go into labor tonight or not." He puts his arm around her and looks at me. "So we're getting some things set up for when we're gone. I'm going to be working from home, and Cal's..." He pauses and looks at her.

"I'm going to be pulling back a lot," Callie says, her bright blue eyes filled with equal parts excitement and fear. "I'm looking at hiring another secretary to help at the firm." She looks at Dawson, and they have a whole conversation with only their eyes.

I want someone like that, someone I can look at and we can read each other's minds.

"Well, we have another meeting after this one," Dawson says. "Macie? Are you coming in?"

"I didn't know there was a meeting today," I say, frowning at the black plastic door. Coy doesn't magically appear there, despite my wishes that he will.

I meet Callie's eyes, not sure what she sees in mine. "Yeah," I say. "Let's go start this meeting."

CHAPTER TWELVE

COY

I sense Macie before I see her. It's the front of
the storm that foams in the sky before it arrives on land,
and I look up from the stack of papers I've prepared for my
meeting with Dawson Houser, which should be starting
any minute now.

The man is punctual and proper, but he's relaxed a lot
since marrying his wife, Callie. They're the perfect pair,
and they're about to have a baby together.

So I'm shocked to see the pregnant woman leading the
way into my microscopic office. I leap to my feet to greet
her. "Callie."

Her husband follows her, with Macie bringing up the
rear. We'll barely fit in here together, and I only have one
extra chair.

"I'll get my chair," Macie says, her eyes spearing

straight through mine, practically pinning me to the wall behind me. "Don't start without me."

My pulse hammers at me, beating as loud as steel drums in my ears. She leaves, but I can't slam and lock the door. Not with a pregnant woman in here who could go into labor at any moment.

"I didn't know you were all coming," I say. "How are you, Callie?"

"Doing great." She takes the chair and takes a bright pink briefcase bag from her husband. "We'd like to get everything we need from you for the next few weeks, as we're both going to be working part-time once the baby comes."

"Sure, yes," I say, turning to the stack of papers on the desk. I reach for my cherry Chapstick to buy myself some time. I don't actually want to start, because Macie told me not to. No, I hadn't told her about this meeting, because I wanted to talk to Callie and Dawson about the *idea* of a new logo and slogan before bringing it to her. If the marketing experts don't think it's a good idea, I can avoid the conversation.

Never mind that I've been thinking about a new logo for Legacy Brew for eight-point-three months, and drawing for about all of that time.

Macie returns with her chair, and Janice is carrying a folding one that I've never seen before. "Dawson," Macie says as she pushes the chair toward him. She takes the one from Janice and unfolds it right in my doorway.

I guess she's not leaving.

My throat closes, because I'm not ready to show her my drawings. I don't want to show them to anyone.

My father's voice sounds in my head, and I draw my shoulders up and then back. They relax there, and I remind myself I own this company. If I want to change the logo and slogan, I can. I don't need to show these people, even if I trust them and know them and...love them, that I'm afraid it'll be the wrong move.

Doing nothing is worse than doing something wrong.

I'm holding the folder of things Callie and Dawson need, and I look down at it. I sink into my desk chair and turn it to face them all. My knees practically knock against Dawson's, but at least Macie is further away. Out of reach, judging by the swirling anger on her face. Maybe irritation. No matter what, she is *not* happy I left her out of this meeting.

I clear my throat and turn the folder so the pages inside will be upright for the audience across from me. "I first wanted to ask you for your opinion on whether or not getting a new logo and coming up with a new slogan would be worthwhile." The top page is our current logo and slogan. "My dad came up with these almost forty years ago, and I'm thinking forty years in the future."

Callie and Dawson both peer at the logo. Macie doesn't move a muscle, not even a twitch.

"A new logo is a great idea," Dawson says.

Relief I wasn't expecting floods through me. "Really?"

"Yeah." He takes the page out of the folder and holds it up in front of him. "I can see how this is older. It's got some classic designs, of course, but we can update it."

Every cell in my body riots. "I've, uh, been drawing out some ideas."

"You've been what?" Macie asks.

We all look at her, probably because of the incredulity in her tone. I ignore her, sending her my best *this-is-a-meeting* look, and refocus on the people we pay to give us marketing advice, run our marketing campaigns, and who can probably find someone to clean up my ideas.

"I did some graphic design in college," I say. "I've always loved to draw. I never finished, of course, because my daddy died, and I was almost running Legacy before that anyway."

I look at the next page, which is all of my brain vomit for the slogans. "I've been brainstorming new slogans. Things I really want Legacy to stand for. I'm sure you guys can take these and run with something that will fit my vision."

Dawson takes that paper too, but he doesn't look at it for longer than four-point-four seconds. Mostly because his wife sucks in a breath, causing everyone to look at her next.

She plucks the next page from my folder. "You drew this?" she asks.

It's the logo I like best. The one that's the most

complete, with shading and everything. "Yes," I say simply.

"I can't believe you can draw," Macie says, and I'm not sure if she's irritated anymore. I don't have time to get a true read on her, because she stands to look at the logo Callie's holding out in front of her, her face tipped down.

"I have a couple more," I say, and Dawson takes one, leaving the last one for Macie. The third one isn't as good as the others. I haven't had time to really flesh it out.

She holds it with reverence, and I'm not sure what that means. I feel naked in front of them, even when Callie looks at me with pure kindness in her eyes.

"This is all great, Coy," she says. "We can take these to a design team that does amazing work with logos and see what they come up with."

"This one is wonderful," Dawson says, tapping Callie's paper toward himself. "I mean, I like all of this, but that one has the bold lines, the classic lettering. It says legacy without saying legacy."

"I thought so," I say, glad he can see what I do. "I mean, it's a sketch. I'm sure the team can make it crisper and cleaner."

"Yeah, they will." He takes the page from Callie, giving her his. "I like that it's an oval and not a circle. That'll stand out, and it gives us more versatility when it comes to brand placement."

When he starts using marketing lingo, I generally tune out. He and Callie really have done an amazing job since

Macie hired them, so I don't need to know all the terminology. I don't need to babysit them. Macie does a lot of work with them besides, only looping me in when it's time to pay for something.

I suddenly understand why I should've told her about this meeting. I'm not sure why I didn't. Probably for the same reason I didn't confess my crush on her for so long.

She makes me nervous, and her opinion carries a lot of weight for me. I have to be vulnerable in front of her, where my relationship with Callie and Dawson is more professional. If they'd told me the idea of a new logo was stupid, I wouldn't feel nearly as hurt as if Macie had.

She looks up and meets my eyes. "I'm sorry," I blurt out.

She glances over to Callie, who hasn't missed anything. "It's fine," she says, laying the page back in the folder. "I didn't know you went to school for graphic design."

"A couple of semesters," I mutter. My pulse is almost louder than my voice, especially because Macie retakes her seat and folds her arms. She's not done talking to me yet, but she's not going to make a scene in front of her friends.

I'll hear it all whether I want to or not, I'm sure. Part of me wants to engage with her, really get her yelling at me the way she has in the past. That'll lead to some amazing kissing, no doubt.

Another part of me is instantly irritated that she

doesn't trust me to have business meetings without her. That she thinks she has to know everything about me right now, on her timetable.

I'm not as forthcoming as her, but who is? I'm not as blustery or as outgoing. There's a reason she's the public face of Legacy Brew while I work in the back, at the desk, all day long. We have very defined roles here, because they're what we're individually good at.

And because we can't get along, I think. Having such delineation between what she does and what I do has allowed us to work together without having to interact as much. And the reason we don't want to interact as much is because she won't agree with my ideas for a new slogan and logo.

"We'll get these to the team." Dawson stands. "Do you have a list of things you absolutely don't want?"

I gather the papers and place them back in the folder. "In here." I hand it to him. "My budget is in there too. Color ideas."

"This is great, Coy." Callie uses Dawson's hand and arm to stand, and Macie scrambles to get out of their way.

"I'll be in touch," Dawson promises before he gently leads his wife out of the office. Macie stays out of their way, but I don't think for a moment she'll let this go.

Sure enough, she re-enters my office a moment later, gives me a death glare—a legit look that would cause my death if eyes alone could achieve such a thing—and grabs her chair.

"I can get that," I say.

"Don't bother. I've already got it." She makes a big show out of grunting to lift it and then laboring under the weight of it as she leaves.

I roll my eyes before I remember I've been out with her a couple of times now and that we've shared at least five extremely hot kisses.

"Macie." I follow her into her office and close her door. It's dark in here except for a nightlight that shines a pale blue light. Neither of us make a move to flip on her overhead fluorescents, and I'm not sure why.

"Don't be mad."

"If you have to start a conversation with those words, I get to be mad," she says.

"Why? Because I wanted to have a meeting with Dawson and Callie about something that doesn't concern you?"

"Doesn't concern me?" She scoffs and folds her arms, pushing out that oh-so-desirable hip. "Coy, I own forty percent of this company!"

Fire blazes inside of me too. She might be all wind, rain, and hail, but I can be just as destructive if I need to be. "And I own the majority of it," I say. "Not only that, Miss Madsen, but I wasn't even sure a new logo and slogan would be a good idea. I wanted to ask the *marketing experts* you hired before I brought anything to you."

"You were scared I'd see your drawings."

"Yeah," I fire back. "And why do you think that is?"

She opens her mouth to retort, but nothing comes out.

My chest heaves. Her office is so much smaller than mine, and there's not enough air in here for this argument. "Not very many people know I draw," I say in a much calmer voice. "So no, I wasn't ready to show you something I've spent a lot of time and energy creating. They have...some of me in them, and I didn't want to listen to you make fun of them."

"That is so not fair," she says. "You don't know I would've made fun of them."

I concede her point with the wave of my hand. "I wanted to know if a new logo was even a good idea. I would've brought it to you then."

"I hate that you don't share things with me," she says. "And not just work things, Coy, but Life Things. *Real* things."

"I do."

"You don't!" She throws up her hands in frustration. "You know what tartlets I like best, and where to get them. You know I don't like being alone to think through hard things. You know what I like in an applicant to a T. You know all of my pets' names and what kind they are, and I think you have a trio of lizards or snakes or something."

"Bearded dragons," I say. "And I only have two of them."

"Fine, two of them. My point is, you know so much more about me than I know about you."

Something bursts inside me. Maybe my sanity. "That's

because I've been in love with you for years!" I don't mean to yell, but I do. "I'm observant is all. And I swear, I can't look away from you. So who cares if I know what tartlets you like? That makes me pathetic; nothing else."

She fumes, smoke practically seething from her nostrils. "You are not pathetic."

"I am *not* you, Macie," I say. "You're like this amazing, perfect storm. Everyone loves you, because you've got this big, live-out-loud personality. I'm not like that. It takes longer for me to open up to someone, and we are very, *very* new."

She looks like she's going to contradict me again, but she doesn't. Instead, she does something worse. She nods in two tight movements of her chin. Up-down. Up-down. So she's not really agreeing with me at all.

"Are we done?" she asks.

I want to pinch the bridge of my nose and question all of my life choices, especially the one where my heart decided it only beat for Macie Madsen, the barista who has never liked me.

But I've already said too much and grated on her nerves for too long. So I simply turn, open her door, and walk out of her office.

In mine, I turn around and glare at her as she stalks by on her way back out to the front of the shop, and then I close my door and sink into my chair.

I stare at nothing for a few seconds, trying to make sense of the past half-hour. "Well, Dad," I say. "They think a new logo and slogan would be good for Legacy Brew, so I'm going to do it."

I then wake my computer so I can put in the order for the print of the old logo. I'll frame it and put it behind the ordering counter, along with the other two we've used in the past hundred years. It'll show our legacy, and I was excited to tell Macie about this part of a logo redesign.

I still can. Later, when she's blown out her anger and has more mental space to actually listen to me.

Hopefully.

I've moved my mouse a few inches when my brain catches up to something I yelled in her office.

I groan and put my head down on my desk, banging it softly. "Did I really tell her I've been in love with her for years?"

Holy shrimp and grits—in swear words she uses —I did.

Great.

Just when I'd started to feel like she and I were on more equal ground, I've once again fallen at least a couple of stories below her.

CHAPTER THIRTEEN

MACIE

"Coy Cochran," I say in a scoff as I leave the shop that afternoon. I've made it through the late-day rush, and I've covered the shift for tomorrow morning. It's my day off, and I plan to work a very little bit by doing the three interviews I've set up from Coy's choices from the applicants.

Coy's choices.

He really does know me so well, and I should be happier than I am about that. The moment I slide behind the steering wheel of my car, my phone rings.

"Hey, Tara," I say after the call has connected through my Bluetooth.

"Callie called," she says without even saying hello. "She said there's something weird going on with you and Coy?"

I sigh, because of course Callie saw something no one

else can. The woman does not miss anything, I swear. It makes her an excellent friend and a killer marketer. But when I'm trying to keep my new boyfriend under wraps, it's not so good.

"Nothing new," I lie. "We're fighting again."

Tara doesn't say anything for a few seconds. "I think you're a big, fat liar," she says. "Are you on your way home? I'll come over."

"You don't have to do that," I say.

"Of course I don't, but I made this enormous vat of beef stew, and Alec is threatening divorce if I try to feed it to him for a third night in a row. It's the kind with barley, and I know you love that stuff."

"Barley beef stew," I say, enunciating it like I'm cursing.

Tara laughs and says, "I'll be over in an hour. The cracked wheat rolls will be done by then."

"Bless you," I say. "And next time, lead with the carbs."

"I have some Amish butter too," she says. "It's *incredible* on freshly baked bread, and I can't seem to get enough of this wheat bread."

I'm sure I won't be able to either, and if it were up to Tara, I wouldn't be able to tie my apron around my waist. She loves feeding people good food, and since I'm a fan of eating, I always let her feed me.

My dogs act like I'm a serial killer trying to break into the house, and when they see it's me, they're instantly following me everywhere, clearly begging for their dinner.

I've only just finished feeding them their gourmet meals when Tara arrives. "Girl," she says. "You better start talking, because Bri says you're seeing someone new, and Callie says you and Coy were acting weird—I mean, weirder than normal—and." She grunts as she sets a massive crock of stew on my countertop. She's wearing black from head to toe as well, and I want to step into her tall frame and let her hold me.

I miss my mom so much sometimes, and I don't get as many hugs as I would like.

She starts back for the front door, unaware that she has three new doggy friends. "Let me grab the bread and butter. Be right back."

I corral the dogs in the living room before she returns with the yeasty bread that makes my whole body warm and gooey. She puts it on the counter and faces me. "Well?"

"Well what?"

"What's going on with you and Coy?"

I reach up and release my hair from its ponytail. I shake it out and scratch along my scalp to get some relief there. "Honestly?"

"Are we ever dishonest with each other?" Her eyebrows go up. "Because that's news to me if we are."

"We're dating," I blurt out. "Okay? I put up that video asking someone to take me to Bri's wedding, and he texted me. We went out that night, and then again last night, and I kissed him." I pace away from Tara. "And that wasn't even the first time. Last year, when Andy broke up with me—remember how he moved to Philly without even telling me?—I went to the shop and cried myself to sleep on the front couch. Coy found me there, and I kissed him then too."

I spin to face her. "I call it The Kissing Incident, and Tara, he is a really, *really* good kisser."

She stares at me, her eyes getting wider and wider with every passing second. In the living room, Susan barks, probably because she can feel my tension now riding the airwaves in the house.

"You are dating Coy?"

"Yes," I whisper.

Tara's face slides into a smile. "Oh, honey, that's so great!" She rushes at me and gathers me into the hug I wanted a few minutes ago. She's so much taller than me, and so warm, and I sink into her embrace.

"So great?" I repeat. "Really?"

"Of course," Tara says. "Haven't you liked him forever?"

"What? No." I step out of her hug. "I mean, I think he's smart. He's obviously gorgeous. But like him? We barely tolerate each other."

"Clearly not." She grins as she turns to start serving dinner. "I mean, kissing him in the middle of the night on the coffee shop couch? Wow."

"It was a mistake," I say. "I was very upset about Andy."

"I know you were, honey. But it's been months. Do you think you're rebounding?" She moves around my kitchen effortlessly, the way she does in any kitchen.

"No," I say slowly. "We really don't get along that great, Tara."

"Sure you do," she says easily. "He respects your opinion. He trusts you. He obviously thinks you're gorgeous too." She faces me. "Wait. Is this a fake relationship? Just for show for Bri's wedding?"

"No," I say quickly.

"Then you're already ahead of me and Cal." She smiles again.

"He called me a perfect storm."

Tara freezes. "He did?"

I nod and then fall onto a barstool. "My mama used to tell me I was her little hurricane. She warned me that I'd need to learn to control the storm inside me, that it would scare some people away."

"Oh, baby." Tara slides onto the stool next to me. "I'm sure he meant it as a compliment."

I nod, because I think he did. "He calms me down," I whisper. "Without even trying, he calms me down." I look at Tara. "I'm scared, Tara. We own that shop together, and what if we can't make this work?"

I can't lose Legacy Brew. And worse, I'm starting to think I can't lose Coy Cochran. But if I don't figure out how to tame myself into a storm that doesn't blow through town and leave everything in matchsticks, that's exactly what will happen.

"So what are you going to do?" Tara asks. She jumps up and goes back to the stove. "Oh, I'm going to burn this."

I don't answer her question as she works in the kitchen. I don't know how, and she's distracted anyway.

Only a few minutes later, she slides a bowl of steaming stew in front of me, and then places the most toasty, golden, crispy grilled cheese sandwich.

"It's not focaccia," she says with half a shrug. "But I didn't burn it." She turns to the stove and slides another sandwich onto a plate before joining me at the bar. "So you and Coy?"

I shrug too, because I'm not sure about anything right now.

"Oh, come on." Tara nudges me with her shoulder. "I told you and Callie everything about Alec, one hundred percent of the time."

I take a bite of beef and barley, the rich broth coating my tongue. Herbs burst to life on my tongue, and I roll my neck back as well as my eyes. "Holy unsweetened tea, Tara," I say, already scooping up another bite of stew. "And you didn't have to make focaccia."

"Bri suggested it, but then she and Jason went to dinner at Bun Boy."

"I do love Bun Boy."

Tara grins at me, her dark eyes shining with happiness. "Guess who makes all of their dough now?"

It only takes me a heartbeat to know her catering company has that contract. I squeal, abandon my bite of stew, and lunge at her. Something hot splashes my arm, but I ignore it as I congratulate her. "Look at you," I say. "Providing food for restaurants now."

She positively beams. "Going places," she says. "The cookbook is coming along too."

"That's amazing." I smile at her, genuinely meaning it. "Then you and Alec will have a baby, and the two of you will have everything in the world."

Tara doesn't deny that she'd like a baby, but she also doesn't say that she and Alec are going to have one right away. They've only been married for a year or so, and they both work for her catering company in the city.

"So if you and Coy get married," Tara says as she lifts a bite of stew to her mouth. "Will you live here or his place?"

"You know what? I don't know; I've never been to his place."

"So he's a gentleman, always coming here to pick you up."

"We've been out twice," I say. "I put up that post about getting a date to Bri's wedding a few days ago, and he texted." I can't help smiling at the memory, and thankfully, I don't drop my phone in the tub like I did then.

I have made a mess of my stew, my spoon dropping

into it and splattering the broth all over the edges, as well as onto the counter.

"But you like him," Tara presses.

"When we're not fighting, he's great." I rip off a corner of my grilled cheese, getting the greatest strings of ched-dar. As I dip it in my stew, I say, "I need to apologize to him. I wasn't very nice this afternoon."

"Do it now."

I shake my head. "No, I'll do it in person." I offer her the warmest smile I can. "That's what we do. We fight and separate, and then when I've bellowed out my thunder, we apologize to each other."

"Maybe a hot make-up kiss." Tara waggles her eyebrows, and I giggle too. I don't have to tell her not to spread this news around to everyone. She won't, and she'll wait until I'm the one who tells our friends what's going on between me and Coy.

If only *I* knew what was going on between me and Coy.

―――

"DADDY!" I call as I hip my way into my father's house. "It's Mace, and I brought your favorite cookies to go with your favorite daughter." I grin at my own lame joke. I'm the middle child, so I'm constantly trying to bring my daddy's attention to me. Oh, and I'm the only daughter.

I visit him most Wednesdays, as I don't go into the

shop that day, and I need something to keep me from going into the shop that day.

I have an older brother who's married, and a younger brother who's not. So I'm not quite the black sheep, despite the fact that they both went to college and I dropped out. Or that they've left the state and I stayed. Or that they're the same type of calm and cool that Daddy is, and I'm the raging hurricane my mama told me I was —like her.

"Macie-Mae," Daddy says as he comes in from the screened porch off the back of the house.

I abandon the bag of Byrd's key lime cookies on his table, and rush into his arms. He holds me tightly while I press my eyes against the tears burning there.

"Hey, sugar-doll," he says, using the nickname he usually does. Macie-Mae is what Mama used to call me, right up until the day she died. "What's goin' on?"

"Nothing," I say through my too-tight throat. "Just... stupid work stuff."

Daddy holds me for several more seconds before letting go. Even when he does, he maintains his grip on my shoulders. "Coy?"

I nod, and say, "But not in the way you think."

"Intriguing." He grins and steps toward the kitchen and the cookies. "Let's get these and some lemonade, and you can tell me all about it."

My visits with my daddy are usually full of me telling him every detail of the past seven days of my life, exclaiming about something amazing in his yard that he's done, and then him assuring and reassuring me that he's okay. Not lonely. Doing great. Still playing cards with his friends on Mondays and Thursdays and doing his bowling club on Saturday mornings. Every now and then, he'll vent to me about a kid's birthday party that interrupted his time with a twelve-pound ball and a group of men who should've given up bowling a long time ago.

I always listen attentively and commiserate appropriately with him. If he's missing Mama a lot, he goes to church on Sunday, and if he's not, he spends the time with himself, the Lord, and the rose bushes in the backyard.

"Got a new chainsaw this week," he brags to me as he pulls a pitcher of lemonade out of the fridge. I catch sight of a couple of to-go containers from somewhere, so at least Daddy is eating good.

"Daddy," I chastise, because Mama would've. "A chainsaw? What are you using a chainsaw for?"

"To get the limbs off that giant oak," he says. "They're getting up under the gutters."

"You're going to saw off your arm."

He grins as he faces me, and he nods to the bag of cookies. "Grab those, sugar-bean. Let's sit outside. It's so nice today."

The sunshine pours through the sky, but Daddy has a fan blowing across the porch. His once-blonde hair has faded completely to white, and his ears keep growing and growing and growing, which always makes me smile.

He sighs as he sits, adding to the sound as he opens the bag of cookies, and completing it as he glances over to me. "Okay, start at the top, sugar-pie."

His sigh says he feels old today, and I want to give him a tight, tight hug and tell him how much I love him.

I smile at the way everything here is the same as it always is, minus the absence of my mother. "Daddy, remember when Mama got those tickets to The Magic Flute, after you told her under no circumstances you would go?"

He looks at me fully now. "Yeah," he says, drawing out the word.

"She apologized later," I say, keeping my gaze out on his pristine lawn.

"Yeah."

I take a deep breath. "I need to apologize to Coy, and I don't know how."

CHAPTER FOURTEEN

COY

I pull up to my sister's duplex in Summerwood, which sits only two-point-seven miles from my house. If the streets weren't winding and serpentine, and I could drive straight here, it would be shorter. A strong urge to honk so Anna Lee will come out fills me, but I text instead. I'm not in a great mood, and I'm not sure if it's because I had to go in early today, or if Macie wasn't there, or if I still haven't heard from her after yesterday's meeting.

I half-expected her to call me last night. At the very least, she should've texted.

I almost texted her this morning during the slowdown, but I'd held back. *I've* already apologized for not telling her about the meeting. It's her turn.

My text to Anna Lee gets answered quickly, but it takes her another five minutes to come outside. By then, I have half a mind to tell her we're just going to dinner instead of going to see our mother.

I say nothing of the sort, and almost pull away from the curb before my sister has her door all the way closed.

"Whoa," she exclaims, and I jam on the brakes. "What is with you?" She looks at me with half-annoyance and half-surprise on her face.

"We're late," I say. "And I'm going to get blamed for it."

Anna Lee smiles, pulls her leg in, and closes the door. "It's fine. I already texted Mom to say we're running late."

I press my lips into a line and say nothing. Anna Lee surely told our mother that we're running late because of me and my "crazy work schedule."

If it's not that, it'll be because I drive too slow, though I've also been accused of driving too fast. My mother has quite the way of making a person feel like no matter what they do, it's not good enough.

Momma lives alone in a house entirely too big for a single person, though she left behind the mansion where she and Daddy raised me and Anna Lee.

She said she simply couldn't live there after he died, and I don't blame her for that. It had been incredibly hard on all of us to leave that house behind, despite its opulence and lack of warmth.

I had eighteen years invested in that house, and it felt like leaving behind my entire childhood by packing some boxes, hauling out my daddy's desk, and relocating a grandfather clock with my surname on it.

Daddy left me that clock, and it now sits in my front hallway. I see it everyday when I leave the house and come home, and I tap the face of it on my way in and out, precisely the way my father did.

He told me he did it to leave coffee shop problems with the clock and focus on home issues while he was home. He could do that sometimes, but in other instances, Legacy Brew definitely bled into our family life.

Anna Lee opens a small bag of cheddar cheese potato chips, the smell of them filling my sedan instantly. She eats one and then offer the open bag to me.

I see it for what it is: a peace offering. I take out a chip and pop it into my mouth. It's salty and cheesy and crisp, and I relax behind the wheel.

"I broke up with Will," Anna Lee says.

I'm not surprised, but my sister doesn't need to hear that. "I'm sorry." I glance over to her. "When did this happen?"

"Just now," she says, looking away. "It's why I was a little late coming out."

"He must not have been happy," I say. "Did he beg you to stay?" I smile, because I'm teasing her.

"He did, actually." Anna Lee tosses her straight hair that barely brushes her collar. She's a pretty woman, with a delicate, pointed chin and lovely brown eyes that light up with her every emotion. She doesn't have any problem getting dates and boyfriends. It's keeping them Anna Lee can't do.

I'm not sure if it's her or the men she goes out with, but I suspect our gene pool. I never have anyone significant in my life either, but for an entirely different reason. I don't even try to date; Anna Lee does. That's the difference between us, but the result is the same.

We're both still alone.

I'd been planning to tell her and Momma about Macie today, but that idea fades to the recesses of my mind, especially without a text from the redhead who dominates my every thought.

"Why don't you like him?" I ask, suddenly genuinely wanting to know.

She shrugs. "He turned boring."

I don't want to lecture my sister, so I look out my side window to keep my voice quiet.

"I hate it when you do this," Anna Lee says.

"Do what?"

"Lecture me without saying anything."

"I wasn't."

"I know that relationships aren't glitter and black tie dinners every night."

"Okay," I say.

"He really was boring," she says. "I wanted to order chicken sandwiches one night, for crying out loud."

A quick look over to her shows the earnestness on her face. "Coy, he wouldn't even do that. He wanted a bowl of cold cereal and to start the next episode of Throne Tower."

I smile, because Anna Lee hates high fantasy dramas. "Your favorite show."

"I could've done it with a spicy slider from Cayenne's." She folds her arms. "I don't get the appeal of that show. Everyone is a bad person. There's no one to cheer for."

"Lots of people like it," I say, though I agree with her. Thorne Tower isn't my favorite show either. In that moment, I realize that it might seem to her that I don't agree with her when I do. I realize that I do this all the time, with everyone, as if agreeing with them is somehow wrong.

I reach over, pure electricity flowing through my veins. "I agree with you, Anna Lee," I say in a clear, loud voice. "Thorne Tower is stupid, and it's completely boring to eat cold cereal while you watch it."

She meets my eyes, surprise in hers. "I know I already asked, but...what is with you today?"

I pull my hand back and shake my head. "I don't know."

I do know, but I'm not ready to vocalize it yet. Guilt and regret slice through me on the rest of the drive, because I've probably made Macie feel like I don't agree with her when I do.

I need to be better about that with her, and as I pull into Momma's driveway, I vow that I will. My fingers twitch to text her before we go inside, but I pocket my phone instead.

Momma's house is a white, two-story colonial with six pillars that hold up the deck on the second floor to create a shady porch on the first.

The door sits right in the middle of the pillars, with a series of five or six steps that start out in a wide fan and go to a near point once you finally reach the top.

She's set out three rocking chairs, as if anyone ever sits there, including her. Momma is averse to the sun, and whenever she goes outside, she's sunscreened and hatted.

The grass rolls in a luxurious emerald carpet toward the road, and it slinks around both sides of the house.

She lives entirely on the first floor, but she goes upstairs and opens the curtains in the windows that face the front of the house every day. And every evening, she walks upstairs and draws them closed again.

"Let's go," Anna Lee says. "We're already late."

"Yep." I get out and follow my sister to the front door. We don't knock or ring the bell, and Momma doesn't have a butler or a chef anymore. She still has plenty of money, but she calls herself "simple" now, and no one else in this neighborhood has live-in help.

She's not in the foyer, and I look right when I catch Anna Lee checking left.

To the right is Momma's outer greeting room for her master suite. Sometimes we sip tea and nibble on store-bought cookies there.

Sometimes Momma has our visit set up in the library, which is the big room I'm looking into. There's actually no books housed there, but Momma has piled all of her stuffy, uncomfortable furniture in there, and she sometimes sits in there and reads texts on her phone. Thus, a library.

The kitchen and dining room sit behind the library and stairs, and sometimes Anna Lee and I perch on barstools while Momma talks about what kind of grapevines she had to tend to as a child or what the local library board is doing with their adult movie collection.

If she's not in the house, we'll find her on the back deck, where I suspect she spends most of her day. She's got a breakfast nook there, and it's shaded in the summer, with a stand-up heater to warm it if necessary in the winter.

"Momma?" Anna Lee calls while I contemplate making a run for the car. We came. We tried to see her. She wasn't home.

"Out back," Momma calls back, and I sigh as I head past the stairs and through the kitchen. Not a speck of dirt or foodstuffs sits out of place in the white-from-ceiling-to-floorboard kitchen. I'm not sure if Momma actually cooks here or not, as the air is smell-sterile just as it is in color.

Anna Lee leads the way out onto the deck, and I'm a few paces behind her. The door doesn't make a noise as it closes, except for the loud *bang!* when it slams very close to my face.

I shove it out of my way, irritated all over again. "Thanks a lot, Anna Lee."

"I thought you were taking a moment." She sinks into the very middle of the loveseat, leaving me nowhere to sit but the second metal chair at Momma's nook.

She's got macaroons covering the table today, in a rainbow of colors. A white teapot decorated with flowers sits at my place, and I dutifully reach to pour it for all three of us.

"Coy's acting weird," Anna Lee says, slouching into the couch.

"I am not," I say. "It's just been a Wednesday." We come visit Momma almost every week, because, like Macie, my sister also has Wednesdays off.

I wish we could come on another day, but I've never suggested it. I make Wednesdays work, though that means there isn't a manager at Legacy Brew. There's never been a problem, and I knock on the metal table as if it's made of wood.

I lean forward and hand Anna Lee her cup of tea. Our eyes meet, and I very clearly tell her to keep her mouth shut. We don't sell each other out very often, and of course she doesn't know what's really going on in my life.

"You look well, Momma." I hand her a cup of tea too, adding a smile to it.

"Thank you, dear." She takes a delicate sip of her tea and sets it down, saucer and all. "What's going on? Something at the shop?"

I shift in my seat, telling myself it's just the hardness of the chair that's bothering me. "I, uh, it's not the shop." I press my eyes closed. "I mean, it's kind of the shop."

Everything between Macie and I is so intertwined, it's hard to know where things stop between us and where they begin at Legacy Brew.

"I'm dating Macie," I blurt out.

Anna Lee chokes and coughs, and she bobbles her teacup so precariously, I'm sure she'll drop it. She manages to save it, but she hisses at the hot liquid that's splashed her hand.

"What?" she demands.

"You're dating," Momma says, making it sound like a statement and not a question. But it's definitely a question. She reaches up to pat her pinned hair, something I suspect she only does when Anna Lee and I come to visit.

She wears a silk robe over her clothes, like she's an heiress waiting for dinner to be served and her husband to walk through the door and sweep a kiss across her recently blushed cheek.

Yes, Daddy's death was hard on all of us, but no one more than Momma.

"Yes." I clear my throat. "It's very new. We've been out a few times, and we're currently in one of our waiting periods before one of us apologizes."

"You or her?" Anna Lee asks, her eyebrows still sky-high.

"I'm hoping her," I say, finally lifting my tea to my own lips.

Anna lee cocks an eyebrow higher, if that's possible. "Coy."

"Stop it," I bark at her. "Just because we're dating doesn't mean *I* have to apologize for everything."

"What happened?" Momma asks.

Now I'm on ground I really don't want to tread. "Nothing," I say. "A work thing. I've already apologized once, in fact." I give Anna Lee a *so-there* look and pick up a pale brown macaroon. It smells like caramel, and when I take a bite, I get salty and sweet and a perfectly chewy cookie.

"Anna Lee broke up with Will," I say.

She makes a startled noise, her eyes going wide again. I simply put the other half of my cookie in my mouth. "These are great, Momma. Where did you get them?"

"Rochelle brought them over," she says, and I swear, she should wave around a cigarette held in a long, silver holder. I'm not sure why she plays this part with me and Anna Lee, but I catch the tail end of my sister's eyeroll.

"Will just wasn't for me," she says, summing up her break-up. "Coy, how did you ask Macie out?"

I spear her with a look that tells her I'm going to chop out her tongue once we get back to the car. "She actually suggested dessert," I say.

"*She* asked you out?"

"No." I frown, because I had definitely volunteered to take her to Bri's wedding. At the same time, *she* initiated that to the whole world.

She'd also suggested we go out before then. "Sort of," I say. "It's a weird story." And I'm not telling it this afternoon.

I look back at Momma. "You said you had some news," I say.

"Yes." She picks up her teacup and sips, then replaces it on the saucer, really drawing out the moment. Momma loves the spotlight, that's for sure.

"Daddy's brother and I are going on a Mississippi River Boat Cruise!" She claps her hands twice in obvious delight. I'm pretty sure my jaw hits the ground, and this time, Anna Lee does drop her teacup.

The hot liquid splashes both of us, and I yelp while she swears under her breath. Thankfully, the cup doesn't break, and she sweeps it off the deck in the next moment.

"A river boat cruise?" she asks.

"With Uncle Gary?" I add. "I didn't know you talked to Daddy's brother." There's been some bad blood in the past. At some point, they stopped talking, and I don't know the whole story there.

"Of course I talk to him," Momma says with an air of importance. "He's all alone in the world. We're all he has." She gives me a pointed look, then switches her Guilt Glare to Anna Lee. "He mentioned that he never hears from you two."

A scoff comes out of my mouth. "Momma, of course he doesn't." I look between her and Anna Lee. "We don't hear from him either. I don't even have his number."

"Neither do I," Anna Lee says. A flush works through her face, and I know why. She hates that the burden to maintain a relationship falls to her. I've heard her say at least a thousand times that phones call both ways.

She's not wrong, but I would've kept the lines of communication open between my uncle and I had I known he cared.

"I can give you his number," Momma said. "Our cruise is in April."

"Sounds fun," I say with a smile. I'm not going to allow this to get me all worked up. I have plenty of other things that do that already.

Momma gushes about the boat, the cruise, the excursions she wants to do on the week-long trip. As per our usual, Anna Lee and I let her talk, and exactly one-point-five hours later, I stand and stretch.

Momma's actually eaten several cookies during her stories, and I pick up the last chocolate one to take with me. "We have to get going, Momma."

Anna Lee steps into her to hug her, and then I take my turn. I do love my mother, Southern eccentricities and all. She won't walk us out, so if I can make it through that door, I'm home free.

I do, and I rush to catch Anna Lee, who's practically sprinting toward the front door. I break into a run after I pull the door closed behind me, and she squeals as I streak past her.

We're both laughing like lunatics as we pile into the

car, and she says nothing about my lead foot on the accelerator as we leave Momma's in the rearview mirror.

Once we calm, we both breathe in and out together, one long combined sigh. "Sorry I told her about Will," I say.

Anna Lee waves her hand. "I told her about you being weird first."

I nod and reach to fiddle with the radio. Anna Lee has asked me about my love life plenty of times in the past. Today, she doesn't, and I appreciate that.

At her duplex, I put the car in park and look at her. "Do you have a date tonight?"

"I just told you I broke up with my boyfriend."

I shake my head. "No, you said you broke up with Will."

Anna Lee's jaw juts out. She says, "Fine. Yes. I'm going out with Len tonight. He's from Sweden."

"Oh, wow," I say between chuckles. "Len From Sweden. Have fun."

She opens her door and then turns back. "You and your barista?"

"She's more than that now," I say. "She's my partner."

"Is she?" Anna Lee stands before I can ask her what that means. "I've tried to get you to go out with her before, and you've said she's just your barista a million times."

"Times change," I say.

"Have fun," Anna Lee echoes back to me and slams the door against my reply—again.

I take the meandering roads from her house to mine, knowing the moment I make the last turn down my lane that something is amiss at my house.

There's an SUV parked in front of my house that's never been there before. I live on a dead-end street, lined with huge trees, and a golf course kept behind a high chainlink fence.

No one comes to this street unless they mean to.

I stare at the vehicle as I turn into my driveway, and I'm so focused on it that I don't see Macie until she stands from where she's sitting on my front stoop.

My heart swoops down to my knees and then pops back into place behind my ribs. "Mace," I say as I get out of my car.

She tucks her hands in her back pockets, giving me the shy, blown out storm version of herself. Her hair is down, but uncurled. Still gorgeous. Her valleys and curves call to me from beneath a multi-colored sweatshirt and blue jeans, and her eyes stay fixed on mine.

"What are you doing here?" I ask. She's never been here before, and I wasn't aware she even knew where I lived. "How did you find out where I live?"

She pauses several feet from me and watches me. "It's chilly out here," she says. "I've been waiting a while. Can we go inside to talk?"

Since I'll follow her off a cliff if possible, I nod. She turns, and I follow, suddenly terrified of what we might find behind my closed front door.

I can't remember if I did my dishes this morning, or what state the bearded dragons will be in.

I want to yell at Macie to *come back. Let's go to dinner somewhere instead.*

But she's at the top of the steps already, her hand reaching for the doorknob. The door opens, and in she goes, leaving me no choice but to go with her.

I reach into my pocket for my cherry Chapstick, but it's not there. I glance back at my car, but I don't dare leave Macie alone in my house for as long as it'll take to get it. I don't even want her to see me using it.

So I go inside cherry-Chapstick-less and pray I'm properly equipped for this battle without it.

CHAPTER FIFTEEN

MACIE

Coy's house is almost exactly how I imagined it would be. Neat and clean, with comfortable-looking furniture that's in good repair. There's no art on the walls, just like he keeps his office pretty bare. He does have a small family picture sitting on the built-in shelves in the corner of the living room, and an enormous glass fish tank sits in the middle of the room, almost like a showpiece.

No wild barking greets us, and that's a marked difference between his house and mine. Ticking fills the air, and I find the source of it in a standing grandfather clock that sees all who enter here. It looks old, like a family heirloom, and a bright blue-and-white rug leads further into the house.

"So this is Elmer and Orion," he says as he steps past me and into the living room.

I follow him and watch as he flips a switch and a red

light flares to life above the glass tank. He's got a series of lights balanced over the tank, so it's obvious he's paid a lot of attention to these lizards and what they need.

"Wow," I say. "Look at all those light bulbs." I round the table where the tank sits and stand next to Coy.

Colored sticky notes decorate this side of the tank, stuck to the bottom couple of inches. I bend to peer down at them, and they look like instructions for when to turn on what type of light and then how long to leave it on.

"This might be worse than my special breakfasts and dinners for my dogs." I bump him with my hip, glad he smiles through the semi-dumfounded look on his face.

I've completely stunned him by showing up here, and I can't blame him. One, I don't normally apologize so fast. Two, I had to call Bri and Jason and beg them to use their legal database to find his address. Bri's convinced she'll be disbarred now, but Jason was laughing when they hung up the phone after providing me with this house number on this street.

It's been quiet and quaint here, and I can't get Tara's question out my head. If Coy and I end up together, will we live here? Or in my place?

His is better, simply from a street perspective. I live across the street from an intersection, with houses lining my side of the street, and two blocks of neighborhoods extending down the street in front of me.

I'm right in the middle, but I don't really belong

anywhere. The physical location of my house sums up my whole life.

"Worse than counting green beans so a golden retriever won't get her feelings hurt and shun you for the whole evening?" He shakes his head, his smile softening into something more casual now.

He sits on the couch, and I drop to it only a moment later. I loop one arm through his and lace my fingers through his too. Then I put my other hand on our already joined fists.

"I'm really sorry, Coy," I say. "For my erratic and standoffish behavior yesterday."

He blinks at me, and I look down at our hands. "I'd love to be involved in the new logo creation and the fine-tuning of the slogan, but I get it's really personal to you." I swallow, not sure what else my daddy and I talked about.

He leans over and touches his lips to my hairline. "Apology accepted."

Relief floods me, and I cuddle into his chest further. "I went and visited my daddy today, and he helped me with the apology."

"I just got done seeing my momma," he says.

I lift my head, my interest piqued. "Do you see her a lot?" I can't remember what he's told me about her, if anything. He's the one who listens to me talk, and I've never asked him too many personal questions.

"Every week, if I can stand it," he says. "Wednesday is Anna Lee's day off too, so we go together. If you try to go alone…" He whistles like a bomb is dropping, and I laugh when he makes his fingers "explode."

"So we both go visit our parents on Wednesday," I say. "I think we finally have something in common."

"Come on, now," he says. "We have plenty in common."

"We do? What?" I don't mean for my voice to come out so challenging, but it totally does.

"We both love the shop," he says.

"Nothing work-related," I say.

He frowns, his eyebrows drawing down in the most sexy way possible. "Coffee," he says. "We both like coffee."

I refrain from rolling my eyes. "We like cute streets with cute little old houses," I say. "Yours is totally better than mine, by the way."

"I like your house," he says.

"It's too central," I argue. "Yours is quaint and quiet."

"All of my neighbors are at least sixty-point-six years old," he says.

We laugh quietly together, though there's nothing wrong with having older neighbors.

"You always say numbers in decimals," I say. "I swear in Southern food. So we're quirky."

Coy lets a beat of silence go by before he says, "I've never had anyone call me quirky before."

"We both like loaded French fries," I continue. "And we visit our parents on Wednesdays, and we both care about Legacy Brew. You so much that you want to plan for the next forty years, and me so much that I've already hired two people to replace Amber."

I beam up at him, glad for the soft, adoring look he rains down on me.

"We both like pets," he murmurs. "Even if my bearded dragons don't bark when I walk in after work."

I lean closer, almost desperate for him to kiss me. He understands my body language, because he closes the distance between us in a slow, planned way.

My lips tingle with happiness, and I easily sigh into his mouth on the second stroke of his lips against mine. He lays me back on the couch, and the weight of his body above mine is deliciously hot. I feel adored by Coy, and for someone who's been bottling their passion for so long the way he has, it's an enormous, all-encompassing feeling I can't get enough of.

His kisses turn more heated, and he slides one hand down to my waist, the other lingering in my hair.

While trailing kisses across my collarbone, he whispers, "Have you eaten dinner?"

My voice is stuck somewhere behind the desire screaming through me, so I shake my head.

"Are you hungry?" he asks next, his lips at my ear.

I nod, and I'd been so subdued waiting for him, but I feel myself coming back to life with every kiss he gives me. I thread my fingers through his hair and say, "I want breakfast for dinner."

"Yes, ma'am," he says, but he doesn't stop kissing me to

go make breakfast appear on the table. He covers my mouth with his, his full of power and grace. He tastes like caramel and something medicinal. He's been visiting his mother, so he probably had tea, and I can't get enough of it.

A sense of claustrophobia envelops me, and I push against his chest. He lifts up and stands, moving away from me and giving me breathing room. I struggle to get up, and as he reaches to help me, my foot kicks out.

A mighty *thud!* fills the air, and I jump to my feet. Sort of. I'm on one leg, the other one attached to his lizard tank. Oops—bearded dragons.

I hadn't seen either of them yet, but now one comes out, and I scream. It's warranted, because bearded dragons are *huge*.

As I hop-stand there, the strap on my shoe caught on the light fixtures on top of the tank, another one comes out from its hiding place. My heartbeat flutters, because those things are two feet long. Each.

"Macie, don't move," Coy says.

Instead of listening to him, I jump, trying to pull my shoe back. The light rigging falls into the tank.

One of the bulbs breaks with an underwhelming *crack*, but all of the lights go out. Tears stream down my face, because now there's no barrier between me and those lizards. They're killers, I'm certain of it, and I try to hop backward and pull on my foot at the same time.

That doesn't work, and I fall onto the couch behind

me. Sort of. My cheeks barely catch so I don't topple to the hard floor.

"Stop it!" Coy yells. "Hold still, and let me get it off." He's got a grip around my ankle, and I can't see the dragons anymore.

"Coy, they're going to poison me. Are they poisonous? Do you have an antidote? Maybe I'll call nine-one-one right now." I'm hysterical, I know, but I don't know how to calm myself down.

It takes Coy another several seconds to get the strap out of the rigging, and my ankle stings from being bent so funnily for the past few minutes. I scoot away from the lizard tank and press into the corner of the couch, still whimpering.

He looks at me in disbelief, and then turns back to his bearded dragons. "Oh, no, you don't," he says in a I-mean-business voice. "Don't you dare get out of there!" He dashes into the kitchen, leaving me *alone* with the reptiles, and I start crying again.

They're both eyeing me like I'm their next meal, and I call, "What do they eat, Coy? They're going to eat me!"

He returns with a cookie sheet, which he plunks down over the broken part of the light rigging. His chest heaves as he makes sure his beloved bearded dragons can't get out, and then he turns to me.

"They're going to eat me?" He starts to laugh, but I don't see anything funny about this situation. I wipe my face quickly, pure embarrassment filling me from my sandals to my smile.

I get to my feet and walk toward the front door as I say, "I can't eat here. Let's go out. Or to my place."

"Macie," he says from behind me. "Mace." He jogs to catch up to me, easily spinning me and taking me into his arms. "I'm sorry I laughed. You have to admit, that was pretty funny."

"They're huge," I say. "You made it sound like they were tiny little lizards."

"I told you they were bearded dragons," he says. "That implies they're big."

"To *you*."

"To most people," he says. Then he backs up a step. "You're right. I didn't realize you wouldn't know how big they were. They don't weigh much, but they are about twenty inches long."

"That olive green one is at least four feet."

He chuckles again, and I hold onto him and let him dance me around in his foyer. "We can go if you want," he says. "But they're pretty sedentary, and they won't be able to move that cookie sheet." He turns to face them again, which is fine by me, because that means my back is to them.

Or maybe I want to know where they are at all times, so they can't attack. Right now, I'm not sure. My adrenaline is still coming down, and my face feels crusty from the salty tears.

"They're caged appropriately," he says. "Elmer's even gone back into hiding."

I nod and keep holding onto him.

"You had a legit panic attack," he whispers. "I've never seen you like that."

"I did," I say. "I don't know why. It just freaked me out."

He dances me into the kitchen so seamlessly, I don't even know he's done it until he says, "Sit down, baby. I'll get you a drink."

The sweet talking version of Coy Cochran can stay, as can the man who just spent ten minutes kissing me like he might be dead if he hadn't.

He brings me a bottle of peach iced tea straight from the fridge and drops into a crouch in front of me. "Okay?"

I take the bottle and pop the top. "Yes, sorry. I just...I couldn't breathe, and then my foot was stuck." It still aches a little, but I don't tell him that. I'll have to examine it for fang marks later.

Coy simply smiles at me shyly as he ducks his head. "Waffles okay? I'll have them delivered."

"With extra bacon," I say, recapping the iced tea as he stands and returns to the living room to find his phone. "I can't stay late."

"Bananas or berries?" Coy asks from his perch across the room. He leans against the wide, arched doorway that connects the living, cooking, and dining areas.

"Bananas," I say, and he goes back to ordering.

Once he finishes, he looks at me again. "Just dinner, and then you better get home to the dogs."

"They'll be upset their food is so late," I say, meaning it. "Justice will probably puke in the night, because she hasn't had time to digest before bed." I roll my eyes, glad when Coy laughs and joins me in the kitchen.

He kneels and wraps me in a hug, and I lean my cheek against his chest. "Feeling better?"

"Yes," I whisper, though plenty of foolishness still ribbons through me.

"Are you going to go to jail for how you found out where I live?" he asks.

I manage to smile as I pull away from him. "No. I asked Bri and Jason to look you up. Did you know you have an unpaid parking ticket from thirteen years ago?"

Shock travels across his features. "I do not." The disgust in his tone isn't hard to hear.

"You do. That's how they found you. It's the only thing you have in the system." I look around his house. "You've been here for thirteen years?"

"No," he says. "Only about four now."

"Well, I don't know how it works. I just know they found you, and I needed to see you, and I knew you wouldn't go back to the shop."

He looks uncomfortable, and he groans as he gets to his feet. He paces away from me, running his hands through his hair. I've seen Coy like this before. He has something to tell me. Something I probably won't like.

"About that," I say, and he faces me again. "I'm wondering if you'd like to..." I clear my throat and seize onto the same bravery that I used to call Bri, get Coy's address, and then drive over here and wait for almost an hour.

"If I'd like to what?" he asks.

"Sit with us in the coffee shop." The words rush out of me. "You know how all my friends and their husbands come hang out in the evenings? I sit with them sometimes; I'm sure you've seen me. I go through the line like a customer and everything."

"Sometimes you do," he says, which ignites my irritation.

I tamp it down. "Maybe you'd like to come, I don't know, hang out. Get to know them. They're pretty much my only friends outside of work." I shrug one shoulder like this is no big deal. But to me, it is. "And I told them about you today, so they know we're dating."

His eyebrows go up. "They do?"

"I mean, I sort of told Bri yesterday, and then today, when I asked for your address..." I cock my head and my eyebrows as if to tell him, *I couldn't just lie to her.*

"Anyway, and Tara came over last night and fed me, because Bri and Callie talked to her and said I was acting weird about you or the meeting or whatever, and so I figured, that's all of them except for Jessie and Lance, but Jess was there before our second date, so I just told everyone."

I take a deep breath, because I've said way too many words for the oxygen I need. Coy blinks a few times, maybe waiting for me to go on if I need to. When I don't, he says, "Okay, yeah. I guess I can hang out in my own coffee shop at night."

I squeal and grab onto him. "It's fun, I swear. They're all *so* nice."

"Yeah, Mace," he says dryly. "I know them all already."

"So you're not nervous at all?" I step back and watch him.

He shrugs, but there's something riding in his gaze. "I mean, yeah, a little." In the next breath of time, his eyes harden into marbles. "Fine, I'm nervous. Does that make you happy?"

"No," I say simply. "Why are you nervous?"

"Because they're your friends," he says. "And no one ever picks the guy their friends don't like."

CHAPTER SIXTEEN

CALLIE

I waddle into Legacy Brew and leave Dawson to order for us. I can't stand in that line. My ankles are like tree trunks, and my feet hurt because of the half-block I walked to get into this blasted coffee shop.

I should've stayed home, but the way every single person—men and women alike—jumps to their feet when they see me testifies of the opposite. I start to weep, which is about my standard these days.

See, I'm a week overdue with my first baby, and I honestly don't know how I can survive another day.

"Cal," Tara says. "Sit down, honey."

"I'll get you some lemonade," Macie says, rushing off to do that before I can tell her Dawson was planning to order me some.

Jessie fixes the pillow behind my back for me, because Lord knows I can't do it. I can't put on my shoes or bend over and pick anything up off the floor either. I can't lay down without something hurting, and I can't eat more than three bites before the baby presses painfully against my stomach, signaling that I'm totally full.

Bri turns the fan toward me, and I give her a grateful smile. "Thank you," I say. "All of you."

"Help her with her shoes, Alec," Tara says, and her husband helps me take off my slip-ons. Relief spirals up my calves, and I lean back in the chair Jason gave up for me.

"Sorry I took your chair," I tell him. "But thank you."

"When are you getting induced?" Lance asks, and he hands me a gold-foil-wrapped sucker. The sight of it makes me start weeping again, and he gives me a sympathetic smile.

"Friday," I say. "If the baby doesn't come before then."

"What are the final names again?" Jessie asks. We've gone over a list of names, and Dawson and I have to discuss both boys and girls every time, since we don't know the gender of our baby yet. I'd opted not to find out during the sonogram, and most of the time, I'm happy with that decision.

As uncomfortable as I am right now, I hate deciding things, so I wish I knew. Then I can purchase bedding in the right color and have a name picked out before we leave for the hospital. Then I won't have to wonder which first name will go with the middle name, and how that all sounds with Houser.

Macie returns with my lemonade, and I take it from her gratefully. "Tell Dawson I don't need more," I say. "Then I'll be up all night in the bathroom." As it is, I'll take four sips of this and have to go three times before we leave the shop.

"We're thinking Hilde is the winner for a baby girl," I say, watching Macie step over Bri's legs to get to the middle of the couch. Jason has taken the arm of the couch, and Bri drapes her forearm lazily over his leg. I remember them fighting like feral cats for the same turf, and they're now only a handful of weeks away from getting married.

Macie squeezes into the small space between Bri and Coy, and her coffee shop partner and new boyfriend lifts his arm and pulls her tighter against his side. She looks at him with stars in her eyes—I'm assuming, because I can't actually see Macie's face right now—and then turns her peppy smile in my direction.

Tara's on the end of the couch, four of them smashed in a space for three, and Alec has gone to stand with Dawson in the ordering line. Jessie sits in the other recliner opposite me, the big, wide, square table between us. She scoots over as Lance returns to her, and they cram themselves into the chair together. I love the sight of them, because Lance needs someone who loves him as much as Jessie does, and he finally found her.

Dawson pulls a chair over from a table and sits beside me while Alec goes and sits on the floor next to Tara. She leans over and says something to him I can't hear all the way over here, especially when a couple of guys at the table behind me start laughing about something.

I love watching Tara and Alec together too, because they're the cutest couple in the world. All of us met at work. All of us still work together—well, except for me and Dawson, as he absolutely refuses to let me go into the office or do much more than text a client or a courier. He's handling it, and I know he's just as nervous as I am to become a parent.

He hands me a blueberry muffin top and says, "It was the last one, sweetheart," before he looks at the others. "What are we talking about?"

"Your baby," Jason says with a smile. "Callie says Hilde is the female choice." He lifts his coffee cup to his lips and sips. Jason has come a long way from his player days, because I think he's drinking out of a cappuccino cup, and those mugs are often more beautiful than the drink inside.

"Yeah, I think so," Dawson says, meeting my eyes. We've talked names to death, and I just want this little human to arrive so we can start talking about something else. Oh, and so I won't be swollen from neck to big toe. That will be nice too.

"Hilde Houser is adorable," Tara says with a smile.

I think so too, and we've had this conversation before. Sometimes I feel like I'm living inside a rut, and I do the same things day after day after day. That's not always a bad thing, and coming to the coffee shop tonight was my idea. It's the first time I've been out of the house today, and it forced me to get dressed. All wins, in my opinion.

"I don't know on a boy name," I say, taking a tiny sip of my lemonade. I want to guzzle it to satisfy my parched throat, but I don't. I've done that, and it was a painful lesson learned. "Baby?" I look over to Dawson, who reaches over and runs his thumb along my left eye, catching some unshed tears.

His fierce gaze tells me he doesn't like it when I cry, but he doesn't understand the hailstorm of emotions I have swirling through me. Heck, I cried during a car insurance commercial today, and I cried when Claude Monet came and laid beside me on the bed, because he's been stand-offish since my belly started growing, almost like he knows there's going to be another wailing creature in our house very soon.

"We have two favorites," he says. "Mine is Theodore, after my father. I think Teddy Houser is just about the cutest thing ever." He smiles as he talks, and I marvel at how far this man has come in the past couple of years. He still runs Dawson Dials In, his self-founded boutique marketing firm, but he can't do that and manage all he does for his massive family company, Fowler International.

He's transitioning to that full-time in the next year, and we're hiring more managing directors for the marketing firm. He can't stand to give it up, and I don't make Dawson do anything that'll kill his dreams—except be kind to me and everyone else. Kindness is never a dream-killer.

"Callie's is Knox."

"It's a strong name," I say in defense of myself.

"Knox Houser," Coy says, trying the names out together. "It's not bad."

"I kinda like it," Tara says. "I thought you liked Harrison for a boy, Cal."

"I decided two last names is kind of obnoxious." Another sip of lemonade slides down my throat. "Now, enough about us and the baby. We're going to be stuck home changing diapers and napping whenever we can, but you guys are all going out for Valentine's Day, right?" I look around at all of them. "I ordered some all-red, heart-shaped Skittles. Grumpy Pants here won't let me deliver them, so you'll have to come see the baby to get your treat."

Dawson simply smiles at me, despite me calling him grumpy. I don't disagree with him, but it's very hard to feel like I'm not allowed to be...me. I don't like sitting around and doing nothing, and I keep telling myself that as soon as this baby comes, I'll have plenty to do.

If only the baby would come.

Jason starts, and he tells us all about this amazing cruise he booked for him and Bri. He gazes fondly at her and says, "I'm pretty sure I fell in love with her on a boat, so it feels fitting."

We all "aw," and then the attention gets turned to Coy and Macie. They've only been dating for maybe a week and a half, and when I see the panic streak across Coy's face, I want to spare him. "You can pass," I say quickly.

He meets my eye with relief. "Okay, good." He chuckles, and I can see why Macie likes him. He's tall, dark, and handsome, with a voice as deep as the ocean and a delicious flush crawling up his neck.

"I pass then," he says. "I want it to be a surprise for Mace."

"A surprise?" she asks. "You can tell me just a little bit. I'll still act surprised."

"Don't ruin it for him," I say at the same time Tara does. We meet each other's eyes, and then look at Macie. We've known her for years now, and she does tend to be on the higher end of the maintenance scale. I mean that in the best way possible.

She's got a lot of energy, and she expects her men to keep up with her. Sometimes I can't even keep up with her, so I want to give Coy a real shot. He obviously likes her a whole lot, and Tara reaches over and pats her leg. "We just mean, he's planning something special for you. Let him do it."

"Yeah, the way you let me make that ice cream cake for your birthday?" Alec asks in the driest voice I've ever heard.

Tara whips her attention to him. "You did not tell me not to go in the walk-in freezer."

"I did too," he shoots back, his dark eyes twinkling with a tease. "There was even a note—printed on bright yellow paper—taped to the door." He looks around at the rest of us. "Did she see it? She claims no. Did she hear me say—four or five times—not to go in there? Again, she claims no."

"I didn't," Tara says feebly, her eyes wide, desperate for us to believe her. I grin and try to hide it behind my lemonade cup.

"I believe you, Tara," Jessie says, and that makes Lance burst out laughing. His voice gets the rest of us going, and in the end, Tara throws her arms in the air and laughs too.

"Just let him surprise you," Alec says as we quiet down. "Us men don't get to do that very often, and it's nice when it can happen."

"Fine," Macie says. "If you even so much as *breathe* a word of what we're doing on Valentine's Day, we're done."

I blink, wondering how she goes from hot to cold so dang fast. This is what I mean by not being able to keep up with her.

"Oh, brother," Coy says, rolling his eyes. And that's how he tames her. "What about you, Jess? What are you and Lance doing?"

She looks over to him, and he looks at her. "We don't know," they say together.

"I'll probably finish Cha-Cha's sweater," she says. "And Lance will get me all the pink things in the world." She beams at him, and he kisses her gently. "And that's it. We're easy."

They are easy together, and I love hanging out with

them. We double-date with them sometimes, and some-times with Tara and Alec, and sometimes Dawson goes out with just the guys, and I go to Tara's for lunch with just the ladies.

It's a good life, and I wonder what kind of crazy I am to bring a baby into it.

"Sounds amazing," I say.

"Tara and Alec got skipped," Dawson says, to which Alec throws him a darted glare. "Oh, Tara and Alec wanted to be skipped. Never mind." He grins, and none of us presses either of them to say anything.

Finally, Tara sighs and blurts out, "We're lamely catering for a pop-up, Valentine's-Day-only restaurant, okay?" She looks over to Alec. "Alec wants to open a restaurant, and we're going to see how it'll actually work on the busiest night of the year."

That throws the rest of us into silence. Alec has wanted his own restaurant for a long time. When he first started working for Tara, he thought catering beneath him. He knows better now, but his dream of owning and oper-ating a restaurant hasn't died. It's only grown, and while I know Tara's worried about it, she also wants her husband to be happy.

"That's amazing," I finally say, and several others murmur their assent. "So you'll celebrate another day."

Tara wears worry on her face once more. "Yeah." She clears her throat. "I really need you to have this baby, Cal, because Alec and I are going on a cruise on February sixteenth. To recover from the pop-up."

"A cruise?" My eyebrows shoot up. I need my best friend here. What if I have no idea how to be a mother? How will I feed myself if Tara isn't in town? She's already filled my freezer with a variety of soups and stews, as well as more bread than any woman should ever eat.

I quickly remind myself that I have a mother in town, along with a sister, and of course, Dawson will be right at my side every baby step of the way.

"You're a week overdue," Tara says. "It wasn't supposed to interfere."

"It'll be fine," I assure her quickly. "The sixteenth is still more than two weeks away."

The chatter moves on to something else, and I love sitting here, listening to my friends and being part of their lives. I sincerely hope a baby won't change that, though I'm quite certain a baby changes everything.

I can't worry about that right now. I simply want this baby to come, and then I'll figure things out one day at a time.

———

I WAKE up in the middle of the night to go to the bathroom. Nothing new there. Dawson's breathing evenly, and he doesn't stir as I heave myself out of bed and pad into the bathroom. I sit down, and instantly a huge gush of water rushes out of me.

Embarrassed, I'm glad I made it to the toilet first, though I swear I didn't have to go that badly while lying in bed. My stomach starts to cramp, and it takes me a couple of seconds to realize what's happened.

"My water broke." My voice echoes in the tiled bathroom, and I groan as the cramp becomes a contraction. "Dawson!" I call. "My water broke!"

He comes running, wearing only his gym shorts. I'm on the toilet, and though we're married, that's still not an image I want him to have in his head, ever. I whimper and say, "I can't move."

"Stay there," he says. "I'll get dressed and be right back."

"I have to get dressed too," I say, but he's already gone. The contraction subsides, leaving me wondering if it really happened. I've had random aches and pains before.

I get to my feet as he returns, and he frowns mightily at me. "I said to stay there."

"The contraction stopped," I say. "I need to get dressed too."

He helps me every step of the way, which he has to do during daylight hours too. I don't feel any discomfort at all, and I pause and look at him. "Maybe this is stupid. Nothing's happening."

"You had a contraction, right?"

"Yeah, but aren't they supposed to be close together before you go to the hospital?"

"Your water broke," he says. "We're going."

"I guess it broke," I say. "I had to go to the bathroom."

"You're not thinking clearly," he says.

That irritates me, and I cock my hip the best I can with my giant belly. "Really? I'm not thinking clearly?"

"Callie, sweetheart." He puts his hand on my belly, but I want to back up to make it fall. "Even if you think I'm wrong, I need you to do this for me. It's fifteen minutes to the hospital. If they turn you away, we'll be back here and asleep in under an hour."

Most of my irritation subsides. "Okay," I say.

"Okay." He takes my hand and leads me outside to his SUV. The moment I lift my leg to get in, another gushing happens. Horrified, I freeze.

"Come on," he says.

"I can't," I say as the tightening happens all across my abdomen and down into my legs. I start to sweat, and the world tilts like I'm about to pass out. "Dawson."

He grabs me and helps me into the car, then rushes around to the driver's side. "We're on the way, baby," he says, and since he never calls me baby, I assume he's talking to the baby. I'm not sure that fifteen minutes have passed before he's yelling for a nurse and a wheelchair, and not much time passes before I'm out of my wet clothes and into a gown.

I'm hooked to machines and an IV, and with all the

bright lights in the hospital, it's impossible to tell what time it is. I hadn't looked at my phone when I'd gotten up, and I honestly think I dozed on the way to the hospital.

I'm not dozing now, as every contraction comes harder and faster. Dawson holds my hand and lets me squeeze as hard as I want, and our doctor arrives in the eleventh hour, seemingly having been woken up just for this.

I'm suddenly not sure he's qualified to deliver my baby, but no one else seems to think anything is wrong. Things seem to happen in snatches and blurs, and then the doctor is telling me to push.

"I can't," I tell him. I've never birthed a baby! How does he expect me to know what to do?

"Callie," Dawson says, ever the rock in the raging sea of my life. "You know how to do this. We took a class." He moves and leans down so he's right in front of me. "Look at me, sweetheart. The baby is here. It's time to push."

I nod in short little bursts of movement. "Okay." I grit my teeth and let Dawson shore me up from behind. "Okay."

The lights are so bright. The doctor's voice is so grating. The machines beep too much. It smells so sterile.

And then, the most joyous sound in the world meets my ears. The wail of a tiny baby. My baby.

"It's a girl!" the doctor yells, and behind me, the softest sigh escapes my husband's lips.

"A girl, Cal," he whispers.

I'm already crying, because it's what I do these days,

and I reach for my daughter as the nurse brings the tiny infant to me. She's all wrapped up, her eyes squeezed shut, clearly unhappy at being pushed out of the warm, dark cocoon she's been in for the past nine months.

"Oh, baby," I coo at her. "Hello, baby." I press my lips to her forehead, afraid to break her. Thankfully, she doesn't break, and some of her ire fades as she snuggles into my chest. "Look, Dawson," I whisper.

"I'm looking," he says, pure wonder in his voice. He leans over too and kisses the baby girl's head. "Hello Hilde Anna Houser."

A WEEK LATER, I come down the hall from our master suite, expecting to find Hilde asleep in her swing and Dawson doing something at his computer. He was supposed to be making lunch for us while I showered, but I smell no evidence of food.

He's not in the kitchen, either, and Hilde isn't in her swing. I turn in a full circle, wondering where my family has gone. I don't even see Claude Monet, and he's been stuck to me like feathers on tar since we brought Hilde home.

I hear a soft snore, and I spin toward the front room. Sunshine floods in through the open windows where Claude likes to sit and watch the magpies, but he's not at his post now.

Oh, no. He's curled up on Dawson's hip, the traitor. That orange tabby has liked him more than me since the first time he laid eyes on my boss. We were fake dating back then, but Claude didn't care. He rubbed along Dawson's legs and purred up a literal storm.

Hilde is snoozing face-down on Dawson's chest, and he's got one hand resting protectively on her little bitty baby back. Claude has nuzzled right into his fingers, and seeing the three of them there, all asleep on the couch together, makes me the luckiest woman in the world.

CHAPTER SEVENTEEN

COY

It takes Mack forty-four-point-seven seconds to get my coffee during one of the busiest times in the morning. Not bad for someone who's been at the shop for just over a week. "Here you go, Mister Cochran," he says with a grin as bright as the sun.

I take the coffee and give him a smile in return. As I head over to the flavoring station, I catch Macie watching me. She thinks my "customer checks" are semi-lame, but I don't care. He's our newest barista, and I want him to do a good job.

She sidles up to me while I stir cane sugar into my coffee. "So," she says. "How'd he do?"

"Good," I say.

"Oh, catfish," she says. "It's the busiest time of day, and he had to wait for the machine. He got you that coffee in less than a minute." She flashes dangerous, green fire from her eyes, and I kinda like it. Fine, I really like it.

"He did fine," I say.

"Fine is worse than good," she says back. "What's your rubric? Great: coffee in less than twenty-point-two seconds. Good: anywhere from twenty-point-three to forty-five-point-seven. Fine is forty-five-point-eight and above." She folds her arms and glares.

I give her attitude right back to her. "There's one better than great, Mace."

"You can't be twenty seconds for a cup of coffee," she says. "The machine doesn't even put it out that fast."

"It does if you tamper with it." With that, I walk away from her, her scoff of disbelief following me toward the black plastic door that leads to the back of the house. It's pure chaos back here today, because it's Friday, and we do a ton of baking in prep for our evening crowd and our Saturday morning crowd. The scent of baking quiche crust meets my nose, and I don't mind that.

I do mind the way Macie pounds the door open with her fist as she follows me. I keep my pace slow just to irritate her, which it totally does. She's growling by the time we reach my office and I fit the key in the lock. Everything here is a little old and a little clunky, so it takes me an extra second.

"You're taking this long on purpose," she says.

"I am not. My key is warped."

"I'll show you warped," she mutters.

I glance at her. "What is wrong with you today?"

"Nothing, other than I've trained Mack to perfection, and you said he was doing *good*."

The door finally unlocks, and I push it open. She follows me inside and flips on the light when I leave it off. "I wanted to follow-up with you on a couple of things."

The scent of sugar and her perfume mixes with my coffee, a trio of my favorite things. It's been a long week, but it's fine. Macie takes off Sundays and Wednesdays, and I'm gone Mondays, and I work reduced hours on Tuesday and Wednesday. Our system has been working pretty great, and we leave Janice in charge when neither of us can be here.

"All right." I sigh as I sink into my chair and face her.

She narrows her eyes. "Did you not get enough sleep last night?"

I am tired, but I'm not sure how she'd know that. "I... how did you know?"

"That was a tired sigh."

"A tired sigh?"

"Yeah." She perches on the edge of my desk. "I can always tell how a person feels by the way they sigh."

I blink, because I'm not sure what to do with this information. She gives herself a little shake before I come up with anything, and she starts talking fast. "I wanted to check on the logo and slogan. I know you might want to go over them yourself, but you haven't said anything about them for weeks, and yeah. I'll be really open to whatever, and I'll listen to what you think, and I just...I own part of this place too, and I want to *feel* some ownership in it."

My office door sits open, the noise from the kitchen easily coming inside. This feels like a conversation we need to have behind a closed door, so I get up and push it closed. It's not locked, and it doesn't latch all the way. Someone could open it by pressing on it with a couple of fingers. When I turn back to Macie, my suspicions are confirmed.

"You're nervous." I retake my seat and push the power button on my computer. "Why are you nervous?"

She folds her hands around themselves, seems to realize she's doing it, and stops. "I don't know."

"You are an owner of this place, Mace." I pull the payroll files toward me, because I've got to get those submitted today so people can get paid next Friday.

"I don't feel like it."

That gets me to stop setting up my office for the day. "What do you mean? You don't feel like you own this place?" That can't be true. She's the public face of Legacy Brew, and everyone knows it.

"I..." She sighs, and since I'm not the Sigh Master, I can't categorize it. I know Macie sometimes has trouble expressing herself, and if I wait long enough, she'll order the words and start talking.

"When I look around, I see invisible things that yes, I'm responsible for."

"Like?"

"The flavoring station," she says. "The colored aprons. But none of it is really anything I've done. The logo and branding feels like...well, it *could* be something that brings us together. Makes us a new company, with new ownership."

I turn toward her and take her onto my lap. She yelps and tries to stand up again as the chair starts to roll. "No, stay," I say. She settles onto my legs, but I can tell she's not resting her full weight on me. "It's always going to be Legacy Brew, my pudding."

I've called her *doll* and *baby*, but they didn't feel right. *Pudding* feels perfect for her, and she even likes it.

"I know." She leans her head against my shoulder. "But I want to look at something and go, 'that's me. There I am. I said we should do a star above the coffee cup, and isn't it so cute?'" She exhales again and wraps her arms around my shoulder.

"Do you want a star above the coffee cup?" I grin at the door across from us.

"No," she says. "I mean, maybe. Maybe a heart." She sits up suddenly, and the chair rocks again. "Did you draw a heart above the coffee cup? You know like a swirl of smoke, but it can end in a heart."

I start to laugh, which isn't the right thing to do. I can't help it. She's just so enthusiastic about everything. She darkens, like the sun going behind a cloud as a storm rolls in—the Macie Madsen Radar goes off in my head, and I quiet down.

"We can try it with a heart," I say.

"No, it's stupid." She tries to get up but her feet don't quite reach the ground. We roll some more, and the wheel goes right up to my foot, where it jams. I grunt; the chair twists violently; Macie pitches in my lap.

She goes sprawling onto the concrete floor, her hands out in front of her. A cry fills the office, and I'm on my knees in a flash, ready to help her. "I'm so sorry," I say. "The chair bucked you right out."

Macie turns from her knees to her backside and looks at me like I pushed her over a cliff. I reach out and slide her ponytail through my fingers. "Dinner tonight after we close?"

Shock covers her face, and I find it pretty laughable. I manage to tame it into a chuckle, and I get to my feet and help Macie up next. She doesn't confirm for dinner tonight, and I encircle her in my arms.

"Everyone's coming about five-thirty," she says. "Callie and Dawson are bringing Hilde for the first time."

"Ah, her first visit to Legacy Brew," I say. "We should hire a camera crew."

"Don't think I haven't thought about it," Macie says dryly. "Callie would kill me, though."

"So no camera crew."

She runs her hands up my chest. "What about Valentine's Day?"

"What about it?"

"Coy."

"Macie, I'm not telling you what I have planned." For how much I'm playing up this surprise, it better be the best Valentine's Day on the planet—especially for someone like Macie.

She pouts, pulls her ponytail tight, and picks up something from my desk. She examines it and sets it back down. "Dinner tonight after coffee," she says, turning back to me.

I wonder where she goes in moments like these, but I don't ask. Maybe at some point I'll know everything about her, but that day is not today. I nod and kiss her quick before she heads out the door, leaving it open behind her.

"Baby," I call after her, and she turns back to me at the black plastic door. "When the mocks come in, I'd love to go over them with you."

Her entire being lights up, but all she does is nod before she heads out to the service area. I watch her go, then return to my office, where yes, I have to do the payroll. But first, I have to make sure I don't fall on my face next Tuesday night.

———

LATER THAT NIGHT, I'm sitting on a stool next to the couch where Macie is chatting with Jessie. Lance had a late call, but he should be here any minute. Bri and Jason have just walked in, and Tara arrives with a tray of cupcakes that have bright purple frosting.

I don't normally allow outside food in the shop, and

Macie throws me a look. No one else does, and I say nothing.

"I just have to put the little booties on," Tara says. She puts the tray on the table in front of the couch and drops to her knees. Alec comes inside with a bin, and Tara starts plucking pale yellow pre-made baby booties out of it, sticking them down into the frosting until they're supported by it.

Once she has them all done, she leans back and proclaims, "Done." She looks over to Alec, who's put the bin by the recliner and then claimed it.

"Those are so stinking cute," Macie gushes, all smiles and sunshine tonight.

Tara stands, groans, and says, "I'm going to get some green tea. Baby? You want anything?"

He shakes his head, and I'm not sure, because Alec isn't my bestie or anything, but he doesn't seem super jazzed to be here. I meet his eyes, and he raises his eyebrows as he folds his arms.

I nod and shoot a glance over to Macie. "I'll go grab some plates and napkins." I don't know how far out Callie and Dawson are, but Tara's in line, so I probably have a few minutes. No one else has come in, so when I join the line, I'm behind one of Macie's besties.

Alec joins me, and the three of us make a little huddle. "So," he says. "Did you get in touch with Flo?"

"Yes," I say without moving my lips. "We're all set. Thank you."

"She's going to lose her mind," Tara says, grinning. "She loves pink, furry things."

Alec chuckles, but I've seen Macie's social media and the velvety ties she puts in her hair. She also has some custom aprons she wears around the shop, and I send up one more prayer that I won't ruin hers this weekend.

We make it through the line, and Macie looks over to me as I slide back onto my barstool. "What's going on with you and Tara and Alec?"

"Nothing." I fold my arms and refuse to look over to them. Tara's sipping her tea from the bin, leaving the couch for Dawson and Callie.

"Oh, good," Lance says as he breezes into the shop. "I didn't miss them." He collapses onto the couch with Macie and Jess. "The Roundys are going to be the couple that forces me into retirement."

He pulls at his tie in disgust, and when he gets it off, Jessie takes it from him. Lance looks over to me. "Coy, can you fill in on Saturday for basketball again?"

"Sure thing," I say, and Macie's gaze whips to mine.

"You play basketball?"

"I mean, I know how." I meet Lance's gaze again. "I just have to be done about ten-thirty. I have...something else."

"No problem," Lance says, but Macie hooks her eyes into me. "What 'something else'?"

I wish I had a cup of coffee, but I don't. I'm already a little too keyed up, and nothing I do seems to be right for

Macie today. "You're so nosy," I tell her. "I used to do things by myself all the time."

"Ohhhh, wow," Tara says, and both she and Alec are staring at me. Even Lance and Jessie have frozen and watch me.

"What?" I ask.

It's Lance who clears his throat and says, "Yeah, sure, you can do things by yourself still. Right, Jessie?"

"Sure?" she guesses.

"Uh oh," Bri says under her breath. Even the lawyer thinks I'm in trouble. Great.

"I'm going to play basketball in the morning," I say. "What difference does it make if I have another appointment after that?"

"So while I'm here holding down *our shop*, you're off playing basketball and going to appointments?" She makes air quotes around the last word.

"I don't come in until the afternoon on Saturdays." I blink at her, not quite getting it. "You hate it when I'm here 'hovering over you.'" I can do air quotes too, thank you very much. "You've never asked me what I'm doing on Saturday mornings. Or any morning, for that matter. You won't leave the shop and come watch me play basketball anyway."

No one says anything, and I'm not sure if I've just dug my grave or not.

"Maybe I would," Macie says, lifting her head.

"Oh, please," I say, apparently satisfied to start

throwing dirt on the hypothetical coffin. Thankfully, before I bury myself alive, Callie and Dawson walk in.

The women gasp as if they've never seen a baby before, and all of them jump to their feet. I know for a fact that they've all been over to Callie's house to see baby Hilde already, and I'm probably the only one who hasn't met the infant yet.

Dawson's got the baby carrier in his arms, and Tara pulls the blanket back. I look over to Lance, who's stayed on the couch, and we lean toward each other. "What in the world was that?"

Lance keeps his eyes on the women as Dawson puts the baby carrier on the table and comes our way. He sighs as he takes Macie's spot on the couch. "Hey, brother." He holds out his fist, and I bump it before he extends it toward Lance.

"Coy's in trouble," Lance hisses.

"Oh, yeah?" Dawson looks at me, genuine concern on his face. "Work trouble? Or Macie trouble?"

"One impacts the other," I say.

Dawson grins. "I get that."

"We all get that," Alec says as he slides into the recliner on this side of the coffee table. Jason hands me a cup of coffee, and I don't even care what's in it. I take a big gulp, not sure what to do next.

"So what are you doing tomorrow after basketball?" Jason asks.

I don't want to tell them, and I squirm on the stool.

"This is bad," Lance says.

"It's not bad," I say. "It's a thing I'm doing with my sister. We're actually making a gift for Macie for Valentine's Day." I take another swig of coffee.

"Oh, that's great," Dawson says. "What's wrong with this?" He watches as Tara slides his baby into Jessie's arms. His eyes soften, and I switch my gaze to the baby too. She's a pretty little thing, with plenty of soft, brown hair.

No one answers Dawson's question, because we've all followed his gaze to where the women stand with the baby. I suddenly see this scenario from up above. Men clustered together on the corner of the couch, and women gathered around their best friend and that precious baby.

"She's amazing, Dawson," I say, everything zooming back in to regular focus.

"Yeah." He clears his throat. "Yeah, she is."

"You know, now Jessie is gonna want a baby," Lance says under his breath.

Dawson chuckles and says, "Go for it, bro. You won't be sorry."

I still don't know what's wrong with me having something on Saturday morning, even if it's not a gift-making class for Macie's Valentine's Day present.

Alec clears his throat and stands up. "We have an announcement." He meets Tara's eyes, and she comes to stand next to him. I think for a moment that they're going to announce that they're expecting a baby too by the way they come together, their hands interlocking.

"Are you going to tell them?" he asks.

"You tell them," she says. "It's your nomination."

"Nomination?" Callie asks. "What nomination?"

"It's your catering company."

"With your dish, with you as the chef."

He grins and ducks his head, his tattoos poking up from underneath his collar. "Well, since we can cut the tension in here with a knife, what between me and Coy, I'll just say it."

"He combined a cliché with a knife joke," Bri says. "Jace, did you make him say that?"

"He loves knife jokes," Tara says as she cuddles into him.

"There's a time and a place for every cliché," Jason adds.

"Someone just say it," Lance growls.

"I can't." Alec looks at Tara.

"He's been nominated for a James Beard Award." Tara squeals and bounces on the balls of her feet. "Best Regional Chef."

The group of us around her and Alec burst into whoops and applause, which draws the attention of the other patrons in the shop. Part of me pushes against this scene, but I'm clapping along with everyone else. I even clap Alec on the back, though I still feel like I don't quite belong with these people.

We quiet down, which somehow soothes me, and I step over to Macie. She's got the baby now, and I put my hand on her lower back. "She's amazing," I say.

"Isn't she?" She looks up at me, pure softness in her eyes. "Do you want babies, Coy?"

I look back to the sleeping baby. "Yeah, I think I could stand to be a father."

"I love babies."

This doesn't surprise me at all. How Macie slides Hilde into my arms in the next breath does. "Oh, uh, I haven't—" But now I'm holding her, and I can't just drop the newborn even if I'm not sure how to hold her. She grunts and cuddles right into my chest, and I bring her close the way I'd hold a football I don't want to lose.

I look over to Macie. "I'm making a gift for you for Valentine's Day on Saturday. With Anna Lee. If you want to come—"

"I don't," she says softly. "I'd love to properly meet Anna Lee as your girlfriend, though."

I nod, though a hint of fear tugs through me. Meeting my sister... Anna Lee can either eat Macie for lunch, or Macie will tear my sister limb from limb.

Either way, it should be interesting.

CHAPTER EIGHTEEN

MACIE

WHEN THE FIRE ALARM GOES OFF IN THE BACK OF THE shop, I don't immediately run for the door. This is how I know I'm not getting out of Legacy Brew in time for my Valentine's Day date.

Only a few customers get up and head for the exit. That is, until Coy comes bursting through the black plastic door and yells, "Evacuate! Everyone out! It's protocol, and we don't want to get closed down by the fire department!"

I kind of do, because it's been a long week already, and it's only Tuesday, right near the end of our morning rush.

Shawny looks at me, as does Mack, and I nod toward the door. "Outside." They start to go, and I tap in my code for the registers and grab the cash tray from the first, then the second. I shove them at Coy, who takes them into the back, and then I make sure everyone is out in the front of the house before I follow them into the blazing February sunshine.

It's a little misleading, because the wind whips down the block between the buildings, and it's not exactly warm despite the cheery light beaming down from the sky. Sirens reach my ears, but I don't see or smell smoke as I slide my arms inside the front of my apron to be slightly warmer.

"What's going on?" Mack asks.

"I don't know," I say. Hardly any customers have stuck around, so I'm standing on the sidewalk in front of the shop with five employees who expect me to know what's happening. "Maybe there was a little too much smoke out of an oven or something."

I've baked here, and once, the muffin batter overflowed and burned on the bottom of the oven. When I opened the door, a plume of smoke had come out and alerted the fire department—and Coy.

One of my midnight stress-baking sessions that had gone wrong. Most of them don't, and since I started dating Coy, I don't find myself at Legacy Brew in the middle of the night, trying to sleep or trying to figure out what I'm doing with my life. I'm not sure what that means, and I push it away as the enormous fire engine arrives in front of the shop.

Firemen rain from the railings of the truck and go right past me and inside the building. I can't help but stare after them; I can't help that I appreciate hometown heroes, especially the kind with muscles for miles and scruffy beards and big hands.

They don't get the hose off the truck, which I find a little odd. Then again, what do I know about fighting fires? Maybe they assess a space first and then come back for the water.

A couple of minutes pass—or at least what feels like that long. I don't really know, because I don't wear a watch. I shiver, meet Mack's eyes, and decide I better act like the girl-boss I am. "I'll go see what's going on," I say.

Inside the shop, it feels eerily quiet. All the lights are on, but no one's there. This literally never happens except in the two minutes before we open. Even then, the place feels like it has life. Right now, it's flatlining.

"Coy?" I call. We're going to have to adjust our plans. We'd been planning to leave right before our mid-day rush, because he's booked us lunch somewhere he won't tell me, but that he promises I will love. Given how observant he is, I don't doubt him.

He doesn't answer right now, and I glance down the aisle between the registers and the coffee machines like there might be a flame there I can put out with a perfectly tossed cappuccino. There's not.

There's nothing.

Nothing, like no scent of smoke.

Nothing, like no sound coming from the back of the shop.

Nothing, like no people there either.

I stand in the doorway, my hand on the black plastic and take in the place. It seems like a busy kitchen, with various pans, bowls, and ingredients sitting on the stainless steel prep stations. The ovens stand against the wall, and from here, I can't even tell if they're on. The fire alarm has been silenced, and a quick glance to Coy's office door shows it closed.

Hopefully locked, with our tills inside.

"Coy?" I try again. I take one step before the loudest music I've ever heard blasts into the shop. We have a speaker system throughout, and we normally play one-step-above elevator music so our patrons can relax as they sip their caffeine.

This is more like the sped up version of that, but from the eighties. I recognize the song, because I love eighties pop. Looking around wildly, I can only stare as the firemen come back into the shop from the back door. One, two, three, four—the same number as entered the shop through the front door a few minutes ago.

They're no longer wearing their bulky pants and jackets, but aprons from Legacy Brew in a variety of colors. No shirts underneath, which I can admit I appreciate. The top part that ties around their necks barely covers any of their broad chests.

They start singing and dancing, and my smile pops onto my face and won't leave.

Coy is the fifth man through the door, and he's still wearing black from head to toe, unfortunately. I haven't seen him with his shirt off, but I've felt his muscles that he claims he's gotten by rowing on a machine in his second bedroom at home.

His apron isn't from Legacy Brew, and it only goes around his waist. It's bright pink, which only makes my heart happier, and it's fluffy and furry over the pockets and sports a cheetah print down the front.

I love it instantly, and I laugh as he and the firefighters do a bad rendition of a ballet move I don't know the name of. The song ends, and they hold up both hands and shake them, jazz-hands style.

I whoop and laugh and applaud while Coy jogs forward. He's grinning from ear to ear too, and he pulls off the apron, folds it, and hands it to me. "Happy Valentine's Day, Mace."

"This is for me?"

"Yes, ma'am," he drawls out. "I made it for you myself, so, uh, don't look too close at the stitching on the pockets, and there might be a little too much glue under some of the sequins."

I stare down at the apron in all of its perfection. And imperfection. Then I'm falling, the ground vanishing right beneath me, as I realize how much Coy means to me. More than that, I know but I'm afraid to admit—I'm falling in love with him.

"You made this?" I lift my eyes to his as the firemen close ranks.

"Happy Valentine's Day, Mace," one says, and he

hands me a perfect, pink rose. He smiles with dimples and heads for the door.

"Happy Valentine's Day, Mace," the second says, giving me an identical rose as the first. Then the third, and the fourth, and so focused on this surprising turn of events was I, that I didn't see Coy move.

But he now stands in front of me with at least two dozen additional pink roses, his face lit up by the overhead lights reflecting off them and making his skin a bit rosier. He smiles and says, "There's been no blood yet, so I think we're off to a great start."

"These are for me?"

He gives me the roses and then places a kiss on my temple. "All for you."

"You pulled the fire alarm."

"It was a risk I was willing to take."

"I thought you wanted a date without an alarms or body slams or spilled drinks."

"I do," he says. "And we haven't had any of those yet."

"No, just dancing, singing firemen."

"You like firemen."

I burst out laughing. "You seriously did not stage a very serious incident to get a few firemen down here for me and..." I trail off, because he seriously *did*. "How'd you do that?"

"The Fire Chief is a friend of my father's," he says. "He did me a favor."

I lean down and smell the roses, buying myself a moment to think.

"Come on in, guys," Coy calls and our employees start streaming back inside.

"Happy Valentine's Day," rings through the air, and I smile and nod and accept all of their well-wishes.

Coy pulls me toward his office, which he does unlock. "Stay here, okay?" He grabs the tills and heads for the door again.

I look at the roses and the apron hanging from my arm. It's so...me. It's like he's captured exactly what I love without making me feel silly for loving it. He really does know me so much better than I know him, which only makes my chest pinch too tightly.

He returns, all smiles, and says, "Let's get out of here while we can."

I nod, my voice curled up in a ball somewhere in my stomach. I shed my Legacy Brew apron, get my purse and jacket, leave behind the new, pink, sparkly, fluffy apron, and join him at my door. "Coy," I say, which causes him to turn back to me.

"Yeah, Mace?"

"Thank you." I tip up onto my toes and kiss him, right there where everyone can see. They all know we're dating; we haven't been shy about it, though we haven't been so explicit either. Especially not during work hours.

He holds me close and keeps the kiss from accelerating

too much. He breaks it and sways with me. "You're welcome."

"My gift for you is going to be really lame."

"I doubt that," he murmurs. "Come on. We'll be late if we don't get going."

"Do I need to change?" We're both wearing black from head to toe, and I'm not sure what kind of restaurant we're attending.

"Not for this." He smiles and takes my hand. "Maybe for dinner." Outside, he opens my door for me and gets behind the wheel of his sporty car.

"Tell me your favorite food," I say.

He glances over to me. "You know this one."

I nod, because I feel like I should. "Steak, right?"

"Yes."

"Favorite color is blue."

"Yes."

"You love those cheesy Christmas movies too." I smile just thinking about the holidays with him.

He chuckles and says, "I can't deny that."

"So I know you," I say.

He sobers. "Of course you know me. Did you think you didn't?" He glances over as he makes a turn, then focuses on the road again.

"It's just...you do everything so perfectly. You make me feel...seen. You make me feel like you know me so much better than I know you."

"I don't know what that means," he says.

"Like, if I were going to make you an apron to wear around Legacy, what would it be like, you know?"

He looks at me again, easing to a stop at a red light a moment later. "Macie, you're not making sense."

I shake my head, frustrated with myself. "Yeah, probably not."

"I'm not perfect," he says.

"I know."

"Is seeing you a bad thing?"

"No." I slump and lean my forehead against the passenger window. "It's perfect."

His fingers thread through mine, and I let him hold my hand. I let him drive us wherever we're going, and I let the silence come between us too. I don't know why I'm ruining this. It's Valentine's Day, and he got firemen to come sing and dance for me, for crying out loud.

I take a deep breath and squeeze his hand. "Thank you again. That was the most amazing start to any date I've ever been on."

"I'm glad." Coy makes another turn, and I realize where we are.

"You are kidding me," I say, nearly twisting my neck I spin my head toward him so fast. "The aquarium?" I search his face, but he's ultra-focused on driving in a parking lot right now. "Coy Cochran, now is not the time to go silent on me."

"We're going to the aquarium," he says.

"I thought we were going to lunch," I say.

"We are." He's not even looking for a place to park. He's not going down any of the aisles. The only thing ahead is the valet parking, and that's obviously his goal. I have a lot more questions I decide to keep to myself, because there is something exciting and romantic about a surprise.

"I haven't been here in a while," I say.

"Me either," he says. "I figured it was time we came." He pulls up to the curb, where two men approach the car. One opens my door, and one rounds the hood to talk to Coy. He says something to them I don't catch, because the Summerwood Sea Center and Aquarium looms before me.

The entire front of the building is one gigantic fish tank, and I stand slack-jawed as I look up to the tropical fishes swimming above me. "What a view," I say to myself. I love the beach, but I don't get to enjoy it very often. It's not super warm right now anyway, but I suddenly want to be in my swimming suit, running toward the surf as Coy tries to catch me.

Then I'll squeal when he does, and we'll both hit the water running. Everyone knows you can't run in water, so we'll fall down, right into each other's arms, and we'll let the ocean rock us back and forth as we kiss.

It's such a perfect picture, and I grin like a lovesick fool. *Don't let the magic of Valentine's Day make you live in a fantasy-land,* I tell myself.

Coy comes to my side and says, "Ready?"

"I guess so." I go with him toward the entrance. "What are we doing here?"

"You'll see."

I'm getting really sick of that answer, but I don't comment on it. Inside, he hands the security guard a couple of tickets, and he steps back from a roped-off area and indicates we go that way. My eyebrows lunge up in surprise, but the gentle pressure from Coy's hand on my back gets me to go down that hallway.

"Where does this go?" I can't help asking. "I didn't see a sign."

"To where we're eating lunch," he says, and at least it's not "You'll see."

Through another door we go, and the hall turns to the right. It's long and our steps echo off the walls, which are covered with pictures and posters of manatees, whales, sharks, and brightly colored tropical fish.

"I feel like we're on a field trip," I say with a smile. "You know how you got to go upstairs in the grocery store? It was like, so off-limits."

He chuckles, and I grin, and I'm loving everything about this non-traditional Valentine's Day. Yes, I got flowers, and I can only hope there will be candy later. But a day-date? At the aquarium? After a firemen show?

Things can't get better.

And then I see the sign.

"Lunch with Luna?" I spin toward him again. "Coy, this better not be a joke."

He grins at me. "It's not a joke."

I scream and start running for the door at the end of the hall, just as a woman comes out of it. She's dressed in professional clothes, what with her gray pencil skirt and violet blouse. She smiles like a crazy thirty-something woman isn't sprinting toward her. I catch just a hint of shock before she wipes it away and says, "Can I see your tickets, please?"

Coy hasn't broken into a run, and his laughter joins him as he catches up to me. He shows the woman the tickets while I bounce on the balls of my feet. "Luna is my all-time favorite sea turtle," I say.

"That's wonderful," the woman says. "Let me show you to your seats." She opens the door and goes through it first. We're not the first to arrive, but it hardly matters. Miss Thing takes us toward a wall of glassed-in water—a tank I've never seen from this side—to the very front row of tables.

There are only two chairs at each one, and they both face the ginormous fish tank. "Here you are," she says, her voice muted in here. Or maybe that's just the vibe I'm getting. It's reverent here, like if we make too much noise, we'll disturb the sea life. "We'll begin in about ten minutes."

I sit down, ignore the menu in front of me, and watch in wonder as three sea turtles swim by right in front of me. Mere feet away. "I can't tell if that's Luna," I say.

"You'll get to find out," Coy says.

"I will?" I tear my eyes from the water in front of me, though another animal swims by. I jerk my attention back to it. "Was that a dolphin?"

"Probably," Coy says with far too much forced falseness in his voice.

"Coy," I say again, plenty of warning in my voice.

He looks at me, his dark eyes dancing with joy. "You can't scream in here."

"You booked Lunch with Luna," I say. "That required a scream." I sigh. "I've always wanted to do this. This is like, a dream come true." I meet his eyes again, and I can see that's exactly what he wanted to do: Make my dreams come true. "Coy," I say again, this time with a completely different emotion running through the single-syllable name.

"Mace," he says. "Don't scream, okay? But also, try not to eat too much, because one, we have dinner tonight too, and two..." He glances back to the tank. "We get to swim with Luna and the other turtles, and yes, there's a dolphin in the tank today too. Her name is Pookie, and they'll do a demo with her and then you'll get to swim with her."

I open my mouth, and even if I wanted to scream, I can't. The air has left my body, every last particle of it. People say a perfect man can't be found, but I think they're wrong. They just haven't met Coy Cochran yet.

CHAPTER NINETEEN

COY

"Breathe, my pudding," I murmur to Macie. Honestly, I'd prefer the screaming to the staring. Her lips are starting to turn blue, or maybe that's just the reflection from all the water in front of us.

Macie pulls in a breath, her wonder like that of a child. It actually infects me and makes me so dang satisfied that I've pulled this off so far.

"Are you going to swim too?" she asks.

"Yes," I say. "We'll be here for a while. All afternoon. Then we'll go home and shower and get ready. We have reservations at Alec's pop-up at seven-thirty."

"I thought you couldn't get reservations for a pop-up." She shifts in her seat, her attention wandering back to the tank as more turtles float by. "Isn't that the definition of a pop-up?"

"You can when you know the owner," I say.

Her eyes come back to mine. "Is that how you got into this? Because Valentine's Day? Lunch with Luna? We've only been dating for a few weeks. There's no way they had space for us."

"I called in a favor."

"Wow." She leans back in her chair and folds her arms. She's not trying to be combative; she's truly surprised. Still, she seems a little defensive. "You're calling in a lot of favors today."

"It's Valentine's Day," I say. She doesn't need to know I've fantasized about this day—with her—for years. I've had plenty of time to come up with ideas for what we might do, what she might like, how I might somehow convince her that we'd be so, so good together.

"And this wasn't really my favor. Flo, the booking agent for this event, is good friends with Alec. He gave me her number, and I called her. Got it all arranged. It's *his* favor."

"Sure," Macie says right before her face splits into a grin. "I don't care how you did it. This is amazing." She scoots her chair closer and links her arm through mine as she leans her head against my bicep. "Thank you, Coy."

I touch my lips to her temple. "You don't have to thank me all day."

"I'll thank you as much as I want," she fires back.

I shake my head and laugh lightly. "All right. Simmer down. You don't want to upset Luna."

"Mm, no," she murmurs. "I don't."

A waiter arrives and says, "Have you had a chance to look at the menu?"

Macie grabs the paper in front of her, and I look down at mine. "Not yet," I say.

He starts to tell us what they've got, and since it's a small group of people for a special event, the options aren't plentiful.

"We can start with drinks," he says. "We have an amazing selection of mocktails, because we don't allow guests to drink before they swim with the animals."

"Seems smart," I say. "I'll have the Mango Peach Paradise, please."

The waiter looks at Macie. "I'd love the Strawberry Fields Forever." She smiles at him, and he leaves to take care of the tropical drinks.

"What are you going to get?" she asks, and I know why now. Macie is a food-sharer. She loves ordering several things and eating bites of all of them. Once, last week, we went out for dinner after coffee-hour with her friends—*our* friends—and she ended up eating all of my pasta instead of hers.

I don't mind; I'm just glad I know now. "I'm thinking of the mushroom Swiss burger," I say. "What about you? The salmon BLT?"

"It's on the radar," she says, still studying the menu. "But they have crab cakes..."

"You love crab cakes."

She looks up. "You love red meat."

"Guilty." I smile at her, but hers is already fading. "Macie." I cover her hand with mine. "I don't like how you think I know you better than you know me."

"I'm still learning a lot about you," she says. "That's all."

"I'm learning about you too," I say.

She shakes her head, but she doesn't argue with me. I frown at the top of her head, because she's looked down at the menu again. "Macie."

"Mm?"

"Tell me the names of my pets."

"Elmer and Orion."

"And they are...?"

"Bearded dragons." She gives me a little push with her shoulder. "And they are poisonous, by the way. I looked it up."

"They are not."

"They totally are. They can give you salmonella poisoning from their bacteria."

I blink, sure she's wrong. I'm not going to look it up right in front of her, because that's rude. But later, when I'm home alone with my possibly-poisonous pets.

"What's my sister's name?"

She raises her eyebrows. "I know what you're doing."

"Then play along."

She sighs like I'm the most insufferable man alive. "Anna Lee."

"Why not just Anna?"

"Because your daddy wanted Lee, and your momma wanted Anna. But your momma couldn't stand to have your daddy's name first, so Leeanna was out. They went with Anna Lee. Two words. No hyphen."

I grin at her. "See how much you know?"

She rolls her eyes. "Yeah, and your momma's name is Amanda, and she's never gone by any nickname for a single day of her life."

"That she has not."

"And your daddy is Charles, but he passed away about eleven years ago now." Her expression turns a little vulnerable. "That's when you got the bearded dragons."

I've never told her that, but it's true. I did tell her my oldest bearded dragon was ten years old. I nod and say, "Yes."

"Why don't you ever say 'yeah'?" she asks. "It's been 'yes, yes, yes,' all day today." She lowers her voice to mimic me on the word "yes" every time she says it.

"I say yeah," I say. "Maybe not every time, but I'm not a yes-exclusive person." I shoot her a look, and thankfully, the waiter returns. Macie quickly ducks her head to look at the menu again, and I say, "I'll have the mushroom Swiss burger with onion rings, please."

"And for you, miss?"

"What's the pizza crust here like?" she asks. "Is it stretchy?"

"Sure," the waiter says. "It's great."

"Hmm." She consults the menu again. "Is the salmon fresh-caught today?"

"Yes, ma'am," he says.

I smile as she opens her mouth to ask another question. She always does this; she can't just order something. She has to know all about several things first. "And the crab in the crab cakes? It's not that imitation krab-with-a-K, is it?"

"No, ma'am, it's real lump crabmeat."

"Okay, I'll..."

"She'll have the crab cakes," I say. "And the pesto and prosciutto pizza." Macie looks up and meets my eyes, and I raise my eyebrows. "Right?"

"Yes," she says, and I swear her voice pitches lower, mimicking me from earlier. My eyebrows perk up in challenge, and instead of answering, I reach into my pocket for my cherry Chapstick.

Macie laughs even as she rolls her eyes, and I'm pretty sure I fall for her a little bit more in that moment.

"ARE YOU GETTING THIS?" Macie asks, the joy pure and radiant on her face. She looks over to me from where she stands, ankle-deep in water, with a dolphin poking its nose up toward her waist. We're both wearing wetsuits, but we haven't gotten all the way in the water yet. We'll get to ride the dolphin, and then they'll take her out of the tank, and we'll be able to snorkel with Luna and the other turtles.

Macie hasn't stopped gushing since she saw the sign for Lunch with Luna, and I'm just glad things haven't gotten bloody yet.

"Yeah," I say. "I'm filming. Wave to everyone."

Macie flings her hand back and forth like she's seven years old, which makes me laugh. Then it's our turn to put away our phones and pay attention so we can swim with Pookie. I put them on a towel off to the side of the tank and join Macie to learn how to stand, how to grab the fin, all of it.

"Who wants to go first?" the instructor asks.

Pookie emits a loud whistle-call, which delights all six people in our group, myself included. I suddenly don't care how much this cost—and it wasn't cheap—because this is easily the best date I've been on in a long, long time.

Another couple steps up to take their turn with Pookie, and she dives under the water and boogies away. Macie's hand slips into mine, and I squeeze. We wait our turn, watching the first couple as they get to have a once-in-a-lifetime experience.

Then it's Macie's turn. She steps down into the water further and stands right next to the female instructor, who wears a giant grin. "Slap the water," she tells Macie, who doesn't go into question mode. She does exactly what she's told, and four seconds later, not only one dolphin, but three, leap out of the water. Their noses point straight up, and everyone cries out.

Even me. I've seen dolphin shows before, but we're indoors, and this isn't a theme park. They flip once each and head back into the water.

"That was incredible," I say.

Macie reaches back and tightens her ponytail, her smile so big I can see a lot of it from the side of her face. The instructor has her edge out further, tells her to get her hands ready, and a moment later, she grabs onto Pookie and they're swimming.

It's a glorious sight to see the dolphin towing her alongside it, and after about fifteen feet, Pookie turns, and Macie releases. She goes all the way underwater and comes up a moment later, sputtering and laughing at the same time.

She doggy paddles over to the side, where another instructor motions to her and helps her out of the pool.

"Sir," someone says, and I focus my attention away from my hot, sexy girlfriend who just rode a freaking dolphin. My heartbeat kicks into high gear, and not only because I can't wait to kiss her later.

It's my turn. I step down and take my position next to the instructor. I don't get to slap the water, but Pookie comes right up to us and pokes her head out.

"Good girl," the instructor says. "What do you say?"

Pookie emits her whistle, which I've learned is unique to each dolphin, her face full of that goofy, dolphiny smile.

"Yep, go," the instructor says, and off Pookie goes. She circles the way she took Macie, and she'll come back around for me.

"Out a bit," the woman says, and I move out further. "Hands ready."

I put them right along the water, as instructed, and I look over my left shoulder for the dolphin. I see her coming, and I latch on at the right moment. My feet get yanked out from under me, and for a horrifying moment, I think I'll be the one who can't hang on.

But I do, and the water is rushing at me, and I'm flying along the surface, my feet behind me. Everything is amazing in those few moments, and then Pookie turns, and I lose my grip on her fin. I splash face-first into the water in what I'm sure looks like a belly flop, but when I come up, I don't even care. My smile feels etched on my face, because that was *fun*.

I get out of the tank too and step over to Macie, who hands me a towel. I wipe my face and put my arm around her as she wraps both of hers around my waist. "This is so great, Coy," she says.

"Best date ever," I say, immediately wishing I can suck the words back in.

"Yeah," Macie sighs. "It sure is."

So maybe I don't need to hide how I feel. In the beginning, I thought maybe I was practically buried in feelings for her, and she was still trying to decide if she had any for me. Every time I worry about this, I think of that kiss on that orange couch, months and months ago.

No woman kisses a man the way she kissed me if there's nothing there.

Satisfied that she likes me as much as I like her—and that she might be falling for me the way I'm definitely falling for her—I smile and keep her as close as I dare while we stand in a public place.

So far, so good. All we have left to put this date to bed without any body slamming is dinner, and I say a little prayer that luck will continue to be on our side.

CHAPTER TWENTY

TARA

I'm so nervous, I feel like I might throw up. I haven't eaten anything since last night after Alec and I got home from Saucebilities, so there won't be much coming up. Still. I don't want to puke before we even open the restaurant.

Alec and I have been prepping for this moment all day. All week. All month. Our whole lives. We arrived in the kitchen at seven-thirty this morning, where he started braising the short ribs, and I got baking everything that could be baked for the dessert course tonight.

It's Valentine's Day, and we know people will be ordering more expensive items than they normally would, and plenty of people save room for dessert—especially if their dates are going well.

In front of me, the pop-up restaurant spreads in an array of white tablecloths, deep, dark-wood chairs, golden utensils, and fresh flowers in crystal vases on the edge of every table. Those make me nervous, because it's only a matter of time before a waiter or waitress bumps one, and we'll have roses down and water everywhere.

I didn't decorate this place; a good friend Alec and I met the first time we went to the Miami Food and Wine Festival knows chefs and restauranteurs all over the country, and she found this building for us. Jane has been in the industry for decades, and when she asked the owner of the building if we could have it for one night for a restaurant trial, he'd said yes.

Things had spiraled from there, and anything Jane told me to do, I did. Anyone she sent my way, I listened to. Anything we had to do to make this night happen, Alec and I did.

I want this to be the huge success for him that he deserves. He had to give up his restaurant in Atlanta a few years ago, and it's been his dream to own and operate his own place, serving his inspired dishes, since.

This is a tiny taste, and it's already been the most overwhelming four months of my life getting ready for it. I can't even imagine finding the space myself, decorating it, designing the menu—Alec actually did that for tonight—and running it day in and day out.

Alec's done it before, and I trust him to the very core. So we *could* do it. I'm not sure I want to give up everything I've built at Saucebilities in order to do it, though. If Alec leaves the catering company, I'll need two chefs to replace him, and I turn away from the waiting dining room and retreat into the kitchen.

Alec has just called the staff together, and he's going over the menu for tonight. It's simple and elaborate at the same time. Pan-roasted salmon with a balsamic reduction, Brussels sprouts, and endive, and a wild rice and mushroom risotto that makes my mouth water. I prepped all the veggies, so all they need is a quick sear on the flattop in the last two minutes to bring them up to temperature and give them a nice browny crisp.

The risotto has to be made upon order, and Alec has one person doing that all night long. That's why I don't like restaurant work. I don't want to make wild rice and mushroom risotto for eight hours straight, while some chef yells at me to do it faster.

Risotto is hard work, and if it's not exactly right, there will be a lot of complaints.

We asked the staff at Saucebilities to come work for us tonight, and they all agreed. So Barley, Jared, Henry, and Karla are all here. They're all aproned up and ready to go. Alec also hired two more chefs just for tonight—Alyce and Rich—and of course, I'm here.

Because we won't be home until late, I've got my neighbor going over to get the dogs. He should've gotten them already, and Alec hired not one, but two people to come babysit Peaches.

That Quaker parrot is so temperamental, and she still doesn't like me a whole lot. When Alec and I got married, and he moved into my house, she squawked every time Tommy or Goose, my dogs, even came in the room. She cried when the chickens clucked or gobbled. Peaches has settled a little bit, and I've even noticed that she's starting to bark the way Tommy does.

Alec goes over the short ribs, then the half-chicken. Our veggie option for the main course tonight is a rata-touille made with eggplant and zucchini, onion and garlic, and served alongside a saffron rice pilaf with almonds and peas.

I want all the dishes, and I've tasted them all. My stomach growls as Alec moves down the counter to the desserts, the chefs still tasting the main dishes he's put together for them. That way, they know what to talk to the guests about. I missed the appetizers, but they're beautiful, upscale versions of Caesar salad, a roasted beet salad, and a wood-oven baked bread with rosemary and sun-dried tomato olive oil.

The desserts are a chocolate mousse cake that I spent most of the afternoon perfecting, as well as a strawberry shortcake and a tiramisu that nearly had me in tears when I used the wrong dishes the first time.

In the end, everything has turned out spectacularly, and I move to stand beside Alec as he finishes with the presentation. The waitstaff move in to taste the desserts, and I slip my hand into his.

"We'll see if this makes the cut," he says, always with the knife jokes.

"It's going to be amazing," I tell him. I haven't told him that Jane and I have been collaborating on the side, without him. She knows everyone in the foodie business, and with her suggestions and help, I reached out to the best in the local media and invited them to come try out our one-night-only pop-up version of Saucebilities. Alec didn't want to give it a different name, and I fall more in love with him every time I think about it.

Six reporters confirmed, and the first three will be here in an hour. I didn't schedule them for the opening of the restaurant, because I'm hoping any hiccups will be ironed flat before they arrive.

We're open in five minutes, from five o'clock to ten-thirty tonight, and while it's only five and a half hours, it feels like I need to strap on another pair of my thick-soled black beauties, because I'm about to run a marathon.

We have two people working the front of the house tonight. Our hostess, who is our secretary at Saucebilities, Lydia, is wearing a gorgeous little black dress that hugs all of her curves exactly right, and since all of my friends now have significant others—and very little experience in the restaurant industry—I asked Callie and Dawson's landlord to come help manage the front of the house.

Jillian Redstone has been managing rentals around the city for a while now, and she runs her own day spa and yoga studio right next door to Dawson and Callie's marketing firm. She owns their building too, and they rent from her.

Maybe not for much longer, I think, a creeping sadness edging through me. I'm not sad for Callie. She has a baby now. A family. A child requires a lot of attention, and while I know she loves her job, they don't need the money.

I can't imagine anyone else working for Dawson, and Callie's told me he'll be moving to Fowler International—his huge family conglomerate worth billions—full-time in the coming months. The future of Dawson Dials In is out in the ether, and I don't think even Callie or Dawson knows what will happen to it.

They have dozens of clients too.

I feel the same way about Saucebilities. If Alec leaves, if our attention is divided between the catering and a restaurant, will we be letting down our current customers? Will all the work I've put into building my company for the past several years end up being for nothing?

I really don't like how life can change so much, and in such a short amount of time. I much prefer the day-in, day-out type of work. Get up. Feed the chickens, listen to their warbling while they have their pasteurize. Eat breakfast. Feed the dogs. Go into the kitchen for whatever needs to be done that day.

It sounds easy and casual, and sometimes it is. Sometimes, like tonight, it's anything but.

"We're open!" Jillian calls, and I once again turn away from the doorway that bridges the gap from the front of the house to the back. I'm on desserts tonight, which means I probably have an hour before I have to plate anything. In the interim, I'll be helping with appetizers and expediting, and I head for my spot near the pick-up area.

My eyes lock onto Alec's, and he looks about how I feel—like we'll both throw up. Then I swipe a smile onto my face, go past my post, and straight into his arms. "It's going to be amazing," I tell him again. "You'll see."

"From your mouth to God's ears," he murmurs, and then he faces the door with a look on his face that says he's ready for battle.

A couple of hours later, I personally take the dual strawberry shortcakes to the first reporter who's made it to the third course. "Here you go," I say, placing the perfectly plated desserts in front of her and her husband. "Can I get you two some coffee?"

They gaze at the cakes, which I've arranged into a tall, slim heart. The strawberries have been halved, and they go right down the center seam, with more crimson glaze spilling over the edges of the cake and drizzling down to the plate. Dollops of piped whipped cream line one half of the plate, in the same heart-shape as the cake.

"This is beautiful," they say together.

I laugh lightly. "So no coffee?"

"I'll have coffee," the woman says, and I nod. I don't want to linger too long, and I've only come out for one other table—Jessie and Lance, who had a six o'clock reservation. They're sitting all the way on the other side of the space, so I don't go that way.

"Table twelve wants coffee," I tell their waiter. "She's a critic."

"Yes, ma'am," he says, and he heads straight for the beverage station. I turn and take in the busy restaurant. People are laughing and talking. They're eating, and taking pictures, and having fun. It's the stuff you see in magazines and movies, and I quickly pull out my phone and take a picture of the dining room for Alec.

This is his food doing this. His vision.

As I lower my camera, I see Macie and Coy. They're only an aisle away, but Macie doesn't look my way. She's wearing a bright pink party dress—totally Macie—that seems to make the red in her hair even better. She's showing a lot of cleavage, which means she super-likes Coy—and as I watch, she tips her head back and laughs. She gives him a *gosh-I-like-you-so-much* look as she quiets and reaches for her wine glass.

I head over to them, and as I approach the table, Coy looks up at me. "Tara." He jumps to his feet and takes me by complete surprise as he takes me into a hug. He's always been this...mystery figure at Legacy Brew. Of course, I've only ever known the side of him that Macie paints, and she didn't like him for the longest time.

Or maybe she did and didn't want anyone to know. Or to admit it.

I understand all of that, because Alec and I started in much the same way.

"This is phenomenal," he says as he steps back. "Absolutely amazing." He stays on his feet as Macie stands and hugs me too.

"Thank you," I say. "You guys have wine and appetizers?"

"The beet salad." Macie moans and sags as if her knees have gone weak. "Seriously the best thing I've eaten in a long, long time."

"How was the food at Lunch with Luna?"

"It was good," she says. "But this is next-level."

That makes me smile, whether it's true or not. Macie will never say my food isn't the best in the room, and for that, I love her. "You two having fun?"

They look at one another, and oh, they can communicate without talking now. That makes my heart happy, and seeing Macie so full of joy puts a smile on my face that won't fade.

"Yeah," Macie says slowly. "I think it's our best date yet."

"You said it was the best date of your life," Coy says as he sits back down.

I laugh, because that sounds like something Macie would say. She doesn't have much gray in her life. It's either good or bad. Black or white. Happy or sad. Raining or full of sunshine.

"So far," she says, and that's so her too. She'll never give Coy any extra rope to play with, and I suppose I can't blame her. Plenty of men in her past have tried to hang her with anything extra she gives them.

He sure seems to adore her though, and I make a mental note to tell her so as soon as I can. But right now, I say, "I'm pretty sure I'm supposed to be plating some strawberry shortcake, but it was so good to see you guys having fun."

"Love you, Tara. Tell Alec hi," Macie says.

I wave to them and head back to the kitchen, my heart so full of love for them. For the way Macie has always loved me, even in some of my worst moments. I rush to Alec's side and pull out my phone. He's plating short ribs, but I hold the phone out so he can see the screen.

"Look, baby," I say. "Look at the dining room. Look at how much fun they're having."

He glances, but doesn't look. He finishes by moving a potato and adding another one, then lifting the dish to the pick-up shelf. "Table twenty-four," he yells.

Then he looks at me, and then my phone. His face is pink from the heat and how hard he's working. He's utterly gorgeous, and I grin at him. "Look how amazing it's going out there."

He meets my eye again. "They look like they're having fun."

"They are."

"I thought I might not be *cut out* for this, but I think it's going really well."

"It could be *grater*," I say, rolling my eyes. "If you'd lay off the cutlery jokes."

He blinks at my amazing quick wit and use of a

kitchen item—the way he does—and then bursts out laughing. He grabs me around the waist, causing me to shriek, and presses a sloppy kiss to my lips to quiet me.

"I love you, Mrs. Ward," he murmurs, dancing slowly with me in his kitchen, with orders piling up and people everywhere.

"I love you too," I whisper back as I let my eyes fall closed.

"This is going so well," he says. "I think we should talk more about it after."

"Of course we will." I step out of his arms and nod. "Now, let's not mess things up by getting behind because you want to kiss me all night." I give him a pointed, cocked-eyebrow look and go toward my dessert station, which now has three tickets waiting on it, Alec's laughter following me like a delicious shadow I want to go everywhere with me.

CHAPTER TWENTY-ONE

MACIE

WHEN COY COMES TO PICK ME UP, I'M PEEKING through the window in my spare bedroom. It's not really a spare bedroom, because it's a cat palace. I don't even want to think about what would happen if I tried to have an office where Lizzie and Emma have their towers and toys and beds.

When Bri's stayed with me in the past, the felines have been displaced, and they stalked around like I was pulling out their whiskers one by one.

Now, her wedding is in only three weeks, and I can admit I'm a little surprised to be standing where I am. Not at the window peeking on my boyfriend as he gets out of the car but his sister doesn't.

But the fact that I'm in a relationship with my partner, with a man who I thought didn't like me and who I didn't like, and that I'm meeting a member of his family.

Meeting siblings and parents is what serious couples do. People in serious relationships. I want to be that woman, but at the same time, I feel wholly unprepared to be the type of person who's ready to do what Bri and Jason are going to do: Get married. Settle down. Maybe have kids to go with their pets.

I also want all of those things with my whole heart and soul. Watching all of my friends find their True Love, get married, and have babies has been an emotional roller coaster for me. Theme park rides are fun, and I'm always excited to get on them. There are rushes of enjoyment, but then there are moments of panic, of fear, of not knowing what's going to happen when you get to the top of the tallest hill, or if you'll lose your sunglasses on the loop-de-loop.

My doorbell rings, and I realize I've fallen a little bit too far into my thoughts. My dogs go wild, of course, but I've already caged them in the living room. It's the middle of the day, and Coy's taking me and Anna Lee to lunch.

"Something simple," he'd said. They'll go visit their mother afterward, and I'm sure that's when Anna Lee will gossip all about me. I've told my daddy I'll be later coming to see him, and he only responded with, *That's A-okay, sugarplum.*

I hurry around the corner, my guts in a knot. I want Anna Lee to like me so much, and that alone tells me how far I've fallen for Coy Cochran. My steps slow, as does my mind. "I'm falling in love with him."

I really am, and it scares me. I've fallen first for every man in my life, and it's exhausting to find out they don't feel the same. It hurts my heart when they laugh lightly and tell me they've met someone else at work, or they don't want someone who's going to work in a coffee shop her whole life, or they've already moved to Philadelphia for a job promotion I didn't even know they were up for.

"Mace?" Coy opens the door as he calls my name, and our eyes meet. He smiles like he's genuinely happy to see me, and the crazy thing is... He is genuinely happy to see me. I can feel it flowing off of him as he approaches, his gaze flickering to where the canines are behind me. "Hey, my pudding pie."

I love his term of endearment for me. It's very Southern, and very him, and I wrap my arms around him and lean into his weight. "Hey, yourself."

"You're not wearing shoes." He leans down to kiss me, and every nerve ending in my body clues into my lips. Nothing else matters, and I can have whole systems fail in my body and I wouldn't know. Not while Coy kisses me.

He pulls away after a few seconds. "You'll need shoes, Mace. Unless you made lunch here?" He glances toward my kitchen, knowing full-well I didn't make lunch. My proposed idea of a dinner in has never happened either.

"They're right here." I step into the kitchen and into my Crocs—a bright pink pair of tie-dye footwear that makes me smile.

He doesn't comment on them, and I don't think there's

a piece of clothing I can shock him with at this point. I think he nearly died of a heart attack on Valentine's Day when he came to pick me up for dinner. I'd had Jess get me a rockin' pink party dress that practically became my skin on top and then flared at the waist.

It may have shown a little too much of my girls, but I didn't hear any complaining from Coy. In fact, he'd stood in my front hallway and slathered cherry Chapstick on his lips like he might eat the whole tube for dinner.

The memory makes me smile, especially now that I know he uses that Chapstick as a way to buy time while he thinks of something to say, or as a way to force himself *not* to say what's on his mind.

He doesn't have the Chapstick right now at all, and I open the gate to let the dogs out. "All right, go say hello," I say. "Be nice. Gracious. Susan, don't run!"

Coy chuckles as Susan does indeed run at him. He's prepared for her now, and he lets her go right between his legs so he can scratch the base of her tail. Darcy is not happy to be left out of the scrub-fest, and Justice growls and whines for attention in the same breath.

"You guys go on," I tell them in a very commanding voice. They don't listen to me at all, and Coy continues to shower them with pets and pats and love. "Coy."

"Yeah." He straightens. "Yep. We have to go, guys. You guys go take a nap on the couch or the bed or wherever."

They listen to him, sort of. Darcy does, because he can really only handle excitement for a few seconds. Susan is an attention-hog, and she'll take anything she can get. In the morning, she follows me into the bathroom and looks at me in earnest while I try to figure out what she wants.

Usually, it's food, but she's sometimes just as happy for me to scratch around her ears or scrub her jowls. She trots into the living room and dives for a pair of old socks she carries around just for purposes like this. She loves showing off her claim for guests, and Coy plays right into her doggy paws.

"Susan," I warn her.

She doesn't care at all, and Coy finally heads for the front door. I follow him, and we make it out of the house without any canine incidents. I approach the car and a dark-haired woman with a pair of celebrity sunglasses on her face rises from the passenger seat. I can't see her eyes, and yet I can tell she and Coy are related.

A blip of panic moves through me. For some reason, I thought I'd be able to meet her...not in my driveway.

"You are beautiful," Anna Lee says, her lips curving up into a smile. "Coy, you didn't say she was beautiful."

"You've seen her before." Coy speaks in a tone as dry as the desert, which makes me smile.

"Hey, Anna Lee." I step around the front of Coy's luxury car and embrace her. We have seen each other before. I'm always behind the service counter, and she's ordering coffee with her brother. They chat to each other, and we've always done a really good job of ignoring one another until they've paid and can move on.

"It's great to finally meet you-meet you." She steps back and glances over to her brother. "Coy's told me a lot about you."

"Anna Lee, you promised."

"Oh, now I have to know what he's said."

"You really don't," Coy says. "Besides, I'm sure you can guess."

"How relentless I am about wanting to buy into Legacy Brew?" I guess.

"That's come up a time or two," Anna Lee admits. She turns to get in the back seat, and I meet Coy's eye over the top of his car.

"We weren't always as friendly as we are now," he says.

"I know." I give him a smile. "It's fine, Coy. My friends have been very good about setting aside all the things I've said about you."

He pauses with his hand on the door handle. "What have you said about me?"

Surprise darts through me. "Nothing." I open the door and slide into the passenger seat.

Coy drops into the car too, his eyes glued to me now. "Macie."

"Like you said, we weren't always as friendly as we are now." I reach up and tuck my hair behind my ear. I wear it down on days I don't go into the shop, and I use it to hide behind for a moment. "Coy, it was never bad."

"It doesn't sound good."

"You play basketball with Lance and Alec every weekend," I say. "They like you. Don't you like hanging out with them?"

"Yes," he says, and I hate that he's gone back to his formal affirmations.

"Okay, then." I can push this issue, but I decide I don't want to. Coy pulls out of my driveway, and as I look out the window on my side of the car, I realize I've changed a little bit. The Macie Before Coy would've pushed the issue. She'd have fought with him until her point got made.

The Macie I Am With Coy doesn't want to hurt his feelings. I'm not afraid of hard conversations, but I don't have to be right all the time. I don't have to have the last word in every discussion we have, including this one.

A small smile rises through my soul and touches my face. I like being with Coy, and I look over to him and reach for his hand. "Where are we going for lunch?"

"Anna Lee found this cool new food truck," he says, lifting his eyes to look in the rearview mirror. "Where am I going?"

"It's called The Big Red Wagon Wheel," she says. "Turn right up here."

"Can't you just put it on the speaker system?" he asks. "I don't want you to tell me where to go the whole way there."

"Turn right up here," Anna Lee says.

I quickly tap and swipe and type in the name of the food truck. It comes up on my app, and I balance it in the cup holder so Coy can hopefully see it. He looks over to me, and we exchange some words without saying anything.

His gratitude shines through in his small smile and the way he reaches to turn up the radio. He checks the phone every few minutes, and Anna Lee continues to verbally direct him. He only rolls his eyes once, and his restraint is amazing. I marvel at it as he reaches for something in the console, knocking my phone to the floor.

"Dang it," he says while I say, "Pimento cheese and crackers."

"Pimento cheese and crackers?" Anna Lee asks.

I start fishing around my feet for my phone, but I can't find it anywhere. My shoulder starts to twist, and my neck kinks, but I hate not knowing where my phone is.

"We're almost there," Coy says.

"How do you know?" Anna Lee asks.

He lifts his cherry Chapstick to his mouth, but he still answers after he swipes it on. "Because Macie put it on her phone."

"Why'd you put it in your phone?" Anna Lee asks. "I'm getting him there."

I can't find the stupid phone, and now I'm in trouble with Coy's sister. This isn't good. "I, uh..." I look over to him, but he says nothing. "I could just tell he wanted to be able to see the route for himself."

"He's too much of a control freak."

"This control freak is the one driving through the city

during the lunch rush," Coy says, plenty of irritation in his tone.

"You're the one who told me you were a control freak," she says from the back seat. "That's why you wouldn't let Macie buy into Legacy for so long."

"Anna Lee," he says, plenty of exasperation in his voice. He sighs, and it's the frustrated kind. "I don't want to do this."

"It's fine, Coy," I say. I knew he had a lot of reasons he didn't want to let me buy into Legacy, and of course I know what a control freak Coy is. He oils his rowing machine, for crying out loud.

The Big Red Wagon Wheel comes into view on the right, and it's nowhere Coy would ever go. It's a giant pioneer wagon stained a bright red, with white-painted letters that spell out the name, half of which aren't lined up with each other.

Coy would never allow such a thing at Legacy Brew, and I glance over to him. He sighs again, this one telling me he's going to eat as little as possible and stop somewhere better later. I know that won't be until after his visit with his mother, which he also doesn't want to do.

My heart goes out to him as he pulls into the gravel parking lot that only holds a few other cars.

"I don't know about this place, Anna Lee," Coy says.

"You have no sense of adventure," she tosses back.

He doesn't respond, and I can't stand the way his jaw

tightens and juts out. My protective side rears up, and I say, "That's not true."

"Mace," he says under his breath.

"Did you tell her about the swimming with the dolphins?" I ask him. "Or how you've taken a ton of risks in the past year since I came on at Legacy? Or that you've drawn a new logo for Legacy—and that's like stepping out onto the wild frontier." I twist in my seat, the fire inside me raging hot. "He has plenty of adventure."

Anna Lee simply looks at me from behind her sunglasses, and Coy stays likewise silent. Irritation floods me, and I reach for my door handle to get out of this tense situation. "I don't get why you won't say something."

"It's not worth it," Coy says. "Anna Lee knows how to rile me up, and I know how to shut her down. This isn't helping."

I feel two inches tall, and my pulse vibrates through my body. "There are a million restaurants in this city. We should be able to go somewhere we'll like."

"They're supposed to have amazing wings here," Anna Lee says.

"You don't even like eating things with your hands," I say, looking at Coy.

He glares at me like this is my fault. Something tells me to drop this, but instead, I dig my heels in. "Come on. Let's find somewhere else."

"You don't like wings?" Anna Lee asks. "What kind of Southern boy are you?"

"I'm fine." He gets out of the car, and I scramble to go after him.

"Coy," I say.

"Macie, just drop this," he says. "I don't care where we eat."

"Yes, you do," I say. "Why won't you tell your own sister you want to go somewhere else?"

Anna Lee joins us, and it's probably a good thing there aren't many people here. That's never a good sign, by the way. A good restaurant should have people clamoring to eat at it during a busy mealtime. This place is dead, and I'm not sure I can put anything in my mouth that comes out of that wagon.

"Do you want to go somewhere else?" she asks.

"Yes." I face her. "I'd love to go somewhere else."

Coy comes to my side, his hand sliding along my waist. "Macie, you know I love your fire, but it's fine."

"Is this how you guys are?" I look from her to him.

"No," they say together.

This is obviously a losing battle, and I take a deep breath and face The Big Red Wagon Wheel. "All right. Let's go eat some wings." I take a couple of steps and add under my breath, "And hope we don't get salmonella."

"Macie," Coy says behind me. His feet crunch in the gravel too, but I'm marching, and when that happens, I'm fast. He grabs my arm, but I pull it away without turning. "Will you stop?"

I come to a dead stop and twirl to face him. "She's not

your momma," I say. "I can't believe you don't disagree with her about anything."

"We disagree about plenty," he fires back. "I just thought we could have a nice lunch without...this." He gestures to me, as if I'm the problem.

"This?" My voice pitches up to match my eyebrows. My forehead feels all crinkly, and my heartbeat crackles through my veins.

"Coy, we can go somewhere else," Anna Lee says as she arrives on the scene.

I wave toward her. "Now she wants to go somewhere else. That's two out of three." I start back toward the car, my short legs eating up a lot of distance in a short amount of time. I'm walking through gravel, but I still hear Coy say, "This is how she is."

Everything slows down. My body goes cold. The sun is shining, and there's traffic noise from the cars that continue to pass by on the street. I want to turn back to him and ask him what he just said.

But I know what he said. The words echo in my ears and sting their way through my whole body.

This is how she is.

Their footsteps approach, and they both flow by me. It feels like someone has wrapped me in a mummy-suit of plastic wrap, and everything is warped and blurry.

"Mace," Coy says, and the world moves at the right speed again.

I pull out my phone, getting very much reminded of

another time I had to use my phone to call for a ride when I was out with my boyfriend.

Coy gives me a few seconds, and then he says, "What are you doing? Are you coming?"

I look up at him. "You know what? No. I'm not coming. I'm calling a Carry." I turn away from him, but my options here are a diving rental place and the fugly wagon wheel place. There's no refuge here, and I have serious doubts that Coy will just drive away the way Andy did.

"A Carry?"

I finish putting in my pin and tap to request a car at my location.

"Macie, talk to me."

I face him, the fire inside me near bonfire level. "How am I, exactly, Coy?"

"How are you?"

"You just told your sister, 'this is how she is.'" I poke him in the chest, and he falls back a step. "What does that mean?"

He sighs, and it's the tired, *I-don't-have-time-for-this* kind. It sums up how he's always felt about me, and another piece of my heart grows cold.

"It's fine," I say. "I know how I am." Hurt pinches through me, but I will not cry in this horrible parking lot with a horribly loud red wagon as a backdrop. "You and Anna Lee enjoy your lunch."

"I didn't mean to cause a problem," Anna Lee says

from several feet behind Coy.

He draws in a breath through his nose and meets my eye. "I just meant you're like a storm," he says. "It's nothing I've not said before."

"You think I'm a storm?" I didn't question him on it before, and I'm not sure why it bothers me so much now.

"You like to thunder and lightning and...blow like the wind." He reaches for me, and to my surprise, I let him hold my hands. "You storm and boil and then the eye of the storm comes through, and everything calms down. You're more rational, and we can actually talk."

He's not one-hundred percent wrong, but I hate the words, *This is how she is.*

"Pudding, it's a compliment," he says. "I really do love the storminess inside you. Sometimes, I wish you'd slow down and listen to me."

"I listen to you." I've actually been working really hard on doing that.

"I said I didn't care about coming here."

"But I knew it annoyed you," I say. "Just like the map thing, and you were okay with that."

"I'm a grown man," he says. "I can take care of myself."

I settle back on my far foot, pulling my hands with me. "So you just don't like that I tried to stand up for you." My stomach feels like I've swallowed the fluorescent red wagon.

"It's not that," he says. He gently takes my phone from

me. "I'm going to cancel your Carry, and we'll drop Anna Lee off at home, and we'll just go to lunch." He raises his eyebrows. "Okay?"

"She's going to hate me," I say.

"She won't," he says as he taps on my phone. With my ride canceled, he hands the device back to me. "Macie, can you look at me?"

I hadn't realized I wasn't looking at him until that moment. It takes a lot of energy and several long moments for me to bring my gaze to his. He gives me a soft smile. "I don't mind the storm inside you," he says.

"I don't want you to just 'not mind' it." I shake my head. "I don't want to be a storm at all." That's the real problem, and this conversation isn't going to fix it. Coy's not going to fix it. Anna Lee's never going to like me now that I've blown like the wind.

I don't even know why I want her to like me. Probably because she's Coy's only sibling, and she's important to him.

"Let's just go to lunch." I step past him but not angrily. Well, I am angry, but not at him. Fine, sort of at him. I still slide my hand into his so we can walk back to the car together.

"I'm sorry I upset you," he says.

"I'm the one who obviously upset you," I say. "Don't apologize. And I'm going to have to apologize to Anna Lee."

"She'll be fine."

I don't say anything, because I feel like whatever might come out of my mouth will be the wrong thing. I don't want just *fine*. I don't want my boyfriend to put up with me. I don't want him to have to tell his friends and family that that's "just how I am."

I'm not sure why that bothers me, but it does. Once I figure out how to communicate why it does, I'll talk to him about it.

CHAPTER TWENTY-TWO

COY

The building could burn down around me, and I wouldn't know. My heart lodges so far up my throat, I can't swallow. I also can't look away from the computer screen where Dawson has included the mock-ups of my drawing.

He works with some fantastic designers, and while the three logos that have come in are all different, they're all exactly what I want. "How do people choose?" I mutter.

My head pounds, as I've been a tick or two under the weather in the past week or so. It has nothing to do with the lecture Anna Lee gave me about letting Macie dictate my life, though if you ask Macie, she'd say Anna Lee bosses me around.

It has nothing to do with the fact that things between Macie and I have cooled off considerably since the Lunch That Never Was. Macie had apologized several times, and

I'd dropped Anna Lee back at her duplex, and she'd gone to see our mother herself. That alone cost me something major with my sister, but Macie's important to me.

No matter what it is, I don't feel well, and I'm tired of making decisions. No amount of cherry Chapstick can solve my problems, and I don't even reach for the tube I keep in my top desk drawer.

These are all genius, I type out to Dawson. *I'll go over them with Macie and get back to you. Do we need to meet again? What do you and Callie think as far as where we want to take Legacy?*

I love having a team that comprises a "we." It's so much easier to shoulder the business when I'm not doing it alone, and that's the biggest thing I've been wrong about all these years. In the beginning, I thought I needed to keep Legacy to myself to honor my daddy. I've realized since then that it's not about holding her hostage. It's about being able to help her grow, and I'd taken her as far as I could on my own. With a team, we've gone so much further, and I get up from my desk and call, "Mace!"

She won't have heard me, as she's working out front, as usual. Not only that, but I've only been at my desk for twenty minutes. Long enough to take a few sips of coffee as I went through my email.

I push through the black plastic door. The rush isn't anywhere near over, but I locate Macie quickly. She's out on the floor, delivering something with a sunny smile. She did not like me calling her a storm last week, but I haven't been able to get her to tell me why. She says she doesn't know, and she won't talk any more about it.

Honestly, the distance between us feels the same as what existed after that orange-couch kiss. She'd put me in my place, changed the subject, and refused to come back to it. It's almost exactly the same.

I watch her pat the shoulder of an elderly woman she's obviously friends with, clear some trash from a nearby table, and walk back toward me. Our eyes meet, and I gesture to her that I need her. She nods, and I retreat to my office.

It takes her several minutes to finally join me, at which point, I'm annoyed. "What's going on out there?"

"Well, while you're back here sipping coffee and doing your little drawings, some of us are serving fifty customers an hour." She perches on the lip of my desk and folds her arms. "You have three minutes, because that's when the coffee will be gone, and I'll need to make more. Oh, and it took a few extra minutes because Amber stopped by with her wedding announcements." She tosses the thick paper invite on my desk. "Yay for June fifth."

I'm not sure how to unpack everything she's just said. My lungs leak air from the tiny holes she punched in them by calling my art "little drawings." She's asked me over the past several weeks to show her more of what I've done, but I haven't yet. Now I'm never going to.

That makes my heart shrivel, because I want to share

everything with Macie. But not if I can't trust her not to throw it back in my face, and I obviously can't.

She's also implied that I don't work as hard as her, and that I don't have as many emotional situations to deal with as she does. Both might be true, but at the same time, they're completely untrue.

So I blink, trying to make everything align in my head. "We can talk later," I finally say.

"No, I'm back here now."

I look at my computer, but I've replied to Dawson's email, and the mocks aren't showing. "I shouldn't have asked you to come during the rush."

She turns to look at the screen too, and my hand shoots out, turning off the monitor. "Hey," she says.

"Let's go finish the rush." I get to my feet and start to leave my office. She doesn't follow me, and I'm not surprised one whit. We're one-hundred percent back in that horrible place where she shelved us after that forbidden, midnight kiss.

I bent to her will then, just like I normally bend to my mother's and Anna Lee's. I'm far better at standing up to Macie than I am them, and I always have been. Before, I didn't want to scare her away in case we could be something.

But now we are something, and it's exactly the same. I thought we'd changed. I know I have, as I don't fire back at her immediately the way I used to. She'd stopped doing it too—until last week.

I leave my office, because if I don't, I'm going to say something I'll regret. I don't work the front of the house very often, but I can certainly do it. I have the menu memorized forward and backward and sideways, and I reach for an apron hanging on a hook just inside the black door and tie it around my waist as I enter the fray out front.

I make more coffee for our huge canisters, check the flavorings bar, and go to check the tickets. I prep cappuccinos and macchiatos and lattes, no problem. Macie doesn't join us, and every employee out front keeps shooting me side-eyes and furtive looks like I've chopped her up and stuffed her in the freezer in the back.

The rush trickles and slows, and I wash my hands and then start wiping down all the counters. This is what Macie does, and for some reason, I want to prove to her and everyone else that I can do it too. That I'm not just sitting in my cushy office drawing cartoons.

None of them would get paid without me, and Macie doesn't even know how to login to that system. She's never even asked me how to do it. Our electric bill wouldn't be paid without me, and aprons wouldn't get reordered or sent for cleaning. Our equipment would be broken down, and our taxes backed up for years.

Just because what I do isn't sexy or all that noticeable doesn't mean it's not necessary. It doesn't mean I'm less important. It doesn't mean I don't work hard.

All of these thoughts fuel me, setting fire to my belly,

as I work, and by the time I leave the service area, I'm stalking like a panther toward my prey.

Macie's sitting in my chair at my desk, and the logos are on the screen.

"What are you doing?" I bark.

She turns toward me, her face set in a mask. "I made some notes." She stands and hands me a legal pad covered in her loopy handwriting.

I don't even look at it. "What's going on here?"

"I don't know what you mean."

"I mean, you said we could do this together. You told me you'd have an open mind about these logos. I called you back here so we could go over them together." I take a step closer to her. "Legacy is *ours*, Mace. I don't want you to take notes solo and then hand them off to me." I toss the notebook back to the desk. "The rush just ended. They're cleaning. Can you sit down and talk to me about what you think?"

For a moment, her face crumbles. Then she shakes her head, slides everything back into position, and leaves my office.

I turn and watch her go, completely confused about what's happening. "I don't want to do this anymore," I say out loud. I don't want to be the boss who makes all the decisions. I don't want to be the one everyone tiptoes around. I don't want Macie to be upset with me for reasons I don't understand.

"Your own medicine is bitter, isn't it?"

"What?" I look up from the floor.

Macie stuffs her hands in a regular blue Legacy apron. She hasn't worn her cheetah print one since last week, and she's insane if she thinks I haven't noticed.

"You judge everyone," she says. "It's not so fun to be judged, is it?"

"I—judge everyone?"

"That's why I don't want to be called a storm." She takes a menacing step inside my office. "It feels like you're judging me, and it's not a fun feeling. It feels demeaning, like I'm beneath you."

"I...I have never thought that," I say. "That's not what I'm doing at all when I say that." She's storming right now, I want to point out, but I hold my tongue. If I don't, she'll probably cut it off. "Not only are you making incorrect assumptions, but I've literally only called you a storm one time. One." I hold up one finger. "And you told me you didn't like it, and I haven't done it again. I don't know how to do better than that."

"You're thinking it."

"You have no idea what I'm thinking." I shake my head. "But I know how you are, Mace. You think I'm judging you, so you'll judge me. While you work so hard out front, I'm back here doing my *little drawings*."

I sit down and pick up her notebook. I drop it in the trashcan. "You think I feel like I'm better than you—which I don't, by the way—so you'll throw punches and jabs at me to make me feel small."

"That's ridiculous. I—"

"Congratulations," I say over her. "You did all of the above. I'm a moron. I don't do anything around here. You're better than me." I'm yelling by the last statement. "So just go. I'll handle the logo—just the way I want. Because you promised me you'd have an open mind and help me with it, but that's obviously not true."

I scoot closer to my computer. "At least I don't break my promises."

"You're being stupid."

"Yep, that's what I am."

"Coy, this is—"

"Stupid," I say over her, exploding to my feet. My chair goes flying behind me, and Macie jumps as it slams into the wall. My heart pops like firecrackers, some with loud beats and some quieter. "Yeah, I am stupid, Macie. Because I thought we could actually get along for longer than a few weeks. I thought you could be professional at work. I thought you'd *help* me run this place, not try to take it over. I thought you'd be a bit more mature."

I scan her down to her sparkly sneakers, which I used to love. Right now, everything makes me angry.

"You know, you've dangled me by a string for long enough. I'm tired of caving to you and letting you dictate if we're okay or not. I'm tired of dealing with your moods. I'm tired of rationalizing away the things you do that I don't like, because there's so dang much about you I do." My throat hurts, and I have to get out of here.

I shake my head again and face my desk. "I don't feel well. I *barely work* on Tuesdays anyway, so I'm going to go home." I jam my wallet in my back pocket, rip off the apron, and walk away.

She doesn't say a single word, and she doesn't follow me outside to my car. Part of me wishes she would've, and part of me feels nothing but victory that I've finally taken a stand against the mighty Macie Madsen—and won.

CHAPTER TWENTY-THREE

MACIE

I wake up in the middle of the night, my breath lodged somewhere down in my chest. The water around me undulates, shifting me left and right, up and down. I've been underwater for too long. I can't breathe.

After flinging my comforter off my legs, I stand and realize I'm not underwater. I'm not a big fishing vessel that's lost at sea, a huge hurricane coming toward me. A wall of water. Wind that howls like wolves, and rain that pelts sideways.

A terrible storm no one can stop.

All at once, I understand why it bothers me so much when Coy says I'm like a storm. My mama used to call me one too, but she said it while she smiled. She'd pet back my hair and tell me, "Macie-Mae, you've got to learn to calm the trouble inside you. I know you can do it."

She'd tell me that whenever she made me wear an

itchy dress to church, and I'd throw a tantrum. Or when it was time to leave the park, and I didn't want to. As a child, I tamed those small-kid storms, but the raging tempest has never really died inside me.

I only subdue her for a time.

Mama calling me a storm didn't bother me, because I knew she loved me.

"It was Andy," I whisper to the nighttime air around me. On the bed behind me, one of the dogs shifts. Maybe two. They sleep in a big old pile, and I ignore them as I walk around the bed and toward my master bath.

I don't turn on any lights, because I've traveled this path lots of times in the dark. My heart pounds as I lean my hands against the vanity and take deep breath after deep breath.

"Andy called me a storm," I say. "He said I was a hurricane no one could stop."

That was the whole reason I'd gone to Legacy Brew and run into Coy all those months ago. When we kissed.

The Kissing Incident started because Andy called me a storm. He told me I was the reason he'd left Charleston and moved to Phila-freaking-delphia without telling me.

It was my fault.

Tears sting my eyes, fill them, and fall before I even know what's happening. "I'm the reason everything falls apart," I whisper to my ghostly reflection in the gray light of my bathroom.

I don't want to be this storm that rages through towns

and communities, destroying them. I don't want to wreck everything and leave everyone who comes in contact with me in ruins.

I don't do that—to my girlfriends. Only the men who dare to get too close.

Fear reaches out with its big hand and grips my heart. The fingers close around it and twist, and my chest heaves as I try to breathe through the pain of knowing that I'm just too much for most men.

I'm too loud. I'm too bossy. I'm too argumentative. I'm too opinionated. I'm too much bad and not enough good.

I turn away from myself and slink down to the floor, my tears painting invisible tracks down my face. Susan pads toward me and noses my cheek. I grab onto the golden retriever and hug her tightly. Darcy arrives, followed by Justice. They create a barrier around me, trying to make me feel better.

They can't, but it sure is nice not to be alone. I'm glad I didn't rehome Susan the way I'd planned. I take in strays from time to time and try to find them good homes. Some I just keep.

I'm very much like those strays right now, homeless and wondering if I'll ever belong to someone for longer than a few months, and only myself to blame for it.

When I'm all cried out, I get to my feet. My phone tells me it's two-thirty, and I figure that's not too early to go into work. Coy works a reduced schedule on Thursdays, and I was off all day yesterday.

He didn't text or call, and though our friends hung out at the shop, I didn't go. We haven't exactly broken up, but I feel like the next time I come in contact with him face-to-face, we will. Maybe that's why I don't want to see him.

He's too nice of a guy to break up with me over the phone or in a text, and maybe if I just never see him again, I can pretend I didn't ruin us with thunder and lightning.

I skip the shower and simply pull on my black clothes. I make sure the animals have fresh food and water, but I don't do any of my other morning chores. Dishes can sit in the sink for another day. Who'll care? No one will be coming over.

The streets are empty, the town silent, which isn't unusual for midweek in early March. It's not exactly warm, and the nightlife in Charleston is more downtown and less out where Legacy Brew sits.

As I key my way into the back door, I wonder what logo Coy chose and when he'll tell me. I wonder if I should sell him his coffee shop back, cut my losses, and go find something else to do with my life.

What? I ask myself. *What else am I going to do with my life?*

College dropout. Unmarried. No real skills to speak of, unless you count how amazing of a barista I am.

"You're a people-person," I tell myself as I flip on the lights and reach for an apron. I could do anything that requires me to chit-chat with people. Ghost tours of the city. Historical tours. Another coffee shop, somewhere on the other side of the metropolis so I'll never see anyone I know ever again.

I'm being dramatic, I know. I'm allowed for a little while, and by the time I slide the tray of my mama's chocolate cupcakes in the oven, I'm starting to feel better.

I leave everything where it is—and I'm not a clean baker—and pull out my phone to check what I have to do for Bri's wedding next weekend. I can't believe it's only ten days away. Us girls have a spa day planned for the entire Saturday before she and Jason tie the knot in the backyard of his rustic farmhouse, and I suddenly can't wait.

Callie, Tara, Jessie, and Bri will know what to say to cheer me up. They'll help me grapple with the horrible reality that I might be single for the rest of my life.

My final bridesmaid dress fitting is tomorrow, and Callie texted near midnight to say the shoes she'd ordered for all of us would be here no later than Monday.

Bri's sister is coming from California to do all the food, and she's asked me to be Chelsea's shadow at the wedding. I'd told Bri I could do that. I can help set up. I can help take down. I can help serve dinner.

Both she and Jason want a small affair, so it's lunch, not dinner, and they're not using a wedding planner. Bri can barely match her clothes, and she wears pretty much neutrals with maybe a splash of color in a scarf. But she knows what she likes, and she wants simple.

Jason will do whatever she wants, despite his family

being old and Southern like Coy's. My mind drifts to what our wedding might've been like. I only have men in my family, and they don't really care what my I-do looks like. I used to dream about it all the time, but in recent years, the film's gone gray.

I smell chocolate and straighten as I pull myself out of my discolored fantasies. I didn't set a timer. I've turned toward the oven when the lights go off. Just blazing bright one moment, and pitch black the next.

"What the—?"

"Oops," someone says. A man. In the building with me.

I duck, my hand scrambling along the top of the station for something I can use to defend myself. My fingers close around the leftover bag of brown sugar as light floods the kitchen again.

I blink, trying to get my eyes to work when they've been thrown from light to dark and back. I squeeze the lump of sugar into a tight ball and launch it at the man in the black hoodie who's just come in through the plastic door that leads out front.

"Get out of here!" I yell.

"Hey, whoa," he says, ducking.

It hardly matters. My baseball-sized lump of sugar didn't make it very far. The man flips back his hoodie, and it's Coy.

The world freezes. My body screams at me to run, but my mind is trying to tell it we don't need to. My heart says we do, and the scent of chocolate intensifies, telling me I'm about to burn my middle-of-the-night cupcakes.

"What are you doing here?" I gripe at him as I swipe the oven mitts off a nearby counter and hurry over to the oven. I rescue the cupcakes at nearly the last moment and slide them onto a cooling rack.

When I face Coy, he hasn't moved a muscle. He looks like he hasn't been asleep yet tonight, and maybe he hasn't been. I know he likes to stay up late, because he doesn't have to be here at the crack of dawn.

He blinks, his features hardening as he seems to take in who he's with. Me. "Couldn't sleep," he says. "You?"

"I had a nightmare," I say before I can censor myself.

Something compassionate crosses his face. "Really?" he asks. "What about?"

"Drowning." I remove the oven mitts and toss them back onto the counter where they'd been. "Out at sea, in this huge storm. It was horrible."

"Sounds horrible." He takes a step toward me, thinks better of it, and points toward his office. "Did you want to go over the logos for a minute?" He glances over to the cupcakes and then the mess I haven't cleaned up yet. "Or did you just want to bake?"

I haven't called him. I didn't text him that I'd be here. It makes no sense that he'd think I'm here in the middle of the night, just hoping he'll come in so we can go over the logos. But I say, "I'd like to see the logos," and then I follow him to his office.

I hang back as he unlocks it, and the space inside is about half of what I remember. Maybe that's the sexy cologne clinging to his sweatshirt or the way his tee rides up and shows me a nice set of abs as he removes the sweatshirt.

My whole body heats, and thankfully, Coy doesn't look at me. "Dawson sent over three," he says. "I think they're all pretty final, but I'm sure we can ask for adjustments."

"Okay," I murmur.

His machine takes its sweet time waking up. "Did you really think you could incapacitate an intruder with a cup of brown sugar?" A chuckle rides in his question, and instead of answering it, I hold my head high and pull the extra chair in his office closer to his desk.

"You never know," I say.

He does laugh quietly then, and it makes me want to reach out and brush that lock of hair off his forehead that always falls forward. I do, and we both freeze again.

"I know why I don't like it when you call me a storm," I say. "I know why it feels judgmental, even if you don't mean it to."

"Why?" he asks.

"Because it's what Andy said the night he told me he'd already moved to Philadelphia. He said he always went along with me, with everything I said, because I'm this big storm at sea and nothing can stop me."

Coy searches my face, and I have no idea what I want him to say.

"I came here that night too," I say. "That's the night we kissed."

His eyes drop to my mouth but rebound just as quickly. "He told you that on that same night?"

I nod, not sure why I'm telling him this. Then it all makes sense. "I wasn't sure why it bothered me so much. My mama used to call me a storm too." A smile touches my mouth now, with my quivering lip not far behind. I miss her so much sometimes. "But when she did it, it was out of love. Andy did it as insult, and it sounded like you did too."

"I didn't mean it to be," he whispers.

I nod again, wondering if necks ever get tired of doing that. "Thank you." I indicate his computer. "Let's go over these." A bold, striking logo with the words "Legacy Brew" in sharp, almost jagged letters already sits on the screen.

It looks like I'm seeing through a window with a coffee cup painted on it, the words inside and steam lifting above it.

"Okay," he says. "There's this one. They took one of the cups I'd drawn in another rendition and focused in on it. Added the window. I don't hate it."

"Sounds like you don't love it." I do love the logo sitting on the screen, but with a few clicks, Coy replaces it with another one.

This one is too busy, in my opinion. There's silhouettes of people, which is kind of nice. It makes the image feel alive and vibrant, I'll say that. They're drinking coffee, of course, but it doesn't feel like the thing we sell the most is prevalent enough.

"I like this one," he says.

"You do?"

He looks over at me, surprise in his tired eyes. "You don't?" He goes back to studying the logo. "Of course you don't."

My stomach swoops and catches on fire. I try to tamp it down, but the flames rise anyway. "What do you like about it?" I sit back in my chair and fold my arms, almost like I'm preparing for a fight.

Because I am.

Coy even said it the last time we met here in the middle of the night. We fight about everything.

Not everything, I think. We've actually gotten along really well for the past six weeks. I really like him. I remind myself of these things as he starts to say why he likes this logo.

"It feels like coming home," he says. "Like I could walk into the picture and be turned into a blob-person, grab a cup of coffee, and sit on the couch and belong."

That's essentially what he did when he started hanging out with me and the other couples in the couch area of the shop.

"I like that it shows some of Lavender Street," he says.

"We've been here for eighty years." He shrugs the powerful shoulder closest to me. "I don't know. I like it."

"There's another one?" I ask.

"Yeah." He clicks around some more, and a third logo brightens the screen. It's not a long visual of the shop, nor is it a square like looking through a window. This one is round, with a simple cup of coffee in the middle.

"This one looks the most like one I drew," he says. "I think the lettering is better than the others, but it feels...boring."

I lean closer to the screen, just now noticing that the circle around the cup is actually made up of letters. "What does that say around it?"

"It's the suggested slogan," he says. "I hate that it's around the coffee cup. You can't even read it."

"Yeah, I agree."

"It says, 'You build the legacy. We'll provide the coffee.'"

"Huh."

"Do you like it?" he asks. "I gave them what we'd talked about, but I thought it was too long. This *is* more succinct."

"It is," I say, but I don't say I like it. I don't, and I'm trying to have the open mind he wants me to have. This is an easy choice for me, but Coy's obviously been laboring over it for a couple of days now.

"You don't like any of them," he says.

My eyes cut over to his. "How do you know that?"

"Because your mouth is all bunched up like you smell something bad." He sighs in a way that says *I don't even know why I try*, and he reaches to switch off the monitor. "They're not perfect, I know that. But two of them are pretty close. We can give feedback."

"Great, give them some feedback."

"What would yours be?"

I shake my head, because I already looked at these and wrote out some feedback. He threw it away. "I'm not going to say. This is your thing, and you obviously have a different vision for it than I would."

"It's not me versus you. Or me *or* you. It's me *and* you." His dark eyes glow with the flicker of danger, of irritation. "You said you'd help me."

"I just did. Now you only have two to consider." I stand, because this office is too small, and I still annoy Coy way too much. He hasn't broken up with me, but I fear he will if I stay for even another minute.

It's far easier to breathe out in the main kitchen, but Coy's footsteps behind me land solidly. "That's it?" he asks.

"Coy, I don't want to fight with you." I stoop to pick up my pathetic brown-sugar-weapon. "I think the first one is too jagged, okay? The letters feel like what you'd see on a... a...an ammunition logo. We serve teas and coffees and frilly pastries. The second one is too busy. It has too much going on. The families, the friends, the freaking pets."

"We have people bring their pets in all the time."

"Yeah, I know." I turn my back on him and go back to the station where I made the cupcakes. Normally, I'd stay and frost them, eat half a dozen and fall asleep at my desk. I don't want to do that either.

I simply stand there, staring at the brown sugar, my mind so, so tired and wandering all over. Coy joins me, but he doesn't touch anything either. "Are you okay?" he asks.

"Don't be nice to me," I say, because I really hate being patronized.

He rolls his head, stretching his neck. "So this is it for us, then."

"I don't know."

"You won't talk to me about the business. You won't let me be nice to you personally. I don't know what you want from me, Macie."

"I don't either." I finally get the courage to look up. "Don't you get it? I don't either!"

He grabs my shoulders, his fingers digging in painfully. "Hey," I say, struggling against his grip. "Let me go."

Coy, in all his dark-haired and dark-eyed glory, takes a big breath. "How long until this blows over?"

"I'm not a storm," I say through gritted teeth.

He backs up a step and releases me. I pull down my shirt, my heart pounding. "It's not you," I say. "I need to date a...a...a weatherman or something. Someone who can predict my moods, tell us both when something bad is coming so we can hunker down and ride it out."

He simply stares at me, and I don't know what I'm even saying. "You deserve someone better than me, Coy." I throw my hands up into the air, already crying again. "You really do. I'm sorry you've wasted so much time on me. You deserve so much better."

I shake my head, my nose hot and tight, and all of my systems in agreement that we need to get out of here, pronto.

I take off at a run for the back door, despite Coy's protest. I slam through it and keep going toward my car. He can lock up. He can clean up. Legacy is *his* legacy, and I wonder for the first time in twelve long years if it's mine.

Behind the wheel, I wipe my face and get the car started. I sense more than see Coy standing at the back door, so I don't look that way. I just jam the car into drive and go.

I drive, and drive, and drive, thinking I may never go back.

CHAPTER TWENTY-FOUR

COY

I BEND OVER AND TIE MY SHOES, MY CHEST A HOLLOW tin that can't take proper care of my vital organs. My heart somehow keeps beating. The shop has carried on without Macie for two days now. She's texted me to say she won't be back until Monday, but part of me even questions that.

When I tried to get more information out of her, she said she just needed to get away from things for a while. When I asked her where she was and if she was safe, she said, *At my brother's in North Carolina. I'm fine.*

Both of her brothers live in North Carolina, but I hadn't pushed the issue. Macie doesn't want me to push her, and now that we're not together anymore, I don't have that luxury anyway.

"Coy," Dawson says, plenty of brightness in his tone.

I look up and into his eyes, a quick smile darting across my face before it gets too heavy to hold. "Hey."

He and Lance sit down on the bench beside me and start lacing up their high-tops too. Alec is already out on the court, and Jason isn't coming this morning. He and Bri are doing something for their wedding next weekend, and once again, my robotic heart flops against my metallic chest.

The wedding.

I have to go, and Macie wouldn't miss it for the world. She's nothing if not loyal, and I used to think she'd never go back on her word. The problem is, she has a couple of times with me.

Sort of, my mind whispers. She did give me feedback about the logos, even if it wasn't in the format or quantity that I wanted. She's covered her shifts, but I know that's not because of me. It's because she loves Legacy Brew as much as I do, and she will never compromise the shop.

I'm expendable, able to be tossed aside while she figures out what she wants in her life, but the coffee shop? No way.

"Can you pick me up for Copperhead's tonight?" Lance asks, leaning past Dawson to look at me.

My mind blanks. "What?"

"Copperhead's," they say together. "The ladies are doing a fashion show in their bridesmaids dresses," Lance adds. "Jessie wants to do like a photo shoot or something at the house." He looks at Dawson for more details, but Dawson only shrugs one shoulder.

"We're all going to Copperhead's for wings and

drinks," Dawson says. "You said you were in, and Lance needs a ride."

"Oh, uh, I don't know." I stand as Alec jogs toward us. He passes me the ball, and it feels too big and too hard in my hands. "I don't think I can come tonight. Macie hasn't been at the shop, and…" I trail off, because this is a stupid excuse. Macie wouldn't be at the shop on a Saturday night anyway, and everyone standing here knows it.

"You're not coming tonight?" Alec asks. He bends over and plucks a towel from his gym bag and mops up his face with it. "You have to."

"Why?" I ask.

"Because." Dawson stands too and claps me on the shoulder. "You're one of us now, Coy."

"Am I, though?" I survey the three of them, and yes, I really like them. They're good men, and they're good to their wives. They have good jobs, and they're living good lives. I'm very lucky that they've allowed me to graft my way into their friendship, and my cold, tiny heart actually beats normally for a moment.

They're the first friends I've had in a long, long time. Since taking over the shop, when I let it consume me day and night. I lost a lot when I gained what I thought I wanted, because it's too hard to maintain friendships and relationships and run a business when you're only twenty-four years old.

"Of course I am," I say at the same time Lance says, "Of course you are."

"What's happening here?" Alec asks.

"I broke up with Macie," I say. "Or she broke up with me. We broke up. She's not going to stop hanging out with y'all at the shop, and—"

"She hasn't been there for the past few nights," Lance says.

"I haven't been around either," Alec says. "Too many evening clients lately."

"Cal and I don't come every night," Dawson says. "But I did notice Macie wasn't there yesterday."

"She's apparently in North Carolina," I say. "She hasn't been to work either." I'm not going to say anything bad about her, but if Jessie is doing a fashion show photo shoot at her house tonight...Macie will be there. I rationalize that she always has Sundays off, and she didn't tell me she'd be at her brother's until she returned to work. She said she'd be back on Monday.

"It'll be easier if I just yield to her," I say. "She can hang out with you guys in the evening." I lift the basketball. "But maybe I can still come play with you on Saturdays?"

Dawson grins and slings his arm around my shoulders. "Definitely. And you're coming to Copperhead's tonight. It's not like Macie will be there."

"So are things like, over-over?" Lance asks, tugging a headband into place.

"Yeah," I say. "I'm pretty sure they are."

"I'd be sure-sure," he says. "Women like Macie sometimes just need some time to cool off."

"We've tried that," I say.

"What happened?" Alec asks, exchanging a look with the other guys.

"What?" I ask, rounding the ball on all of them. "What was that look?"

"Nothing," they all say in tandem, and they sound like a poorly harmonized version of the Chipmunks.

"I don't want to play today." I bounce the ball back to Alec, who scoffs in protest.

"Listen," Dawson says as I sit down and start to remove my shoes. "We know you love her, man. She's just…"

"Amazing," Lance says loudly. "Intense sometimes. But like, this amazing version of intensely amazing."

I narrow my eyes at him. "What?"

"Don't listen to him." Alec sits heavily on the bench on my other side. "Coy, I'll be straight with you."

"Can't wait," I say dryly.

"I love Macie, but she's a big personality. That's what Lance means. She's…"

"A storm," I say.

"Yes," Alec says, seizing onto the word. "That's perfect for her. So you just need to get a thicker raincoat, and she needs to…"

"Blow herself out faster," Dawson says. "She always does, though, Coy. Callie's been friends with her forever.

She always *always* calms down, and she's sweet, and you obviously think she's gorgeous and sexy and—this feels so weird to say about someone besides my wife." His face starts to redden. "*I* don't think she's gorgeous or sexy."

"I do," I say miserably.

"Then maybe it's not over-over," Lance says, plucking the ball from Alec's hands. "But you two are gonna be if we can ever get this game going." He grins as he shuffle-steps backward, bouncing the ball in front of him.

Dawson jogs out onto the court after him, and I look over to Alec. "I can't play without ya, buddy," he says, both eyebrows cocked up.

"Fine," I say with a sigh.

He grins and pulls me to my feet. "And Coy, come to Copperhead's tonight. All you have to do is tell everyone you don't want to talk about Macie, and we won't talk about Macie."

"Does that work with you guys?"

"It does with us," he says. "We're not our wives." He turns and follows Lance and Dawson out onto the court, leaving me to join them last.

"MOMMA," I call as I walk into the mansion ahead of Anna Lee. She'd gotten a phone call just as we'd arrived, and she lingers out on the porch, talking to someone named Dagen I haven't heard of before.

Things between us have been a little strained, to say the least. I was ticked at her for making a mess of lunch, and she thought it was all Macie's fault. In the end, she admitted she would've rather eaten her own shoe than order from that hideous red wagon, and that she actually found it kind of cute the way Macie stood up for me.

They definitely got off on the wrong foot, and they haven't had a chance to try again. Now they never will.

I feel like a droopy-eared dog who's been kicked, so going to see my momma in such a mood isn't a good idea. But I can't tell her why I'm so low, so here I am. It's a no-win situation, and I tell myself to do the same thing I did last week.

Say as little as possible.

"Coy, darling," Momma says as she breezes out of the kitchen in a mint-green dress that looks like it belongs in an episode of *Leave it to Beaver*. It's got a big white sash around the waist and everything.

She sweeps into me and hugs me, and I wonder if this is the result of the absence of her medication or because she's remembered to take it for more than one day in a row. "Hey, Momma," I say, because she's my mother and while she tries my patience, I love her.

"Come see what I have in the backyard." She looks past me to the front door. "Where's your sister?"

"She had a phone call."

"Oh, okay. Let's wait for her in the library." She's wearing black pumps today, which is so strange, and she clicks into the foyer and through it toward the room in the front corner of the house.

"All right." I follow her, tucking my hands into my khakis. "What's going on with you?" I ask. "Did you have a meeting this morning or something?"

She flicks me a look over her shoulder. "As a matter of fact, I did."

"With whom?" I ask, really holding onto the M in the last word.

"A real estate agent." She laughs like this is great news. It sounds false to my ears, but everything about my mother is a little off today.

"A real estate agent?" I ask.

"Sort of."

"Sort of? Momma, you're not making any sense."

"Just wait till Anna Lee comes in, and then I'll show you."

I sit in the wingback beside her, but I don't relax. "In the backyard," I say. "You were going to show me something in the backyard." I look that direction, but there's half a house in my way.

"Yes."

"Usually it's just another flavor of lemonade." I fix her with a look that I hope tells her to start talking. "I have a feeling this is more than that."

"It is." She grins like the news will just be wonderful.

My gut pitches like it won't be. "I'll get Anna Lee." I lunge to my feet and fly from the library amidst my mother's protests. I yank open the front door and find Anna Lee three feet away, just standing there.

"Get in here," I hiss. "Momma has something to show us in the backyard, and it sounds like it might be a llama or something."

Anna Lee turns to me, surprised. "A llama? Momma got a llama?"

"No," I say, but then my eyes widen. "I mean, I don't know. Anything is possible." Our eyes meet, and the moment turns grim. She comes inside the cavernous foyer, and we both look toward the library.

"Momma," I call, my attention already moving through the house and outside to the screened-in porch. "We're ready."

"What do you have back there?" Anna Lee asks as Momma comes out of the library. "Why are you dressed like a housewife from the fifties?"

We never do anything without a proper Southern greeting, so Momma hugs Anna Lee and says, "Your hair is so straight," like it's a compliment. She clicks past the staircase and through the kitchen, Anna Lee and I hot on her heels, literally.

Outside, I crowd up next to her, but I don't see anything amiss. "Momma?" I ask.

"I'm going to build a shop," she says with delight. She even claps her hands a couple of times. "Right over there." She points to the far left corner of the yard.

"A shop?" I ask.

"A shop for what?" Anna Lee adds.

"To make my hats," Momma says with crispness. "I've been getting quite a few requests for them from the ladies in my sewing club, and I think it's time."

"To build a hat shop," I say slowly, because the words don't make sense. Yes, she's always loved hats, but a shop in the corner of her property? That's so unnecessary.

"Momma, I don't know," Anna Lee says. "How many is 'quite a few'?"

"Well, MaryBeth said she wanted one for the Derby this year. Then Glenda got on that bandwagon." She trills out a laugh and moves over to her regular spot on the deck. Sure enough, the lemonade has frozen raspberries floating in it today. I'm just glad it's not tea, as the weather has started to get quite a bit warmer.

"So two hats," Anna Lee says, shooting me a look.

I say nothing, because Momma has plenty of money, and if she wants to build a shop in the corner of the yard, I say let her. I have enough of my own problems to deal with.

"And then the twins, Ethel and Edith. They both want one for their son's wedding. I mean, it's Ethel's son. Edith's nephew. They're getting married on a boat in July. Ugh. Can you imagine?"

"No," I murmur, my thoughts automatically settling on Macie. She returned to the shop on Monday, as she'd promised. We've been experts at avoiding one another in the past, and we simply picked that practice right back up again.

I've only spoken to her a couple of times, and only out of necessity. If any of our employees have noticed, they're not talking to me about it. They wouldn't either, and as Momma continues to prattle about her hat orders and what the ladies in her clubs are doing, I'm extremely grateful I didn't skip out on wings and drinks with Dawson, Lance, Alec, and Jason a few nights ago.

They're the only friends I have, and I have to share them with Macie when all I want to do is share myself with Macie.

"Right, Coy?" Anna Lee asks in a near-yell.

"Hmm?" I blink and lift my still-full glass of lemonade to my lips. I don't even know how I got this glass of lemonade. Some of it trickles out of the corner of my mouth, and I lean forward to catch it before it drips onto my shirt.

"I said, one of us is getting closer and closer to getting married." Anna Lee practically spits the words at me. "So Momma can stop nagging me about who I'm dating." She shoots Momma a glare that should probably stop her heart.

"She's only twenty-six," I tell Momma. "She has plenty of time."

"So you and Macie are getting serious." Momma's eyelashes flutter.

"No," I say. "Who was here this morning, Momma? A real estate agent or a general contractor?"

"Both," she says. "I wanted to know how much it'll be

to put in the shop, and what the increase will be on my property once I do." She picks up a cookie and takes a microscopic bite from it.

"And?" I prompt.

"And they're getting me some numbers." She holds her head high, and I look over to Anna Lee. This shop isn't getting built. We both relax, at least until Momma sighs and says, "This place would be so much more fun with some grandchildren."

Anna Lee gives a dry laugh, but I say nothing. I don't move. I'd love to give Momma some grandchildren, preferably some with Macie's pretty strawberry blonde hair and all that fire inside her soul.

Momma won't know what hit her then, and the very idea makes me grin from ear to ear.

Too bad Macie and I aren't dating anymore.

The visit finally concludes, and Anna Lee and I make it out of the house with two gallon-sized zipper bags of cookies each. I'll freeze mine and eat them in the next few weeks, but Anna Lee tosses hers in my back seat. "A shop!" She shakes her head. "That woman has lost her mind." She stares out her side window while I pull away from the house. "Her dress was cute, though."

I chuckle then, and that only brings my sister's focus to me. "What?" I finally ask when her laser gaze gets too hot for me.

"You and Macie broke up," she says.

I nearly break my neck I twist toward her so fast. "How'd you know?"

"You went quiet back there." She reaches over and takes my hand in hers. "Tell me it wasn't because of me, Coy."

"Of course it wasn't, Anna Lee. I told you. It's just...us. We don't get along."

She nods, and we're almost back to her place when she says, "You're wrong, you know."

"How do you figure?"

"You and Macie are so perfect for each other." She looks at me and sighs. "You just love to hate each other when you need to figure out how to love to love each other."

My jaw clenches, trying to keep back the words that surge up my throat. I can't do it, and I say, "I'm pretty sure I'm in love with her."

"Oh, honey, that's great." Anna Lee actually means it too.

I give a barky laugh. "No, it's not great," I say. "We aren't together anymore. I have no right to love her."

"Then get her back," Anna Lee says like it's so simple.

I shake my head. "I don't think she wants me." The words hurt, but they also feel true. Maybe after she simmers down. Cools off. Blows herself out. Maybe then she'll miss me, and maybe then, we can try again.

It's a hopeful thought, but hope is all I have right now, so I seize onto it and pray I'll know when to act.

CHAPTER TWENTY-FIVE

MACIE

As I turn off the highway and into my daddy's neighborhood, the stacked containers I've been so careful with for the past half-hour slide dangerously close to the edge of the passenger seat. I throw my hand out to catch them, muttering about fried chicken and buttermilk biscuits under my breath.

This is the second time this week I'm going to see Daddy, because the state of his refrigerator had been bad enough to cause me alarm on Wednesday. He'll grump at me, and I'll snap at him about his dietary choices, and then we'll settle down and watch the grass grow.

That's what we did on Wednesday anyway, because I didn't tell him Coy and I have broken up. He doesn't usually ask a whole lot of questions about my life, because I'm thirty-two years old and work at a coffee shop. How exciting can it be?

I usually entertain him with stories of the funny or eccentric or shocking customers who've come into Legacy that week, and sometimes he throws in a fact about one of my brothers.

I haven't told him about my visit to Ned in Raleigh either, even if I was only there for two days. He and his wife have a two-year-old, and I spent a solid chunk of that forty-eight hours cuddled up with my nephew. My brother and his wife had been nothing but gracious and kind, and they'd asked no questions.

If I'd gone to stay with Peter, he would've. Which is why I didn't go stay with Peter.

I pull up to Daddy's house and hurry to circle the SUV and get out the containers of food I've brought him. They bear clear lids, and they don't look too jumbled to me. I stack the ones on the seat into the collapsible tote and lug the whole thing toward the front door.

Steeling myself for a blast of arctic air conditioning to go with my father's icy tone, I twist the knob and kick with my foot. "Daddy," I call. "I'm here."

"Sugar-bug," he says with surprise, his voice coming from my immediate right. His old recliner squeaks and squeals as he puts the footrest down and stands up. "What are you doin' here on a Friday?"

"I'm allowed to come other days besides Wednesday," I say, panting with the effort it takes to haul this much food around. "Help."

He takes the tote and frowns down at the contents. "What is this?"

"Food," I say.

"Macie, I don't need food."

"Yes, you do." I stand firm and plant my hands on my hips. "Daddy, you can't live on take-out and ketchup packets—which was all I saw in your fridge earlier this week." I shake my finger at him. "This is real food. Go on now."

He goes, but he's not happy about it. "Where did you get real food?"

"First of all," I say. "I can cook. I just don't. Second, Bri's sister is in town for the wedding. She's like, this mega-goddess in the kitchen, and she made it for you when I told her what you'd been eating."

He heaves the tote onto the counter and takes out a single container. "I haven't been eating ketchup packets, by the way."

"Why were there so many in your trashcan then? Hmm?" I keep unpacking the food. "I told her what you like and what you don't. How old you are. Your level of physical activity. She made a menu I think you're going to love." I smile and feel some brightness return to my life. My new therapist said it would return, especially if I focused on seeing it when it came.

"Turkey meatloaf?" He holds up a marked container. "Seems like a crime against poultry," he mutters as he puts it in his fridge.

"Daddy." I can't hold back the giggle, and I haven't laughed in several days. It feels good, and I acknowledge that too. The trouble with recognizing when I'm happy or getting uplifted is that it makes me realize how *un*happy I've been.

And this isn't just, *oh, I don't feel good.* Or, *oh, I'm a little sad.*

The past week since Coy broke up with me—or I broke up with him—have been torture. Agonizing days that go on and on, the scent of his cologne mixing with the smells of the coffee house and making my mouth water.

These are not fleeting feelings, and my therapist says that's okay. They just take longer to work through and process. I told him I'm not afraid of hard work, but it's a brand new and unknown kind of work, and I'm not even sure I'm doing it right. Tell me I need to make a cappuccino, and I'm gold. Tell me I need to work through my repressed rage, and I'm floundering like a bird with a clipped wing.

"Now, I'm going to be back here on Wednesday," I say. "This should be almost gone by then, Daddy. So I'll know if you're not eating it."

"Why wouldn't I eat it?"

"Because you're addicted to onion rings and fried chicken," I shoot back.

"I'm an old man," he says with a frown. "I should be able to eat what I want."

"Well, should and reality are two different things."

We both pause for a moment, and everything around me softens. I clear my throat and step over to Daddy to hug him. "That's what she would've said, anyway."

"Yeah, sugar, that's what she would've said."

I draw in a deep breath and release it all out. "I have to tell you something."

"All righty." He slides the last of the containers in the fridge and hands me a bottle of peach lemonade as he straightens. "Do you want to see the roses?"

I smile at him, my heart so full of love for my daddy. "Always."

He leads me outside, switches on the fans, and we both really take our time to settle into our afternoon relaxation positions. "How'd you get away from the shop this afternoon?" he finally asks.

My lemonade is half gone, and I take another slow sip. "I've been trying to work less, actually. So I've been training one of my long-time baristas in a lot of what I do. Then she can fill in for me while I'm gone."

Daddy makes a grunt, and I look over to him, fearing a heart attack. He's staring at me blankly, and I slop my lemonade out of the wide-mouthed bottle as I jump to my feet. "Daddy?"

"You're trying to work...*less*?"

I kneel in front of him, but he's not going into cardiac arrest. My own pulse sprints through my body, much the way it did when I thought Coy's bearded dragons were going to eat me for dinner. "You don't have to sound so shocked." I get up and brush off my knees. Now that April is almost here, it's definitely shorts weather, and since I can't wear them at the shop, I take every other opportunity I can.

"You like working," he says.

"I did." I return to my chair and sink into the flowered cushions over white wicker. "Coy and I broke up. It's tense there all the time."

"You broke up?" Daddy practically roars the question, causing me to look over to him again. Surprise courses through me, because Daddy has never cared who I date. With Andy, he couldn't even remember the man's name. Called him Anthony sometimes and Aaron others.

"What is with you today?"

Daddy shakes his head. "Honestly, Mace, it's you I'm worried about."

I'm suddenly worried too, because Daddy never calls me by my name. Hardly ever. It's always sugar-something, and it feels like the earth is spinning too fast for several terrifying moments.

"I'll be right back," he says.

"Where are you going?"

But he gets up and walks back into the house, leaving his bottle of lemonade on the tiny table between us. It doesn't take long for him to return, and when he does, he's carrying a small shirt box. It's white, untaped and unwrapped, and he hands it to me without a word.

"What is this?"

"It's from your mama." He clears his throat.

I stare down at the unremarkable box, my eyes widening by the moment. "Mama? Why are you just giving it to me now?"

"Because she asked me to," he says.

I look over to him, and he gestures as if to say, *Well, go on now.*

I go on, opening the top of the box. It folds away from the bottom half to reveal a notebook with a cover that shows an oceanfront scene, a piece of nearly clear seaglass polished smooth, and a pendant.

My breath catches in my throat, and I leave the other two items in favor of Mama's pendant. "Oh, Daddy." I look at him with bright tears shining in my eyes. "She loved this pendant."

"She wanted you to have it when you were ready."

I drink it in, the near-perfect circle which has delicate, curved arms spiraling out from the center to portray the rays of the sun. "I loved it when she would show me the pictures inside." I use my fingernail to get in the gap between the front and the back, and it pops open. There's nothing inside it now, and my face falls.

"Where's the pictures she used to keep in here?" She always had one of her and Daddy. One of Ned, of me, and of Peter. She used to tell me that we kept her grounded, no matter what. I wasn't sure what she meant back then, and I'm still not sure now.

"She wanted them buried with her." Daddy clears his throat. "She explains in the journal."

I'm almost afraid to open it, but I lift it out and smile at the warmth coming from the sky. "I love the ocean," I murmur.

"Mama did too," Daddy says, back to his carefree, casual tone of voice.

I open the notebook, and the words there immediately blur again. "Her handwriting," I say, unsure as to why I thought this would have typing inside. Seeing the slanted, careful way she wrote her letters makes me feel so close to her, and I press the journal to my chest and hold it there for a moment.

Then I start to read.

MY MASSAGE CHAIR GOES OFF, causing me to open my eyes, fumble for the remote, and turn it back on. The atmosphere at this spa is so calming, the air scented with lemongrass and grapefruit, I'd almost forgotten about the notebook my daddy had given me yesterday.

Then Callie hands it back to me, her bright blue eyes wider than I've ever seen. Everyone is looking at me, and I don't normally hate the attention.

"Well?" My voice scratches through my throat. I'd told them all I had something to show them, and that I then wanted their honest opinion. They'd put me in the center, with Tara on one side of me, and Callie on the other. Jessie sits next to Callie, with Bri beside Tara, and Chelsea, Bri's sister down on the end by her.

"Well," Tara says slowly, and I switch my attention to her. We're all getting our nails done in the same shade of dark blue, because Bri's wedding colors are silver, navy, and dusty rose.

"My first question is why your *daddy* thought *now* was the time to give this to you." Her eyebrows go up, and she swivels her head, looking from Bri down to Jessie and back to me.

My Macie-Mae. I can see my mama's handwriting in my head. *I asked Daddy to give this to you when you'd fallen in love. Finally.*

No one says anything, and I let my eyes fall closed.

"Because Mister Madsen thinks Macie is in love with Coy," Bri says crisply, her lawyer-tone clipped in place. "And I have to say, I agree with him."

I sigh and deliberately keep my eyes closed. They all know we broke up, and they all know it was my fault—because that's what I told them. Sure, Tara tried to argue with me, and Callie said I put myself down too much.

But Jessie connected me with a therapist, and Bri's already lectured me twice about being the bigger person and apologizing to Coy so we can try again.

"I'm not in love with Coy," I deadpan and open my eyes.

"Then why does your daddy think you are?" Callie asks, and her voice is so much gentler than Bri's.

"I don't know," I murmur.

Whoever he is, he must be something special to have caught your eye. I hope he brings the world to its knees for you, and I'm sure he will. My one regret is that I won't be here to see it, to see you so happy and radiant and in love with your perfect match.

Mace, you'll have to work hard to keep him. I understand the storms inside you, because they rage inside me too. I've found a few ways to calm them, and I hope you'll try these and then discover new solutions for yourself as well.

Remember how I used to carry seaglass in my pocket everywhere I went? My grams gave it to me when I was a little girl, and I found myself rubbing it and rubbing it whenever I got upset. The action of it made me feel less upset, so I'm giving you a piece from my personal collection.

"Do you have the seaglass?" Jessie asks.

I reach into my pocket and draw it out. Callie takes it and passes it to Jess, who admires it. "It's almost clear, but then blue." She smiles. "It's lovely."

Sometimes I forget she comes from Southern money, then she says things like "it's lovely," and I remember. She rubs her thumb along the top of it, and sighs. "It is soothing to rub it."

"I think so too," I say.

"And the pendant?" Callie asks.

I reach up to touch my breastbone, but the pendant isn't there. We've already had a mud treatment today, and I left it in my locker. After this pedicure, we'll get massages and then haircuts in anticipation of Bri's big day tomorrow.

"I have it," I say. "I'll show it to y'all at dinner."

"What pictures are you going to put in it?" Tara asks.

"One of all of you, of course." I smile down the line at each of them, my emotions starting to wobble.

"And Coy?" Bri asks.

I lift one shoulder into a shrug, because I don't know. "I don't really have a picture of him."

"Easily solved," Bri says.

"Objection," Tara says. "You're really being hard on her."

"I am not." Bri spears me with her dark eyes. She is hard on me, but it's okay, and I give her a smile so she'll know. "Sometimes she needs us to be hard on her."

"Sometimes," Tara says. "But give her a few minutes."

"To do what?" Callie asks.

"To think." Tara sighs too. "Honestly, not everyone is you two."

"What does that mean?" Bri asks.

"Yeah," Callie says. "What does that mean?"

"It means you guys are amazing women, and you've always known it. Some of us don't have the same high self-esteem you do. Can you just...give her two seconds to breathe?"

I reach over and take Tara's hand in mind. She squeezes my fingers, and I lay my head back and drop my eyes closed again.

I'm giving you my sunshine pendant. The simple shape reminds me to choose happiness instead of allowing darkness in my life. Additionally, I put pictures in it of the people I love most, to remind me not to treat them badly. To think before I spoke to them, especially when I felt the irritation start to bundle up inside me. Sometimes, when I couldn't cage my sharp tongue fast enough, I had to apologize. Never be afraid to apologize, Mace. No one ever regrets saying they're sorry.

Fill it with pictures of the people you love best. Friends. This man you're in love with. Any children you two might have. Dogs, cats, birds, fish, reptiles. They count too. I know you love animals.

Most of all, my Macie-Mae, remember that not everything has to be said. If you can learn to control the storms inside you instead of letting them control you, you'll be able to hang onto this gorgeous man you love.

Best of luck with this cursed curse inside you. I'm sorry it's so strong within you, and perhaps you might need more help. Get it.

I love you for now and for always,
Mama

"I'm seeing someone," I say.

"What?" Callie screeches. "That's why you're not in love with Coy! You're seeing someone else already!"

"She is not," Bri says.

"She's seeing a therapist," Jessie says.

I point to her and smile. "She's the winner."

Callie's blonde hair swishes as she volleys her gaze between me and Jess. "A therapist?"

"I'm working through my rage." I smile, expecting the question and getting it from Tara.

"What are you angry about?"

"Anything," I say. "Everything. Whatever. He doesn't think I'm manic or anything. I don't have a disorder. I just...*feel* things intensely sometimes. And I get irritated really fast. I'm working on both of those things before I even think about Coy."

I have always fallen in love with my boyfriends way faster than they do me. It's because of this emotional intensity inside me, but I also know I can learn to control it. I can cage it the way my mama did, and I can have the happily-ever-after she and Daddy had.

I can, because I know how to work at something until I get it, and I don't want me to be the reason Coy and I can't be together.

I suck in a breath, my eyes going wide.

"What?" Tara asks.

I cover my mouth with one hand. "Oh, good chicken fried steak." I meet Bri's eyes, then Tara's, then Callie's, and then Jessie's. Then I look past the woman painting my nails to the mirror on the other side of the room and stare straight into my own eyes.

"I'm in love with Coy."

"Aaaand, there we go," Tara says. "Toldya to give her two minutes to think."

"Are you really?" Bri asks, her voice now almost tinny, like a child's.

I nod and meet her eyes in the mirror. "I really think I am."

Callie screeches again, this time a high-pitched scream of joy. Jessie laughs, and the rest of us join in.

The realization is powerful, but I still don't know that I deserve him. I don't know how to tame the storms yet—but I'll learn, and if I'm lucky, I can have him at my side through it all.

"Okay, okay," I say, waving both hands to get everyone to quiet down. Tears splash my cheeks, and I quickly wipe them away. "I need ideas for how to get him back."

Silence descends on us for one, two, three beats, and then everyone starts shouting at once.

SABRINA

"No, I hate the shrug," I say as my sister lifts it off the hanger. It's snowy white and the softest, fluffiest fur in the world. Originally I did want it. Of course I need something to hide the mismatched weight in my chest.

But Jessie's right. She told me this morning that while the shrug is gorgeous, it doesn't match the dress. It's obvious to everyone who'll look at me that I'm trying to cover up something, and I don't need *more* attention in the breastal region, that's for sure.

Standing in front of the mirror in my bridal suite, I look at myself. "This is insane," I whisper. Chelsea steps to my side, her hands on my shoulders chilly and making a shiver waltz through me.

"You are gorgeous," she says, her smile so wide. My mother finishes with the veil, which sticks in my hair with two huge clips that look like they have eagle talons to grip the hair.

"You really are, Bri." She gives me a smile too, and my emotions suck in at me. I pull in a breath to try to tame them, and thankfully, I can.

I can't believe I'm getting married. After everything that happened out west, everything that pushed me here, back to my southern roots...

And not only that, but I'm marrying the hottest man in the entire state. It's laughable that Jason Finch hasn't been snapped up by some blonde supermodel. Nope, instead, he got a dark-haired, dark-tongued woman who challenges him at every turn.

He sure does love me though, and I love him.

My own smile finally appears, and I lean my head against my momma's. "Thank you, you guys."

My hair has been pinned up, but not in my battle bun. Jason teased me about it, because he says he likes to be the one to take my hair out of that bun and kiss me until I relax.

Jitters and nerves bounce through me now, and I'm definitely not relaxed. I'm also determined not to miss a moment of my own wedding day, because this is the only one I plan on having.

My dress has thick straps that go over my shoulders, leaving a nice scoopy area for the diamonds Jessie's loaning me from her family estate. The last teardrop points right at my cleavage, and I definitely like the way the diamonds sparkle with the pearly fabric of the dress. Intricate lace covers that, so there's not too much shine, and the dress zips up the back so it's not horribly hard to get into and out of.

"All right," Callie says, her baby in one arm and a bouquet of flowers in the other. "Oh, you're not even laced." She frowns and looks over her shoulder. "Jess, isn't she supposed to be laced on the side?"

"Yes," Jessie calls from the corner of the room. She dressed me, as well as all of the bridesmaids, and without her, I'm pretty sure I'd be walking down the aisle in my slip.

"Tara," Callie says. "Macie. Chelsea. Lace her up."

"It's too tight," I say. "I thought we were going to just tuck them in."

"I fixed it," Jessie says as she arrives, carrying a pair of bright silver sandals. I almost go blind from a ray of sunshine that reflects off of them, and I turn away quickly. "It won't be tight."

My sister and my best friends drop to their knees to lace up the side of the dress, making it harder to get into and out of now. I don't mind, because it's a nice detail that boosts up my chest, slims my waist a little more, and doesn't detract from the original beauty of the dress.

It fits like a glove all the way to my hips, and then it falls in layers and layers and yards and yards of fabric. It all shimmers like sunlight on white sand, and as Jessie positions the shoes, and I hold my mom's hand to steady myself so I can step into them, everything becomes real.

Very, very real.

Jason adores clichés, but I think we've blown them all out of the water. So far.

We're getting married in his backyard, because I've wanted his farmhouse since the moment I laid eyes on it. We've spent the better part of our engagement cleaning up the yard, clearing debris, and removing all evidence of Timber, his giant great Dane.

The deck was rebuilt, trees trimmed, and a trellis installed. He put a gazebo in the corner, and we're getting married on that, after I walk through the attendee-lined grass and up the steps. I've practiced in a different set of shoes, and since I refuse to wear heels, sinking into the ground wasn't an issue.

Chelsea did all the food, which will be eaten a half-mile down the road in an old barn that's been converted to an event center. Tara made our wedding cake, and it's all set up and ready. Macie and Coy donated the after-dinner coffee to go with the dancing in the barn, and I can't think of a single detail that's not ready.

Except for me.

My heart beats at me like I should flee, but my feet don't move. Of course I don't want to flee. This isn't like the time I exploded eggs all over my apartment or had to sneak a pot of badly seasoned stew to the dumpster.

This is Jason.

His family is a little more refined than mine, but with Jessie's diamonds, her styling, and all of the help with my hair and makeup, I take one last look at myself and say, "I'm ready."

"Yes, you are." Tara links her arm through mine, and we smile at each other in the mirror. Jason is her cousin, and while I've found a family of sisters in Callie, Tara, Jessie, and Macie, we really will be related once I say I-do.

Callie crowds in beside Tara, and Jessie presses into my mom. Chelsea and Macie squeeze in too, and I'm standing in the middle of the women I love most, surrounded by beautiful people wearing shimmery, shiny, navy blue dresses.

They wear silver sandals like me, and we belong together, all of us. After Jason and I return from our honeymoon, we'll meet up at the coffee house to chit-chat about our day, gush over Callie and Dawson's baby girl, and catch up on the latest gossip around Charleston.

It's not what I thought my life would ever be, but it's absolutely the life I want.

Tara holds up her phone, says, "Smile, everyone," and takes a selfie of all of us standing there in a row. The moment holds for another second, and then baby Hilde fusses, which causes Callie to step out of the line to soothe her.

"Come on," Macie says, linking her arm through mine. "I'm supposed to deliver you to your daddy right on time, and I don't want to mess up the only job I have."

"You have more than this job," I tell her. "You're in charge of the coffee and cookies later." I look at her, sudden alarm pulling through me. "Right?"

"Yes, yes," she says almost impatiently.

"You haven't talked to Coy, have you?" I pause as we near the door.

Macie gives me a sour look. It's one I recognize, because I wear it often around the firm. "When would I have had time to do that?" she hisses at me. "Besides, there were too many ideas, and I haven't settled on one yet."

"You just go talk to him," I tell her.

"Sure, like you did." She cocks her hip and lifts one eyebrow. "If I remember right, he brought you a bunch of dip and you tried not to throw hatchets at him."

"Hey," I say. "I wasn't even tempted to throw a hatchet at him."

"Mm hm." She starts moving again, and I go with her. I don't launch into another lecture, because Macie doesn't need to hear it. She never talked at me when I had to stay with her over and over because of my apartment mishaps, and she's never made me answer a question I didn't want to.

We enter the hall just as my father rounds the corner, and I'm hit with another wall of emotion. He grins from ear to ear as he takes in my dress, my hair, the veil.

"Wow, Bri." He kisses both of my cheeks the way proper Southern gentlemen do and offers me his arm. "Right on time. Good job, Macie."

"Thank you, sir," she says. "We'll see you in a few minutes." She steps back into the bedroom in Jason's house where the other women are and says, "Let's go, girls. Our escorts await."

I barely have time to flatten myself against the wall before my friends pour from the room and head for the steps. One by one, they say, "Congratulations, Bri," and "He's so lucky, Bri," and once they're gone, I look at my father.

We both take a deep breath, smile, and then he says, "I'm starting the timer for ten minutes right...now." He pushes a button on his watch, and we go back into the bridal suite to wait.

CHAPTER TWENTY-SEVEN

JASON

"Mother, if you touch my collar one more time..." I leave the words hanging there, because I don't want to issue the verbal threat out loud. Her fingers brush along my lapel now instead, where she's already pinned a white flower dusted in silver glitter.

All of my groomsmen wear one too, from Dawson, Alec, Lance, and Coy, to Vincent Buhler, my boss, and a couple of other lawyers from Farmer, Buhler, and Cason, where Bri and I work.

My secretary and hers are bridesmaids, and we've paired all the legal people together to walk down the aisle. Our married friends are also set to link arms and precede Bri and her father down the aisle, and I toss a look over to Coy.

He looks about the same as always. Calm, completely

put together, and totally professional. He'd fit in at the firm, though I know he'd never leave his family coffee shop. I also know he keeps everything buried beneath all of that coolness—because I used to do the same.

I know he can open up, and I know he has a competitive streak on the basketball court. I know he loves Alec's knife jokes, and he never goes anywhere without his cherry Chapstick. He's a good guy, and I wish I could help him with Macie.

She is a firestorm, but if there's anyone who can tame her, it's Coy. They've worked together at Legacy Brew for years now; I'm not sure how many. A lot. There has to be something that'll bring them back together.

He catches me looking at him, and he raises his eyebrows. I gesture him forward, and every man gathered in my master bedroom must think I'm hand-talking to them, because a bro-huddle forms in only a few seconds.

"What's going on?" Dawson asks. Ever the marketing manager, he usually takes charge of our get-togethers, and I don't mind that at all. Honestly, once I leave work, I just want someone to boss me around, pick a restaurant or a movie, and tell me where and when to show up.

"Coy's got to get back together with Macie," I say.

He makes a startled sound, his eyes going wide. "What?" he asks along with Lance and Alec.

"You have to walk down the aisle with her," I say. "It's my wedding. I don't want a catfight during the nuptials."

"You realize we have literally three minutes to be lined up," Lance says.

"Jason," my momma says, but I ignore her. Well, I don't. I hold up two fingers in her general direction, so she'll give me a minute. If I ignored my momma…I don't even want to know what will happen.

"It's time to line up," she calls anyway, and Lance gestures as if to say, *See? We don't have time for this.*

"There's not going to be a catfight," Coy says calmly. He pulls his jacket down over his cufflinks as if he's James Bond. "Macie and I are civil when we have to be, and we agreed to be perfectly pleasant today for the wedding. It's fine."

"See?" Alec straightens out of the huddle. "They're fine."

Which means they're not, but I don't know what I'm going to do about it. I have a big, loud family, and I quickly put my arm around Dawson on my left and Lance on my right. "Thanks for being here," I say, which is about as emotional as I'm going to get with men.

"Of course," Dawson says, and he pulls me into a hug. They all do as they get set to leave, and then I'm hugging my brothers, my daddy, and my momma, who holds me like she's losing me for life.

I employ all of my patience with her and let her cry for a minute or two before I remind her we don't want to be late. She values punctuality above all, and she steps back and fixes her face before she and Daddy leave the room. They'll lead the wedding party out, with me between them, and we'll be followed by the groomsmen and bridesmaids until all who remains is Bri and her daddy.

My pulse jumps to my throat, where it stays. I can't believe today is my wedding day. I used to be a man who scoffed at marriage and sentimental things. I thought I was happy without ties, without commitment, without lasting friendships.

How wrong I'd been.

Bri is my world, and our friends make a complete family for us in this city where we're building our life together. We'll have each other and them, and it's the stuff happily-ever-afters are made of.

I follow my parents out onto the deck, and we all pause. I frown as I look up into the sky. "No," I say, the word almost a moan. "It's not supposed to rain today."

The weather can be temperamental in March, but the forecast had called for clear skies and not much wind. A beautiful day for a backyard wedding.

But now, the sky is darkening as thick clouds froth across it.

"It won't rain," my mom says. "Those aren't rain-clouds. It's fine, honey. Let's go." She leads me and Daddy to the edge of the steps like her word is law, and Mother Nature will not defy her.

I have my doubts, but all I can do as I step down and

the crowd who's gathered to witness the wedding rises to their feet, is pray.

Pray the weather will hold for another thirty minutes. After that, we'll be in the barn.

Pray I don't trip.

Pray Bri is as ready for this as I am.

CHAPTER TWENTY-EIGHT

COY

Macie stands about halfway back in the line of bridesmaids, behind Jessie and in front of someone I've never met before. Her red hair is pinned up and then curls down, and she's the most stunning woman in the world.

I wonder if I can lean down discreetly and tell her how beautiful she is. If I did, could we kiss and make up? Try again? Start over?

Lance steps up to his wife, and she turns toward him with the brightest smile of love on her face. She fixes his flower, and he kisses her cheek, and the level of comfort they have with each other astounds me.

I move out of the way as one of Jason's lawyer friends moves to stand with the woman behind Macie, and I'm sure she'll be looking for me soon. I can't hide here at the corner of the hall that leads to Jason's bedroom forever, and I get moving to join her.

A relieved look fills her face when I take my place at her side. "Hey," she says, plenty of air whooshing out with the word.

"Hey, Mace." I offer her my arm, and she slides hers through it. I do lean down, the part of my brain that filters what comes out of my mouth suddenly on vacation. "You are stunning in that dress."

Her surprise rolls off her in waves, and she blinks her long eyelashes at me. "Thank you?"

I chuckle and sweep my lips along her jawline, which is nowhere near where I really want them. "You're asking me thank you?"

"No," she says, leaning her head down too. We've created this private bubble where only we exist, and I sure do like that.

"You smell fantastic," I whisper. "I am—"

"All right!" someone calls, interrupting me. I straighten and look toward the front of the line. "Here we go."

The line inches forward slightly, and Macie's hand in the crook of my elbow tightens. "You're what?" she whispers.

I simply shake my head, because I can't say it now. We move through the kitchen and out of the sliding glass doors that lead to the deck. "Uh oh," Lance says in front of us, and Jessie gasps.

"It's going to rain," she says.

I automatically look up, because that's what you do

when someone says it's going to rain. The sky has darkened, but the wind hasn't whipped up yet.

"Bri will be so upset," Macie says in her worried tone. She loves her friends dearly, and she's loyal and true to them. I admire that about her, as well as a whole host of other things.

"I think it'll be okay," I say. "There's no thunder yet."

"Let's keep moving, please," one of the lawyers says, and Lance and Jessie get going. Macie and I follow them, my mind spinning in at least a dozen directions.

"I want this to be us," I whisper to Macie.

She stumbles as she looks at me, and I tighten my grip on her arm to steady her. "Coy," she whispers back.

I should just be quiet. This isn't the time or place for the conversation we need to have, and yet, my heart screams at me to keep going. Macie won't cause a scene here, and I can say everything I want to before we get to the altar.

"I was going to say back there that I'm lost without you." We make it down the steps, and Macie's gone into a state of shock, I'm pretty sure.

"I miss you like crazy," I say. "Even though I see you almost every day, I hate that you're not mine, and I'm not yours, and that we're not an *us.*"

She looks right and left, like the back row of guests we've just passed will care what I'm saying to her.

"We fit together," I say next. "I knew it the moment you slid your arm through mine."

She tightens her arm there, which only makes me smile. "Please forgive me," I say next, my voice getting a little louder. "I won't call you a storm again. You're not a storm. You're exactly what I want."

Jessie turns her head, ducking it down, clearly having heard me.

"Coy," Macie hisses out of the corner of her mouth. "You have to stop it."

"No," I say right out loud. "No, I won't stop it."

In front of us, Lance and Jessie stop, and they both hug Jason, who's been waiting at the bottom of the steps that lead up to the altar in the gazebo.

I look at Macie, then turn fully toward her, letting her arm drop out of mine. I take both of her hands in mine, my pulse ricocheting from the soles of my feet to the top of my head and everywhere in between. "I'm in love with you," I say out loud. Macie's eyes fill with tears as they widen. She looks half afraid and half hopeful.

"Please forgive me. I will work every day to make you happy. I will go to weather school and learn how to read the signs of a storm. I will calm you if possible and let you rage if you need to." I lean down and press my forehead to hers, finally letting my eyes close.

"Please, Mace," I say, my voice breaking. "You are my home. You are who I want. I love you."

"Oh, that's so sweet," someone says in a quiet voice.

We've stopped when we should be moving, but no one tries to go past us.

"Coy," Macie whispers, and I straighten to look at her. Her mouth opens, but she doesn't say anything.

"I think what she's trying to say," Jason says, stepping into both of us. I've stolen time from his wedding, and it might be precious time as the sky continues to darken. "Is that she loves you too."

Macie sniffles, reaches up to wipe her face, and nods.

"Oh, she loves him too!" Jason calls to the crowd, and they start to applaud. My face burns with embarrassment, especially when Alec whistles between his teeth in an earsplitting screech, and Dawson whoops and pumps his fist.

"Now," Jason says. "If you guys could keep the line moving, my momma won't have an aneurism."

"Yes," I say. "Sorry." I tuck Macie against my side again, and we walk past Callie and Dawson, who reaches out to pat me on the shoulder. Then Tara and Alec.

Tara jumps in front of Macie and scoops her into a hug. "I told you he'd take you back." They giggle together for a moment, and then we keep going.

Lance and Jessie hug me and Macie simultaneously, and I'm not sure why Jessie weeps, but she definitely is. Once we're standing behind them, forming a circle around the gazebo as instructed, I take a deep breath.

A few seconds of silence pass while the other couples get into position. Then Macie asks, "That wasn't a joke, was it?"

I look at her, and the world could burn to ashes, and I wouldn't know. "Nope," I say.

Bri hasn't arrived yet, and Macie wears a look like she's been stunned. Her mouth fishes again, and I chuckle to myself that at least I know how to render her speechless now.

Tell her you love her.

"Not a joke," I whisper, feeling some eyes still on me. Lance's for sure. "I love you, Macie Madsen."

She cuddles into my side and says, "I love you too, Coy," just as the bridal march begins to play. The music is far louder than the twinkling stuff that piped through the speakers while we walked down the aisle, and I immediately look toward the house.

Bri descends the stairs with her hand held in her father's, and then they beam at each other for a single beat of time before advancing toward the gazebo. She radiates light in her gorgeous wedding dress, and I can't even imagine being Jason, the man standing at the altar and watching the woman he loves come toward him.

I want it so badly, but only if I can have it with Macie.

"I forgive you," she whispers as Bri reaches Jason. "I know I'm a storm, and I'll try not to be, I swear."

"You don't have to do that," I whisper. "I'll get better at reading your moods, and we'll check our tempers."

"I'm already working on it," she says. "I've started seeing a therapist."

"Shh." Lance hushes us as Bri and Jason go up the

steps with the pastor. The three of them stand in the gazebo, and I struggle to focus on their vows.

Macie's seeing a therapist?

I shelve the thoughts flying around my head, because I want to be part of this friendship-family. That means being there for Jason and Bri, being present.

"At the risk of using a cliché," Bri says with a bright smile on her face. "I guess you could say that I found love in a place I least expected it."

Jason laughs, and I join in. The man loves clichés, and Bri finishes with, "I will be your partner in every way possible. At work, at home, while we throw hatchets. All of it. As long as I'm never *just* your partner."

"Never," he says seriously though he smiles. "My turn?"

"Your turn," the pastor confirms.

Jason, ever the showboat, clears his throat and shakes his shoulders, as if gearing up for a monumental speech. "Sabrina Shadows, you are my favorite person in the whole world."

"You're my favorite person," Macie whispers.

I lean my head toward her, trying to catch her words with one ear while lending the other to Jason. He's saying, "...and my dog likes you more than me. We are perfect together, and I will love you, honor you, cherish you, and cook for you every day of my life."

His grin is as wide as mine when Macie says, "I don't need to forgive you. I need you to forgive me."

"Done," I whisper.

Jason says something else I don't catch, and then he concludes with, "I've heard people say that love means never having to say you're sorry, but I don't think that cliché works for us. I will apologize to you for the stupid things I do, and I expect you to do the same. I know we will, because we love each other. I love you." He smiles and leans closer. "I love you. I love you."

Apparently satisfied with his vows, he nods and faces the pastor. I felt the power of his words in my own soul, and I believe Jason loves, loves, loves Bri.

The pastor pronounces them man and wife, and Jason dips her to kiss her among the shouting, clapping, and congratulating.

Macie steps away from me so we can both clap, and when I dare to look at her, she has tears streaming down her face. I move closer, my hands still adding to the chaos around us. "Those better be for your best friend."

She nods, claps as Bri and Jason come down the steps and get swarmed by their parents and siblings, and then Macie turns into me. She grabs onto me and holds me tightly, and I have no complaints about that.

"I'm sorry," I say with my mouth right at her ear. "Walking down that aisle was torture, and I had to say something."

She nods. "I know. It's okay. I love you." And those become the most beautiful words in the world I've ever heard.

CHAPTER TWENTY-NINE

MACIE

ALL I WANT TO DO IS KISS COY. THERE ARE TOO MANY people and too much going on around us to do so right now, so I simply keep my arms wrapped around his broad shoulders. I never want to let him go.

But I have to when Jessie says, "All right, you two. What's going on?"

I step out of his embrace and fall to his side, where he takes my hand in his. "Nothing," I say.

"Nothing?" Lance's eyebrows fly up. "Right." He scoffs. "It sounded to me like Coy begging you to take him back and you standing there like someone had stolen your voice."

"Lance," Jessie chastises, but he's pretty much summed it up. "She said something."

I didn't though. Not until we'd made it past Coy to our spot around the gazebo. And then, I'd kept my voice quiet enough that no one but Coy could hear me. He's the only one who needed to hear it anyway.

He gazes down at me now. "She said enough," he says, raising his eyes back to Lance and Jessie. "I really didn't mean to interrupt the wedding."

"It was awesome," Dawson says as he approaches. "I'm so glad you guys are back together." He hugs me and Coy as if we're a single person and steps back, grinning.

"I can't believe you're the office grump," I tell him, swatting at his chest. He laughs as he shrinks into himself and Callie pulls him back to her side.

She's beaming at me, as is Jessie, and then Tara, and the only reason I haven't run for the hills yet is because I need to be here for Bri. For the coffee service in a couple of hours.

I look up at Coy.

For him. I reach up to cradle his face in my palm, somehow forgetting that our friends are watching us. I have to be here for *him*.

"Oh, yeah," Tara says suggestively. "She definitely loves him."

I already said I did, and I smile as I let the feeling engulf me. Coy laughs as he picks me right up off my feet and swings me around. I yelp, because a woman of my size, wearing the dress I am, should not be swung.

"Here they are," Lance says, and I stumble to find my balance as Bri and Jason join us.

"Congratulations," I say along with several others, and

when it's my turn to hug Bri, I hold her extra-tight for extra-long.

"I heard you and Coy made up," she whispers.

I nod and say, "I hope it didn't ruin your wedding."

"Not even a little bit." Bri pulls away and beams at me. She looks over to Coy, her expression hardening into her lawyer persona. "So. You two next, is that right?"

"Objection," Jason says, pulling his new wife back to his side. "He just got done groveling, baby. Give them some time to actually make up."

"Yeah," I say. "I haven't even kissed him yet, and I think most of you know how I feel about a make-up kiss."

"That's our cue, guys," Dawson says, and without another word, he, Lance, Jason, and Alec form a wall by standing shoulder-to-shoulder, their backs to us.

Jessie starts to giggle, and Coy's eyebrows go up. "I think they're giving us some privacy from the rest of the wedding guests," he says, easing me into his arms the way I lower myself into a hot bath.

"Oh, yeah?"

"Yeah," Alec barks. "And hurry it up, because I'm pretty sure I just felt a raindrop."

Coy grins as he brings me closer for a kiss, and when his lips touch mine, fire ignites. I can kiss him and kiss him and never tire of it, but after only a few seconds, people start yelping.

"Let's go," Jason says. "Every man for himself!"

I pull away from Coy, drowsy and dizzy from that

phenomenal make-up kiss. When I open my eyes, I see people hurrying toward the house or around it for their vehicles. The wall of men is gone. Raindrops start to splash my arms. Tara cries out as she tries to shield her hair and face with only her hands, and she and Alec make a dash for the farmhouse.

"Dinner is at the barn!" Jason's mother shouts, her hands cupped around her mouth. She turns in a full circle as she yells at the retreating backs of the guests. "We'll see everyone in the barn!"

The whole thing is comical to me, and as the sky really opens up, Coy and I dash for the only hope we have of staying dry—the gazebo. We arrive breathless and laughing, and we're not the only ones who've opted for this roof instead of the one at the house or in our car.

Since we're not alone, I tuck myself into his chest and let his strong arms come around me. He leans down, and in that sexy whisper, he asks, "You're seeing a therapist?"

My voice goes silent again, but I call it back. "Yes," I say. "I am. I have this...this...well, my mama calls it rage. My daddy says it's more like thunder, and I just think it's —unrest?" I don't know how to describe it. "This unrest inside me, and I need to learn how to get it out without losing everyone and everything I love."

I reach up to touch the locket my mama gave me, but it's not hanging around my neck. I've forgotten I took it off because it didn't go with the bridesmaids dress. I turn to face him so we're chest-to-chest. "My mama was the same way. She found solace in writing in her journal, and putting pictures in this locket she gave me. She'd rub seaglass until she wore a hole right through it. She gave me some of that too. I like it. It's pretty, and soft, and Bri was going to help me get a picture of you for the locket, but we didn't have time..." My voice trails off, and I suddenly need to look somewhere else.

"Macie, I don't really know what you're saying," Coy says.

"I know." I sigh out my breath. "Can we talk about it later? I'll show you my mama's letter. She told Daddy not to give it to me until I'd fallen in love."

His eyebrows go up, and I realize how much of the story he doesn't know.

"The rain is letting up," a man says, and people start to leave the gazebo. We need to get over to the barn to receive the coffee canisters and get them set up, so I take Coy's hand in mind and go with everyone else.

As we cross the lawn, I ask, "Can I ride with you?"

"Yes," he murmurs.

"Can we go back to your place after the wedding and talk?"

"Yes," he says, then he glances over at me. "My place? The dragons are there."

I nod, thinking we *should* go to my place. My dogs are so needy, and they'll have been home alone for hours by then. "We'll stop by my place to make sure the dogs go out and get fed, and then yes." I look him right in the eye. "Your place. I'll tell you everything."

"All right," he says. "My place. I'll tell Elmer and Orion to be on their best behavior." He grins at me the way he did while we were dating, and the friendship in the gesture erases all of the loneliness that's built up inside me since we broke up.

Later, he hands me a cup of coffee while the dance in front of me is still going strong. "Here you go, Mace. Macchiato."

"How did you make a macchiato here?" I'm already lifting the mug to my lips. The wedding dinner was delicious, and it's amazing how an old barn can be rustic and chic at the same time. Bri now wears a shorter party dress in dark blue, with a snowy white fur shrug over her shoulders as she clasps hands with Jason and makes her way around the room, chatting with everyone who's come.

The coffee and cookies have been served, and I'm starting to feel like I'll turn into a pumpkin if I don't get home soon. Funny thing is, it's not even eight yet, but my bedtime is approaching fast.

"I have my ways," Coy says, smiling. "Ready to get out of here?"

"Yes." I take a sip of the coffee, and it's fantastic. Maybe not as strong or as milky as a macchiato, but dang close. "But we have fifteen more minutes."

Coy stands and extends his hand toward me. "I asked Alec and Tara to clean up for us. They said yes."

I blink up at him, surprised. "We need that stuff in the morning to open."

"I gave Tara my key."

"You did what now?" I blink-blink. Blink-blink. "You wouldn't give me a key until I gave you my life savings."

He scoffs, the sound turning into a laugh. "That is so not true."

"Oh-ho, it's true." I get to my feet without touching him. "Tara gets a key. Bah." I turn away from him and take another sip of the delicious coffee before setting the cup on the table for someone else to clear. "Let's go. I'd love to get into a pair of pajama pants." And out of this bra, but I keep that to myself.

I give Tara a quick hug on the way out, and she says, "Of course, honey," before turning back to the dancing. She and Alec aren't out in the crowd, and that's about how they are. Coy takes me back to Jason's, where I get my car, and we agree to meet at his place in forty minutes.

I hurry through feeding the dogs and making sure they have enough time outside to take care of their business. Justice wastes at least two minutes barking at some mystery item next door before I can get her back inside, and then they all watch me with baleful eyes as I shoulder my purse. I've tucked the journal, the seaglass, and the pendant into it, and my pulse shudders at the thought of showing it all to Coy.

"I'll be back real soon," I say. I'm tired already, and I'm not sure how many more emotions I can handle tonight.

He answers the door before I knock or ring the bell, and he's gone as casual as me by putting on a pair of black gym shorts and a Legacy Brew tee that looks soft and weathered. I smile at him and point to my own, matching, shirt.

Laughter bubbles between us, and as I step up into his house and past him, I say, "We really should try to wear clothes that don't come from work."

"I like this one," he says. "I like yours too. I didn't realize we had shirts in that shade of purple."

"Just this one," I say. "It was a sample, remember?" I put down my purse on his dining room table and turn to face him. He's leaning against the arched wall that separates the living room from the kitchen.

He's incredibly handsome with all those muscles and that smile softening his soft jaw. "I don't remember."

"It came in that rainbow assortment I ordered to see if we wanted to expand our color selection. You hated the bright colors. 'We're a coffee house, Macie. Our shirts should be black and brown and maybe gray.'" I lower my voice to mimic him, which causes him to laugh.

"So you're saying we argued about it."

"Yes, we did."

"Shocking." He folds his arms as I approach him. The mood between us sobers, but neither of us looks away from the other. "I don't want to argue about Legacy with anyone but you," he says.

I swallow, because that's the perfect thing to say to me

right now. "I love working there with you," I say. "But things are going to have to change, Coy."

A frown troubles his brow. "They are? Why?"

"Because." I slide my hands up his arms and under the sleeves of his shirt. "We work pretty opposite shifts right now. It's hard on *us*." He knows the *us* I mean.

He draws a breath and releases it. "All right. It's not a bad point. I hate getting up early. I'm not an opener, much to my daddy's dismay." He offers me a smile, and I take it right into my heart.

"I can still open," I say quietly. "I'm thinking we need an afternoon-slash-evening manager."

"Then I'll be working like five hours every day," he says.

"No, you'll come in at like eight instead of ten-thirty. And work until four. I'll have the dogs fed by then and we'll have our whole evening together."

"Eight to four," he says.

"Think about it," I say. "It doesn't have to be right away. It would make for a better family life, though."

"Family life?"

I gently coax his arms apart, and he wraps me up in his warm embrace. "Yeah," I whisper against his chest. "Don't you want kids, Coy? Someone to pass Legacy onto when they're your age?"

"Yes," scratches out of his throat.

"Me too." I tilt my head back and look at him. "My mama wrote me a letter before she died. I didn't get it until this past week. My daddy was told not to give it to me until I'd fallen in love, and when I told him you and I had broken up and I didn't know what to do to get you back, he got it out and gave it to me."

Coy's eyebrows go up, but he doesn't ask any questions. I retrieve the items from my purse and pass them to him. Then I wander into the living room to the gigantic glass tank on his coffee table. I study the sticky notes there and switch on the lamps with the red light.

Both bearded dragons emerge from their hidey-holes, and a shiver runs through my body. I'm not sure how he sleeps in this house with the threat of them getting out, but I'm sure I'll get used to it.

A few minutes later, Coy comes to sit beside me. He hasn't brought over anything but the pendant, and he drops it into my hand. "Is this why you started seeing a therapist?"

I look down at the sunshine in my palm. "I started seeing a therapist, because I thought that was how I could calm myself enough to get you back."

"Macie, I fell in love with you before that," he whispers. "All of you."

"No, I know," I say, my voice pitching up with sudden emotion. I don't try to clear it away before continuing. "But I don't like the storms inside myself, Coy. I can be better, and I want to work on myself."

"As long as it's not because of me," he says.

"It's not."

He nods to the locket. "Open it."

I slide my perfectly manicured nail between the halves of the pendant, already knowing what's inside. I gasp at the top picture, though, because I didn't put that one there.

"Coy." I pinch the tiny photograph of him, which he's obviously cut out of another one. I turn toward him and find that love he's proclaimed shining from his face. "Thank you."

"I love you," he whispers.

"I love you too." I meet him halfway and kiss him, glad this has been easier than I anticipated.

"I'll get rid of the dragons if they bother you," he breathes, his lips catching on mine between kisses.

The thought is tempting, but I say, "No," before kissing him again. I pull away, and we breathe in and out together, the slight tang of cherry from his lips in my mouth. "I don't want you to have to change what you don't want to, Coy. Not for me."

"If not for you, then for who?"

"I'm already going to be a lot for you," I say. "You should get to keep your bearded dragons if they make you happy."

"Mace." He lifts my chin, forcing me to look at him. "*You* make me happy."

But I know he loves his bearded dragons. I won't be the reason he gets rid of them. "I like them," I say, gently moving my head out of his grip and toward them. "In a sort of...distant way. Lots of distance."

The olive green one stares right at me, I swear, and I just know if he's ever given the chance, it'll become an attack-bearded-dragon.

Coy chuckles and wraps me up in his arms, whispering, "I'll move them out of the living room, okay, my pudding pie?"

"Yes," I whisper back. "That might be better."

Several seconds pass in silence, and then Coy says, "Talk to me about your dream wedding, Mace. When, where, who, what, how."

I giggle with him and ask, "You sure you want it all?"

"The whole thing," he says seriously. "With you, Mace, I want it all."

Once again, he's found the exact right thing to say, and instead of outlining my dreams for him, I touch my mouth to his and kiss him—this man I love.

CHAPTER THIRTY

BRI

"ARCHIE, NO!" I CRY JUST AS THE VASE STARTS TO topple. Timber bowls into it, which has every piece of pottery and all the knick-knacks in the bookcase teetering and tottering. "Outside, you brutes! Outside!"

I yell at the cat and dog who can't get along and angrily slide open the door. Timber trots out like I've done him a favor, while Archie hisses and growls, his fur still standing at attention, from the top of the bookcase.

"I don't get why you can't get along," I tell the grumpy cat. He and Timber remind me of me and Jason a little bit, but I'll never admit that out loud.

We've been married for six weeks now, and I'm still adjusting to living in this farmhouse I love. The yard is big, and that requires a lot of attention from the two of us. We have a heavy workload at the firm, and then these bickering animals to come home to at night.

Still, I wouldn't trade any aspect of my life right now, and I return to the island to leaf through the mail we got a half-hour ago. Jason's gone to shower, because we're meeting everyone for dinner tonight and he felt "itchy" from being in his brown suit all day.

I don't argue or even try to figure out Jason's shower obsessions. He supports me in wearing my jackets and cardigans to work, though tonight, I'm wearing a little black dress that's appropriate for the steakhouse Jessie chose for us.

Bill, bill, junk mail. Junk mail, junk mail, bank statement. Mail is so boring. I've just flipped to a slim envelope and seen the Farmer, Buhler, and Cason at the top when Jason whistles appreciatively.

"Wow, wow, *wow*," he says as he takes me into his arms. "We might have to stay in so I can get you out of this dress." He smiles as he kisses me, which is the reaction I want with the dress I have on.

But that envelope...

His kiss doesn't distract me for long, and he pulls away. "What?"

"The mail," I choke out.

He smells like spicy aftershave and mint toothpaste, but that fades as he turns and picks up the envelope. "It's your partner letter." He doesn't try to open it but turns to face me. He holds it toward me.

I shake my head, sudden fear overcoming me. "What if I don't get it?"

"Then you don't get it," he says. "There's next year. You're really young to make partner, and you've only been a junior for a year."

We've talked this to death, and I've been waiting to find out if I made partner for weeks now. It makes no sense that I don't want to open that envelope. "You open it."

"You'll regret that," he says, flipping over the envelope slowly.

I snatch it from him. "You're right." I want to open my own mail. I slide my finger under the flap decisively and pull out the single sheet of paper.

Dear Sabrina Shadows,

They haven't changed my name, and that's okay. I don't have my new legal IDs yet, so I haven't even tried to get things switched anywhere.

My eyes fly across the page, right to left, right to left, and I shriek and throw the paper at him. It's a single sheet, so it doesn't go far, and he fumbles as he tries to catch it. "I made partner!" I yell as I start to jump up and down.

"You made partner," he repeats before I grab onto him. He abandons trying to read the paper and holds onto me instead. "I knew you'd make it, baby." We laugh together, the sense of euphoria in the farmhouse the same as it was when I finally moved all of my stuff in and we started our lives together.

We calm quickly, and Jason sways with me in the kitchen of *our* house. "I love this life with you," I whisper.

"I do too," he says.

"We'll tell everyone at dinner?"

"It's your news, sweetheart."

"We'll tell everyone at dinner," I say, and then I tip up to kiss him.

CHAPTER THIRTY-ONE

TARA

I TOSS MORE FEED INTO THE GRASS FOR MY HENS, WHO are out for their pasteurize. The grass is getting long now, and they can usually find plenty of bugs to eat. I just like giving them the extra feed. They warble and cluck their thanks to me, and if anyone ever wanted to feel happier, all they'd have to do is get a handful of chickens.

Hennifer, Nugget, Pot Pie—they're always glad to see me. They know me, and they know I'd do anything to help them be healthy and happy.

"Tara," I hear Alec call me from inside the house. As he opens the back door, Peaches screeches "Bacon-motor-bike!" and even that makes me smile.

He's shirtless and holding up two choices for dinner with our friends tonight. "Blue or red?" he asks.

"Always black," I tell him as I turn away from the chickens. "You're sexiest in black."

He frowns at the shirts. "I didn't bring out a black one."

I go up the steps and into his arms. He doesn't ask what's wrong. He knows. We've been trying to have a baby for a few months now, with no luck. I haven't heard from my editor at Better Gate, which is the publishing house which is publishing my cookbook, and there's been no word on his James Beard Award.

They always tell the nominees before they make the public announcement, and that's in two days. We should know literally any minute now.

"How are the ladies?" he asks in a quiet voice.

"Good," I say. "Did you talk to the rental manager for that place on the Boulevard?" I pull out of his arms. If he's going to leave Saucebilities and open a restaurant, it's probably best that we don't have a baby right now. Opening a restaurant takes thousands of hours and dollars, and right now, we have both. With a baby, we wouldn't.

His face takes on an energy I only see when he talks about opening his own restaurant. "Yes," he says. "Tara, honey, it's the place. The rent is right, and it has a commercial kitchen already."

I smile at him, genuinely meaning it. "All right then. We should secure it."

"I told him I'd call him after I talked to you tonight."

"I'll get the girls back in the coop, and we'll call him." I nudge him back toward the house. "You go find me a black shirt."

He chuckles but fades back into the house as Peaches ding-dongs like the doorbell. It takes several minutes to convince the chickens to get back in their coop, and once they're safe, I head inside.

Alec stands in the kitchen wearing a black polo that pulls tightly around his biceps and shows those sexy tattoos that extend to his elbow. "Mm, yes," I tell him as I approach where he's sorting the mail at the end of the counter.

He glances over to me as I come to his side. "Did you go through this?"

"Nope."

He hands me an envelope silently. It's got my publisher's name on it, and I gasp as I start to rip it open. "This is probably the other half of my advance," I say.

"Probably." He flips through the other things. "I'm gonna check my email for the James Beard Award. There's nothing here."

"Then we'll call Burton about that rental," I say, pulling out several folded sheets of paper. "We want to make sure we get it for Knives Out."

"And I'm going to talk to Dawson tonight about doing marketing for the restaurant," he says. "I know he's moving to Fowler, but he said he can take on select cases."

"Callie's brought on a couple of new guys at the marketing firm too." I look down at the papers in my hands. There is a check there, and it makes me exceedingly happy to be getting paid for my recipes. It's like the ultimate validation for a chef.

I unfold the papers and see they're full-color mock-ups of the interior pages. A handwritten notes flutters out, and I have to bend to pick it up.

Release date of June 6! my editor has written. Just in time for all the summer barbecues. Tara, this book is GORGEOUS. I'm sending a few pages so you can see how the photographs look in all their glory. You should be so proud of this cookbook! I can't wait to share your recipes with the world!

"June sixth," I say to Alec. "They're putting out the cookbook on June sixth!"

He doesn't answer, and I turn toward him. He's sitting at the kitchen table, both Tommy and Goose gathered around him as if he has food and will give them some. He looks up, a dark look on his face. "I'm sorry, what?" He slams his laptop closed.

I leave the papers right where they are. "You didn't get it."

He shakes his head.

I don't pull out the chair beside him. Instead, I crowd right onto his lap. He lays his head against my chest and holds me hard, and I do the same for him. "It's okay," I say, stroking his hair. "You'll get it for Best New Restaurant, or Best Chef, or Best Emerging Chef next year, or Outstanding Chef, Restauranteur, or Restaurant."

I lean back and smile at him, hoping he can see that

this loss doesn't make me love him less. It only makes me love him more. "You're at the very beginning of your career, baby, and you're going to have so many James Beard Awards, we'll have to get a bigger house to hold them all."

He finally cracks a smile and slides one hand up my arm to my face. "What would I do without you?"

"Hmm, you wouldn't have to wait for ten minutes in the morning while I talk to the hens?"

He chuckles, and I grin at him. "No, I know. You wouldn't have to wear a black shirt every time we go out."

I brighten and run my fingers through his hair. "I know. This is it. You'd be able to tell your knife jokes without anyone rolling their eyes."

He touches his mouth to mine, and this kiss is serious though I was trying to be funny. He kisses me and kisses me, and I let him take whatever he needs to heal the hurt this loss has created inside him. He finally pulls away and breathes in the curve of my neck.

"I love you, Tara," he whispers.

"I love you too, Alec."

"My *knife* would be very dull without you." He grins, and I get his meaning, because he's constantly swapping out words like *life* for *knife*.

"Dull," I repeat. "Good one." We laugh together, and then I get off his lap. "I'm going to go change, and then we'll go meet everyone."

"I'm going to call Burton."

I've taken two steps away from him when he says, "Wait. You had news."

"I got a June release date," I say, realizing how close that is. Only about another month. "Just in time for barbecue season." I grin, unable to stop myself.

"That's great, baby."

"Baby," Peaches says. "Baby, baby, baby!"

I just laugh and go to get changed. We'll have good news to share with everyone at dinner despite Alec's loss, because he's getting a restaurant, and I'm getting a cookbook. There really are more opportunities for his award, and we can keep trying to build our family.

One step at a time, I tell myself.

My hands shake as I set the pregnancy test on the back of the toilet. I can't look at it, and I quickly leave the room and wash up. Lance appears in the doorway that leads into our master bedroom, pure anxiety written all over his blond features.

"Well?"

"It takes a few minutes."

He scans the bathroom like there will plus signs or minus signs glowing on the walls. "Okay." He wipes his hands down the front of his slacks and turns around. I follow him into the bedroom, where he collapses onto his side of the bed. I sink next to him and take one of his hands into both of mine.

We don't speak, mostly because I don't know what to say. We weren't trying to get pregnant, but we weren't trying not to either.

"Will your momma be upset?" he finally asks.

"Why would she be upset?" I look at him, but he's studying the carpet. "She's practically begging for grandbabies."

"I guess I'm wondering if *you'll* be upset." He looks at me then. "You didn't want to get married and have babies right away."

I love this man so much, and I love that he's worried about me. "But I did," I whisper.

"We haven't even been married for a year, Jess."

I close my eyes and lean my forehead against his. "Are *you* going to be upset if it's positive?"

"No," he says. "I'll need a new assistant, and that's going to be a trial, but absolutely not. I want you to be our baby's mother and design your dresses and make sweatshirts for Cha-Cha."

I smile, because that sounds like a wonderful life. With capitals W and L.

"ILY," I whisper. "No matter what it says, that's not going to change. Life might change, but that doesn't matter."

"It doesn't?" Lance finally looks up from the carpet.

I shake my head and kiss him quickly. "Can we not afford to have a baby?"

"We can afford it."

"We have the room here already," I say. "You've seen Dawson and Callie with their baby. You'll be the best daddy in South Carolina." I grin at him. "You might have to get a new assistant, but as long as you don't fall in love with her, everything will be okay."

He shakes his head as he smiles.

"A baby will change our lives," I say. "But not *us*."

"Not us," he repeats.

"Besides, you were just saying you were sick of the same-old, same-old at work."

"Yeah," he says. "At work. I'm still figuring out how to be a husband. What if I can't be a dad on top of all of that?"

"You can." I smile at him reassuringly and add, "I mean, Cha-Cha adores you. You've kept her alive all these years."

"She's a *dog*."

"And you're her doggy daddy." I grin at him. "This is not going to change us, okay?"

"You won't be able to drink if you're pregnant," he says. "And we're going to dinner with everyone tonight."

"I don't always drink," I say.

"And the nightly coffee stops?"

"We'll tell our friends, right?"

"Tonight?"

He has a point, so I just look back toward the bathroom. Cha-Cha trots into the room, her happy little corgi face giving me the courage I need to stand. I'm over a week late, and I haven't been feeling well the past few days. I'm not throwing up in the morning, but I'm exhausted even after I sleep all night long. I'm run-down, and I'd finally told Lance this morning that I thought I might be pregnant.

We'd bought the test on the way home, and here we are.

"Here I go." I walk into the bathroom and then the toilet room. The stick sits there, and I reach for it, mentally telling myself that everything is going to be A-okay. No matter what this says, I'll have Lance, and that's not going to change.

I spin to leave the room and crash into my husband's chest. "Oof." I fall back, but he grabs me and hauls me into the bathroom.

We face the mirror together, and I look at the two of us standing side-by-side. Almost instinctively, my hand moves to my belly. "I'm pregnant."

A smile curves Lance's mouth instantly, and he covers my hand with his. "Amazing," he whispers.

I turn into him and throw my arms around him, his reaction to our baby exactly what I want. He laughs and lifts me up, setting me on the bathroom counter. He pushes my hair back off my face and kisses me, this time with far more passion than the chaste union on the bed a minute ago.

"I love you," he breathes into my mouth before he closes that gap again. I wrap my legs around him, knowing we have to leave for dinner soon. Still, I want to be close to him, and he seems to want the same thing, because he keeps kissing me, and kissing me, and kissing me.

CHAPTER THIRTY-THREE

CALLIE

THE MOOD AT DINNER IS FUN AND LIGHT, BUT THERE'S an underlying tension I can feel down in my toes. The ten of us at dinner get along amazingly well, but Macie has been whispering with Bri a lot.

I'm not sure what that's about, but I elbow Dawson and point. Coy catches me, and he says, "It's not what you think."

"No?" I fold my arms on the table, where our drinks and appetizers have been served. "You haven't proposed?"

That gets Macie to look over to me. "What?" she asks. "We've been dating for four months." She exchanges a glance with Coy, and I like how they can have these silent conversations. She used to tell me she longed for that, and now she has it.

I grin at her, then around the table. "All right," I call. "News. Everyone has news, and I want to hear it."

A collective groan rises up, but I won't hear it. "Stop it," I say in my *don't-mess-with-me-I'm-a-secretary* voice. "I know Tara has something up her sleeve. She wears everything on her face. And Bri's been bouncing since she got here, and she hasn't even had anything to drink yet." I look at both of them, my eyebrows up, challenging them to contradict me. They don't, which means I'm right.

"Jessie is...something is off." She looks like she might've been crying, but I can't tell. If Lance did or said something to her... I'll carve out his kidneys myself. He doesn't do that anymore, though, because he worships the ground Jessie walks on.

He too wears some anxiety on his face, but he wipes it away as he looks at Dawson. "Something?" he asks my husband.

"I don't doubt my wife." Dawson drapes his arm around the back of my chair, and I lean into him. "Besides, we have some news." He looks at me, silently asking if he should tell it or do I want to.

I nod, and though we're in a busy steakhouse, we can all hear each other at this table for ten. He takes a breath and says, "We're getting a dog."

Silence pours onto the table, and then Tara says, "You're joking."

"As if a baby isn't enough," Bri adds. "You do know what it's like taking care of a dog, right?"

"We won't get a great Dane," I say.

"Good idea," Jason mutters, and that makes Bri's lasery gaze fire on him.

"He's *your* dog."

"He's really big is all I meant." He grins at her, and their mini-argument wraps up.

"We're not going to get a big dog," I say.

"Yes, we are," Dawson argues. "You literally want it to act as a guard dog against serial killers." He surveys the table and adds in all seriousness. "Now that we have Hilde, we apparently need more protection than the locks, security system, and a blind tabby cat can provide."

"Dogs bark when someone comes," I say.

"The cameras chirp," he says.

I blink at him, stunned he's doing this now. "You said we could get a dog."

He grins at me and presses a kiss to my temple. "We can." He looks down the table again. "So that's our news. Who wants to go next?"

That effectively puts a wet blanket on the table, and our waitress appears. She's got eyebrows that look like caterpillars, and I quickly named one Fred and one Ned when she introduced herself the first time.

"How we doin' here, folks?" she drawls. She waggles her caterpillars at Alec, the man closest to her, and he looks mildly horrified.

I stifle a laugh as Tara says, "Just fine," and the waitress says our meals will be out in a minute. She goes down the table and picks up glasses that need to be refilled and we all sit there silently.

"Come on," I beg. "Tara, please. I know you have something."

"Fine," she says, though she's practically bouncing now. "Alec just put down the first and last month's rent on a space on Southern Boulevard for his restaurant." She gazes at her husband. "We're going to name it Knives Out, and he's going to win a million awards with it once it opens."

"That's because." He clears his throat. "I didn't win the James Beard Award for Best Regional Chef. But Tara got a June sixth release date on her cookbook, so she's going to be a published author-chef in about a month, and everyone in the world is going to be making her recipes for their summer parties and picnics."

They grin at one another, and Tara cuddles into his chest. My heart sings happy notes as I watch them, because I remember Tara at some of the lowest points in her life—after her divorce and a really bad break-up.

Alec completes her, and she him, and seeing them tackle their dreams one at a time is super inspiring to me.

"You made her cry," Bri says. "Great, now I have to follow that."

I reach up and swipe my fingers along my eyes. "I didn't mean to cry. That's just so great." I glance at Alec. "I mean, not that you didn't win. The judges must've had all of their taste buds burnt off. But everything else."

"Thank you, Cal," he murmurs.

Dawson rubs a slow circle on my upper arm, and I lean into him too. We've left Hilde with my mom and dad tonight, and they love babysitting their granddaughter.

"I made partner," Bri says bluntly, about like she does everything.

A pause, the quiet before the storm, hits the table—and then the bomb does. We all seem to roar at the same time, and Bri actually hides beneath both of her hands while Jason laughs and accepts all of her congratulations. Her face goes beet red, but I can tell she's secretly pleased—both by being named a partner and that we're all so happy for her.

My attention turns to Macie, and she looks at Coy blankly and then back to us. "We've got nothing. No proposal. Don't rush me, Callie."

"I'm not rushing you."

"We do have a new logo for Legacy," Coy says.

Macie whips her attention to him. "We're not showing people yet."

"Pudding, these aren't just people. These are our friends."

"I've seen it," I singsong, but that only earns me a death glare from Macie.

She folds her arms and warns, "Callie."

I laugh. "I won't say anything."

"So you've got nothing?" Bri asks.

"I'm taking Coy to meet my daddy," Macie says. "So

some extra prayers this week would be nice."

I laugh again, because her daddy is the softest marsh-mallow on the planet and neither she nor Coy has anything to worry about there.

We're back on our side of the table, with just Lance and Jessie left, and we all focus on them. They look at one another, and Dawson leans toward me and whispers right in my ear, "This is one you might have to skip, sweetheart."

I know instantly what's going on, and I lean forward. "All right, who—?"

"Jessie and Lance haven't gone," Bri says, clearly not able to read minds the way Dawson and I can.

"I think they..." I look at Lance Byers, the man who's been Dawson's best friend for over a decade. I've helped him at his real estate firm. I've stood up to him. I've opened my house to him, and he's become a very, very good friend for me too.

I know with another glance at his pretty blonde wife that she's pregnant, and not just because her arms are clenched around her midsection. She offers a watery smile to everyone and says, "We're like Coy and Macie—not quite ready to share yet."

"I think...we can respect that," Alec says. "Callie?"

"Absolutely." I smile at him and everyone else at the table before swiping on my phone. "Now, I've got pictures of the dog we want to get. Actually, a couple of them, so take a look and tell us which one we should get..."

CHAPTER THIRTY-FOUR

"Open the door!" I yell, my back bending unnaturally backward as I rush toward the back door of Legacy Brew. "Mace!"

Thankfully, the thick black door opens, and my gorgeous girlfriend spills out into the alley behind the shop. She hurries out of the way and holds the door open, yelling, "He's coming in!" to the people in the kitchen.

Janice moves the last muffin tin as I arrive, and I groan and grunt as I slide the heavy box onto the counter. Sweat runs down my face and between my shoulder blades, and I feel disgusting from head to toe.

"Is there more?" Macie asks as the back door slams closed.

I cringe from the sound, but we're not open today. All of our employees are here, but Macie and I closed the shop for two days to do a company retreat and celebration, the first of its kind. It was my idea, but Macie took it and ran with it, and I've never seen her so excited about a project.

She really loves everyone who works here, and we paid them all for two days of work to go to an outdoor retreat and do ziplining, hiking, spa treatments, and eat all of their meals with us. I can admit it was fun to see them outside of work, to get to know them as people and not just employees, and to build stronger bonds.

Today is the second day of that, and we met in the shop this morning to reveal our new logo. We've served breakfast—catered by Tara, of course—and now the moment has come.

"This is enough," I tell her as she steps to my side. I glance over to Janice and Shawny. "You three are going to model?"

"And you," Macie says with a smile.

"I can't model, puddin'. How am I supposed to do that and present?"

She pats my shoulder blade, and it aches from carrying these heavy boxes all over the place. "You'll figure it out. Now, come on. We only have an hour before we have to be loading up to get to the movie."

"Right."

After that, we'll be back here for an intense two-hour cleaning job of the entire shop—top to bottom—and then we've got dinner reservations for our whole staff at Knives Out, which just opened last week.

It's been a huge success from what I can tell, but I

haven't been able to talk to Alec face-to-face yet. He didn't come to basketball on Saturday, and he and Tara haven't been in the shop in the evenings very often as they've been prepping for their big grand opening.

Macie and I went the first night, and the food absolutely blew me away. American, Southern, stuffed with flavor—and the reviews that came out on social media all said the same thing. *Best new restaurant in the city!*

That's what we said in our posts anyway—and it's the truth.

We'll be open for business as usual tomorrow morning, and Macie and I both come in early now. She's here for open, and I arrive by eight. She leaves at two, and I'm done at four. Our night manager is Cutter Keller, and he's run retail shops before. He knows what he's doing, and I haven't had a single complaint in the three months he's been here.

He pushes the door open now. "Boss? You need help?"

"Yeah." I reach to open the top of the box. "You're going to model our men's aprons."

"Coy," Macie protests.

"I'm presenting," I remind her. "And I'm not walking out there in the apron before we reveal the design." I pull out a wad of clothing, and we start to sort through it. Macie wanted bright colors for our new aprons, and I tried. I really did. Even she admitted it didn't fit the vibe.

Everything we have is black or a rich coffee-brown, the logos and words printed on them almost white but not quite. It's probably one-point-two steps away from it, and I'm sure no one can tell but me.

"You build the legacy," Cutter reads from a T-shirt. "We'll brew the coffee." He grins and looks at me. "That's great. I really like that."

"Thanks," I say with a smile, glancing over to Macie. She came up with a simple but profound change. Instead of *We'll provide the coffee*, she made it *We'll brew the coffee*. So our customers build, and we brew. B-words.

That's how she explained it, and we took it back to Callie and Dawson, and they loved it.

The logo is a mixture of the first and second ones they'd sent over. I asked them to take the jagged "ammunition" letters down a notch, and then I asked if we could take some of the elements of the second one that made everything here feel like a community and make it smaller and put it behind the glass of the logo.

They did that, and we ended up showing one table of silhouettes laughing, a dog sitting peacefully with them, as if whoever is looking at the logo is seeing through the window. The logo itself it painted *on* the window, and the slogan runs beneath everything.

"I love this," Janice says, a hint of awe in her voice. "You drew this, Coy?"

"No," I say at the same time Macie says, "Yes."

"No," I say again, giving her a dark look. "The concept. I came up with some of the concepts. Then we turned it over to the experts." We lay out all of the aprons by size—it's amazing how a shorter person doesn't like wearing a long apron—and then I face the black door.

"I guess I better go show everyone." I take a deep breath and get moving. I have a projector set up out in the shop, and our new logo will be painted on the window and the brick wall where I'm shining my presentation while we're at the movie today. Maybe while we're here cleaning. No matter what, it'll be done and ready for our big launch and rebrand tomorrow morning.

I've got two digital billboards that should start showing ads for us with the new logo tomorrow as well, and we're launching a print media campaign in the city's bookstores, consignment shops, and anywhere else that doesn't directly compete with us. The shops that compliment ours. We'll be handing out coupons and flyers for them too.

Dawson arranged all of that for me through his partnerships with other local Charleston business owners, and now I spend most of every first Thursday in meetings with them, learning how they do business here and how we can all help each other.

"All right," I say as I take my position next to the projector. "We'll be leaving for the movie soon, but we have new tees and aprons for everyone." I switch on the projector and open my laptop. "Black pants and shoes are still mandatory, and that part of your uniform will not be provided."

I smile around at them, because I've gotten a lot more

relaxed since Macie and I got back together. Meeting her daddy went just fine. I wasn't even nervous about it. She re-met Anna Lee, and the first visit with my momma nearly had all of us thinking about moving to the West Coast.

I shove those memories away, because Macie is still with me. In my opinion, if there's anyone who can keep Momma in her place, it's Macie, and I kind of really want to see that happen at some point.

I've never told her that, and I'll be taking it to my grave, thank you very much.

"We've commissioned a new logo," I say. "We're rebranding with this new logo and slogan as of tomorrow morning, and I've got T-shirts and aprons for everyone in the back. There is a change with that. Aprons are now a full-length requirement for everyone, even our bakers in the back."

Macie didn't like this change, because she's one who likes to tie one around her waist and be done. I wanted the logo to be front and back, and that looked silly on a T-shirt. Not only that, but a full-body apron just looks classier.

"I wanted to show you the logo and go over the slogan, just so everyone knows what page we're on and where we're going." My hands tremble the littlest bit as I click to open the logo. It shines up on the wall, and I can suddenly see what it'll look like painted.

"Wow," someone says while I'm still staring at it.

It looks so much more detailed when it's big like this,

and I love that I was able to combine two things into one, dynamic image. I grin and gesture to the wall like I'm a game show host revealing a brand new car.

"The new Legacy Brew logo," I say, and to my surprise, the employees—all eighteen of them—start clapping.

I do too, because it is a beautiful logo.

"All right," I say and everyone calms down. "We have a few models who are going to be showing you the new styles." I look to the back door, and Macie pushes through it. She's wearing her black pants and shoes and the new Legacy Brew tee on top.

It's the coffee-colored one, and I say, "Macie is showing you the new tees. Name and slogan on the front. That says, 'You build the legacy. We'll brew the coffee,' and the back."

Macie does a catwalk-model turn, putting her hand on her hip as she cocks it and looks over her shoulder. "Our new logo. This shirt is done in Deep Roast Brown."

Janice comes out of the kitchen, and she's wearing the black tee and a black apron. "Janice is sporting a combination of a new tee in Decaf Black, and an apron of the same color. The logo on the apron matches the shirt, and we'll have it displayed front and back now."

She turns in a much less dramatic fashion as Macie goes back into the kitchen, those sexy hips swaying. I can't believe we're doing a fashion show of tees and aprons in a coffee shop, but it makes my heart warm that we're doing a fashion show of tees and aprons in *my* coffee shop.

My coffee shop that I own with the woman I love.

Cutter comes out of the kitchen, and someone catcalls. He keeps a totally straight face and walks with exaggerated strides as he comes toward me. I can't help laughing, and then I remember I'm supposed to narrate his outfit.

"Cutter's wearing an optional choice of coffee-on-coffee," I say. He's got a brown apron over a brown tee. That's about as spicy as we can make it, because I wanted things to be simple. Classic. Sophisticated.

We're raising prices with this new rebrand, and I want people to feel like they're coming home at the same time they feel like they're getting the very best coffee experience in the city. The logo speaks to both, and I want everyone to peer through the window of the logo and want to come inside.

He turns, nearly falls down, and marches back toward the kitchen. "That concludes," I start to say, but Macie comes out of the kitchen wearing the bright pink, furry, cheetah print apron I made for her at the beginning of the year.

My voice goes mute, and I can only stare at her as she prowls toward me. She comes right to my side, her face as impassive as I've ever seen it. "And then we have the Employee of the Month apron," she says in the silence her entrance has created.

"Anyone who wins our new Employee of the Month

award, which Coy went over in yesterday's meeting, will get to wear this apron." She unties it from around her waist and holds it up like it's a championship heavyweight boxing belt. "It's an extremely important distinction, and all Employee of the Month pictures will be taken in the apron."

"Even for the men?" Mack calls out, and Macie nods very seriously.

"Yes," she says. "See, Coy made this apron for me exactly two hundred and forty two-point five days ago. It signals to anyone who sees it that you're a true leader, one who's building their legacy, even if they're only here for a short time."

She looks at me, and I want to take her into my arms and tell her I love her. Instead, I turn my body slightly so I'm not fully facing our employees. "Is that what this apron means to you?" I ask her in a near-whisper.

"Yes," she whispers back.

I hadn't known that, and I'm not sure why it surprises me. I face the people watching us with interest. "All right," I say. "We're starting a new month on Friday, and our Employee of the Month is..."

I look at Macie, because she wanted to announce this. It was her idea, something that formed as we planned this two-day company training and retreat, and I haven't been very involved. She handles the employees almost exclusively, and I won't even be able to weigh in much.

"Shawny Evans!" she shouts into the silence, and

amidst the clapping and whooping, Shawny comes out of the kitchen, and she's wearing the one and only colored tee I let us purchase.

"She's wearing the Earl Gray tee," I say, jumping right back to narrating the fashion show. "You can only wear this when you're Employee of the Month."

Macie grins and grins as she ties the bright, sparkly apron around Shawny's waist. The young woman blushes mightily, but she still manages to do a full turn so everyone can get a complete view of the Employee of the Month outfit.

I start clapping too, because she deserves this recognition, and I'm beyond proud that Macie and I can give it to her. My emotions seize in my throat, and I put my arm around Macie and press a kiss to her temple.

She looks up at me, and I know we're thinking the same thing. *We've done good.*

I add, *Finally*, inside my own mind, because I've wanted to take Legacy Brew to the next level, but I haven't known how. Bringing Macie on was a huge first step. Getting this new logo spurred the rest, and I know we'll be able to take the shop into the future for years to come.

And that's all I've ever wanted.

Wait. That's not true. All I've ever wanted is Macie Madsen to be at my side while we worked on Legacy Brew together.

And *finally* about sums up our relationship too.

I open the door to Legacy Brew, ready to be out of the late January wind. I swear, it never stops blowing. I'm not here for work, and I drop my oversized purse into the recliner to save it for myself.

Tara looks up as I start to turn to get in line to order, and she asks, "You okay, Mace?"

"No," I throw over my shoulder. "He's never going to ask me to marry him." I stalk away, not sure why I'm taking out Coy's lack of proposal on Tara and Alec. They don't come into the shop nearly as often as they used to, and my little outburst has alerted Bri and Jason to the impending storm too.

In fact, Bri jumps up and joins me in line, clearly trying to head off any lightning that might rain down. "He's going to ask you," she says.

"How do you know?" I ask, cutting her a look out of

the corner of my eye. "We've been dating *forever*." I don't mean to sound like I'm whining, but I kind of am.

Tara leans over the chest-high wall that separates the line from the relaxation lounge. "Honey, you told him you wanted to date for a while."

"A year?" I ask.

"That's not very long," Bri says.

I give her a piercing look. "You dated Jason in a summer and got married a few months after that. Your whole relationship didn't take a year."

"A relationship is far more than just how long it takes you to get to the altar." She shakes her head at me. "Macie, have you said anything to him?"

"No." I study the menu as if I don't know what I want.

"Please don't," Tara says.

I look over to her, having detected something in her voice. "Why not?"

"Because," she says. "I know he's going to ask you, and he probably has a plan." She exchanges a glance with Bri, and I whip my attention to her.

"You two know something."

"No," they say together. Too quickly. Far too quickly. "We don't know any details," Bri amends. "I wouldn't tell you even if I did, because honey, you love a surprise more than anyone, and Coy loves you more than anything. He's going to try to give you the world and the moon and the stars, all on a silver platter." She wears an intensely earnest look now. "Please let him."

I inch toward the register. "I hate that I need you to tell me to let my boyfriend propose to me the way he wants." My neck hurts from looking up, and I bend it down. "But I'm glad you did, because I kind of do need to be told that."

Tara hugs me from behind, as I've reached the part of the line where only plants separate the ordering line from the tables and chairs. I pat her forearm, glad the storm inside of me is already blowing itself out.

"Where is Coy tonight?" Bri asks. "Why isn't he with you?"

"Caramel macchiato," I tell Mildred behind the register. She's not the fastest worker, and she hasn't won Employee of the Month yet. We have almost two dozen people who work here, and only choosing one per month will take us almost two years to recognize everyone. Mildred has been here for a while, and she does far better on the registers than she does the machines, so I try to schedule her there whenever possible.

She puts in the order, adds it to my tab, and I go sit down with my friends. "Coy's visiting his mother today," I say.

"You don't go with him?" Alec asks.

"I do, sometimes," I say. "I wanted to go shopping today. It's Susan's birthday this weekend."

Alec's smile twitches against his lips. He raises his arm and puts it around Tara as she snuggles into him. I pick up my purse and sit in the oversized armchair. "You celebrate your dog's birthday?"

"I told you it was normal," Tara says. "You baked Peaches her own cake, for crying out loud."

"Everyone celebrates their dog's birthday," I say.

"Not everyone," Bri says dryly.

"Hey, we put a hat on Timber and everything," Jason says, looking up from his phone for the first time that evening. "Don't give me that."

"I put a hat on Timber and strong-armed you into taking the photo," she shoots back. "Don't you give yourself more credit than you deserve."

He blinks at her and then shoves his phone under his leg. "It's these eternal custody cases," he says. "I won't look at it again."

She nods. How he knew she was upset about the phone and not celebrating Timber's birthday, I have no idea.

Callie and Dawson walk in, and I jump to my feet. "I want her," I say. Their little Hilde is almost a year old now, and she has the cutest, chubbiest cheeks in the whole world. Her hair is halfway between dark and light, and it wisps along her scalp like cotton candy around the cardboard tube.

She sees me and reaches for me, and we grin at one another like we're long-lost best friends. Callie slides her from her hip to mine, and I sweep my hand through her hair. "Hello, my Hilde-girl."

"Mace," she says, and she cuddles right into my chest.

"Let's go get a treat, okay?"

"Nothing too sweet," Callie warns. "She's been a little sick still."

I nod and head back into the kitchen to find a muffin instead of a cupcake. Our evening bakers coo over Hilde, and we get a pistachio muffin. I pinch off a piece of the top and offer it to her. "How's the doggy?" I ask.

"Doggy," she repeats.

"Is he naughty?"

She just looks at me with dark-as-night eyes, which she got from her father.

"What about Claude Monet? Is he getting along better with the doggy?" Callie and Dawson have had their puppy for about six months now, and based on the stories they tell, he is a naughty little thing. They love him, though, and I understand. I have three naughty little things I could never get rid of.

"Claude," Hilde says, and she reaches for more muffin.

I give her another pinch, and we head back out front. Jessie and Lance have arrived, and all of the seating has been thrown off because of that. Jessie is due with their first baby in only two more weeks, and she looks absolutely miserable.

I want to be in her position so badly, and another round of bitterness coats my throat. It really feels like Coy is never going to ask me to marry him. Maybe I should say something to him...

Maybe just something like, *I'm ready, baby. I want to wear the diamond, and I need time to plan the wedding. When are you going to ask me?*

When he asked me to tell him all my hopes and dreams for a wedding, I had. I want to be married in the summer. I want the sun, and sand, and surf. I want to be married outside, and the more he'd questioned me, the more I'd admitted I wanted to be married on a yacht.

A small affair—forty or fifty people. We'll be married there, have dinner served there, everything. His momma will likely have a fit if I insist on the boat, and I'm not sure I will. Even just the beach would be enough for me.

But I can't get married if I'm not first engaged.

I meet Jessie's eyes and smile. She returns it, though I can tell she's tired. She doesn't drink much coffee anymore, but I ask her, "What can I get you? Anything?"

"I want that oolong," she says. "With loads of honey and the almond milk."

"I can get it, hon," Lance says, getting back to his feet. He wears dark circles under his eyes too, and their baby hasn't even arrived yet.

"Tell them to put it on my bill," I say.

Lance nods, but I know he won't. It's not like he and Jessie don't have money. I would've gotten her the tea is all.

Tara and Alec have crammed into the oversized armchair so Jessie and Lance could have the couch. Callie and Dawson sit there with them, and Bri and Jason have moved to the other chair. I perch on the coffee table right in the middle of all of them, noting there's not really room for me and Coy.

That's stupid, I think. Coy and I absolutely belong here with our friends. We just need another chair or loveseat or couch. I've mentioned it to him a couple of times now, and I focus on Hilde and handing her another piece of muffin.

The coffee shop door continues to open and close, letting in blasts of wind every so often. We chat and chatter, and I'm comfortable and relaxed, dealing with Hilde every few minutes, which is why I don't turn to look at Coy until he says, "Hey, puddin'. Do you want to sit over here with me?"

I twist to find him lounging on a brand-new loveseat on the other side of the table. Shock courses through me. How did I not notice him bringing that in? Callie giggles, and I get to my feet and hand her her daughter.

"Where did this come from?" It's bright pink, and it— "Oh, my holy hummingbird cake." I circle the loveseat, which is mighty small, and press on the back of it. "It rocks."

He tips his head back and grins at me. "Isn't it fantastic?"

"It's like, a hundred years old." I smile at him and circle the loveseat so I'm standing in front of him again. "It's *amazing*. Where did you get it?"

It somehow fits with our modern tables and chairs,

though it's definitely not modern. The cushy furniture we dominate in the evenings is all mismatched, oversized, and eccentric. This fuchsia couch fits right in.

"It's my mother's," he says, still grinning like the Cheshire cat. His lips shine, which means he's already put on his Chapstick, and I want to lick it off.

"What else does Amanda have out on that plantation that we can use?"

He pats the other half of the loveseat, and I don't need to be told twice to go sit beside him. "Is this small enough here?" he asks, his voice lower now that I'm closer.

I look to the sides and behind. The window showing Lavender Street is steps away, and customers can still get from one side of the shop to the other. "I think so," I say. I meet his eyes again. "It's perfect, Coy. Thank you."

"Now you won't have to sit on the hard coffee table." He leans down and brushes a kiss along my forehead. "What did I miss?"

"Nothing." I curl my legs under me and lean further into his chest. "I'm tired, babe."

"Want me to take you home?"

"I have my car."

"Yeah, but I'll drive you, and then I'll get someone to drive it home for you. Tara goes that way."

She'd do it too, but I shake my head, drape my arm across his stomach, and close my eyes.

"Don't go to sleep, Mace," he says.

The demand in his tone gets me to open my eyes. "Why not?"

He glances around at everyone else, and since we're all now sitting in a circle, I can see they're all watching us. How long they've been doing that, I don't know. Coy grinds his voice through his throat and says, "I..."

"Mister Cochran," Mack says. "I need you in the back."

"Be right back." He flies away from us, leaving so fast, I practically fall on my face on the plush pink pad.

I frown at his retreating back, and Dawson audibly sighs. Something is going on. I get up and get my macchiato from the other side of the table, and I've barely sat down again when Coy yells, "Can I have everyone's attention please? Please, just for a few minutes." He waits until all the chatter stops, all the laughter, all the ringing up of orders. The machines still whir and whistle in the background, but otherwise, the shop has gone silent.

He looks at me, and it's then that I notice the overhead music is also gone. He nods to someone on his right, but when I look that direction, I can't see anyone move. Music fills the shop now, and it's a loud club song with a beat that makes my heart throb in time with it.

"What is happening?" I wonder out loud as Coy starts to dance his way toward me. Dance. I've never seen the man dance. Not one time in over ten years.

Our patrons line up like he's a superstar on the red carpet, and they start clapping to the rhythm of the song.

All of our friends are on their feet, dancing too, and when Coy reaches the end of the pink couch, he does a spin and drops to both of his knees.

The music cuts off instantly, and my chest starts to heave the way his is.

Because he's holding a diamond ring. "Macie-Mae," he says, and everything in my vision goes white.

This is actually happening. He's asking me to marry him.

I blink, because I want to see this. I want to remember it for the rest of my life. Thankfully, the blindness was only temporary, and I can see his handsome face again.

"I'm in love with you. I love how hard you work here. I love how you love our employees and our patrons and me. I love that you have good ideas and bad ideas and that you sort of listen to me about the bad ones."

A few people twitter, but it's short-lived. I pull in a breath, because I've somehow forgotten to breathe, my lame body going numb from finally, finally getting proposed to.

"I love you," he says, his voice catching on itself. "I want you to be my wife. What do you think? Will you marry me?"

"Yes," I say without thinking about it. I've waited for this question for my whole life, and yes. "Yes, I'll marry you."

His smile can fill rooms and paint pictures. He looks down at the ring, and adds, "This is my grandmother's ring. My daddy gave it to my momma when they got engaged, but she got a different one later on. Anna Lee said she'd take that one, and I could have this one. For you." He looks up again, pure terror on his face. "If you hate it, I'll buy you whatever you want."

"I love it," I whisper as I hold out my left hand. "I love *you*."

He chuckles and slides the ring onto my finger. I can't stop looking at it, from the way it sparkles in the coffee shop lights, to measuring the weight of it on my hand. It's a square-cut diamond, and since my dreams have turned into black-and-white, I have no illusions of a fairy-tale romance.

He's my prince, even if it took way more and much longer to get here.

He comes closer, and I look up as he slides one hand along my neck. "I love you until the ends of the earth," he whispers. "I really will get rid of the dragons if they bother you. I'll let you get a hundred dogs. Just...be mine."

"I am yours," I whisper back. I close my eyes and wait for him to kiss me, and when he finally does, the stars explode. I'm keenly aware of the cheering and applause, so I don't let myself sink into his touch the way I really want to.

I giggle, and that breaks the kiss. I don't go far, though. "You don't have to get rid of Elmer and Orion," I say. "I like them. I can't even handle the three dogs I have. I'm not getting more." Our eyes meet, and we could melt steel with the combined heat in our gazes. "I love you. I just want to be yours."

"You are," he says.

"I am." I kiss him again, finally getting the proposal, the engagement, and the man I've wanted for my entire life.

Read on for a couple of sneak peak chapters of a slow burn vacation romance - **THE RELATIONTRIP!**

Get a new free book every month, access to live events, special members-only deals, and more when you join the Feel-Good Fiction newsletter. You'll get instant access to the Member's Only area on my new site, where all the goodies are located, so join here: **https://feelgoodfictionbooks.com/book-club**

SNEAK PEEK – THE RELATIONTRIP

CHAPTER ONE:
SLOANE

My mom once told me that to make a marriage work, one had to compromise. "You don't get everything you want," she'd said.

"Ooh, it has a pool," she says now, as she sits at my bar, her plate of dinner long gone. I've washed all the dishes—pots and pans too—and a certain level of exhaustion invades my bones.

"What are you going to do with a pool in Pittsburgh?" I hang up the dishtowel that hasn't seen this much action in months and turn to face her.

She doesn't so much as glance up from my laptop. The one I need to call my best friend and find out the situation with our trip. He'd texted during my last showing, and my mother ambushed me literally at my car as I'd said good-bye to my clients. If my SUV had been unlocked, she'd have been lurking in the passenger seat.

Talking on the drive here. Me cooking something last-minute. More talking. Her going on and on about how the house she's shared with my father for the past twenty-five years is too big now. It feels so empty, she'd said an hour ago. Wistfully.

Other times, she talks about Dad like he's the devil himself. I don't really blame her. I'd had no idea he wasn't happy in his marriage of thirty-three years. I've said very little about Dad since Mom took me to lunch and told me the news.

Some of the things she's said...

I can't go there right now, so I paste a tight smile on my face. "Does it have a gym?"

Mom's been looking at condos and fifty-five-plus communities, which I suppose I can't blame her for. I wouldn't want to do yard work and home improvement or maintenance—things she's literally never had to manage on her own.

"Hm." Mom's eyes glaze over, and I turn, open the fridge, slide my phone off the counter in seemingly one motion. I'm the oldest of three girls, and I'm very good friends with my mother. I don't entertain her nightly—usually—but we talk every day. Most days. I've always liked our close relationship, until this major bump in her life.

I feel thrown back in time five years, and I could say all the things she said to me then. I don't, because I know how harshly words can slice through a person's defenses.

Sometimes those are as see-through as plastic wrap. Though it seems strong and can keep things fresh for longer, it can stick to itself, get twisted, and it's actually very, very easy to poke holes through when already stretched tight.

I know the plastic wrap Mom bears is the stretched-tight kind, so I mind my tongue. I have to get her out of here, and as guilty as that makes me feel, I do have other things to do tonight besides entertain her.

411, I send to Logan. The text flips to *read*, and the tension in my shoulders fades enough to make them finally go down.

"Never mind," Mom says. "It's over by Tree Line."

I turn back to her, Logan's response to me nowhere to be found. "What's over by Tree Lane?"

She doesn't answer, and I'm not sure how much more I can take. "Mom—" I start, a loud, shrill trilling cutting me off.

Praise the heavens.

"Oh." She jumps away from the computer, both hands flying up as if someone has a weapon pointed at her and she needs to show them she doesn't have one.

"That's Murph," I say, doing my best not to grab the computer and flee for my bedroom. "I do need to talk to him about our trip." To my own ears, I sound super sympathetic. My smile feels a bit too wide, but Mom slides from the barstool.

"I should go anyway." She sighs, as if leaving my house

—which she's used some choice adjectives for in the past—is the worst possible outcome for her evening.

"Okay," I say. "It was so good to see you, Mom." I leave the call ringing, because a 411-distress call means I need Murph to call me, specifically on the computer, and if I don't answer, to call my cell only two minutes later.

I'm hoping I can kiss-kiss Mom good-bye and be headed to my bedroom by the time he rings my cell.

"Thanks for cooking," Mom says as she pauses at the front door to get her jacket. "The chicken was surprisingly juicy." Her compliments aren't always compliments, but I keep the smile hitched in place. It rides my face as she turns to me, steps into my embrace, and then leaves.

The moment the door closes, I feel like I've crossed the finish line of a marathon. I'd be one of those runners who put everything forth and then stumbles mere steps from that finish line. Tonight, I made it, and I spin back to the kitchen as my phone rings.

I'd managed to escape to my room for ten minutes to change my clothes and ditch my heels before making a gourmet feast for dinner—wherein the chicken *was* juicy and delicious, I'll have everyone know—so I'm able to jog back to the kitchen.

Jog is a generous term. Maybe a bouncy power walk. Whatever. I know when I swipe my phone from the countertop, it's about to go to voicemail and I shouldn't have attempted any sort of bouncing, power walking, or jogging.

"Murph," I say in a pant.

"There you are," he says, as if I've missed a meeting. "Let me guess. The Smithsonians demanded you show them yet another colonial, you haven't eaten since that gross pumpkin seed bar you have synced to a ten a.m. alarm on your phone, and you've just now made it back to your car."

I start grinning at the mention of my clients. Not so much that he heard me huffing and puffing. I tell myself it doesn't matter. He's my best friend, despite the fact that we only see each other once a year—on this upcoming mid-winter tropical retreat.

I laugh, Logan Murphy's deeper chuckles mingling in with mine. My heartbeat thrums in the vein in my neck, and I feel...happy. So, so happy, whenever I talk to Logan.

"First," I say. "I'll have you know I made dinner tonight. For my mother and I." I raise my eyebrows and turn toward the master suite. When I'd bought the house, it didn't have one. I worked with an interior designer, and now I have a fabulous master suite with a settee in my bay window, a walk-in closet any woman would die for, and more European glass than any single woman should ever own.

"Chicken or beef?" Murph asks, not even letting me get to my second point.

"Chicken." My feet meet the luxurious carpet in my bedroom, and I further relax.

"I bet it was so dry," he says.

"Totally," I deadpan. "Secondly, my clients' name is

Smithson. Not Smithsonian." I can't erase the grin from my lips. Murph never gets names right. He gets close, but never dead-on. I grab my hamper of dirty clothes and continue when he doesn't reply. "Third, I still have to prep the paperwork for that closing tomorrow, I haven't started my laundry yet, and I have no idea where my passport is, so please tell me we don't need it."

He pulls in a breath. "You're gonna need it, Sloane."

I figured as much. "I'm starting my laundry. Start the story." We've been traveling together every winter for the past five years. This is our sixth trip together, all of them stemming from that fateful day I showed up at the airport for my honeymoon...alone.

"You're just now starting your laundry?"

"You said you'd keep it tropical." I heave the basket into the laundry room, open the washing machine, and proceed to dump the entire contents of the hamper into the bowl. I don't sort. Who has time to sort their laundry? Not me.

"I did," he says.

"Then I only need swimming suits," I say. "I've got those laid out already."

"Of course you do." He sounds perfectly amused, which makes me smile.

"I still need other things," I say.

"No heels," he says. "No blouses. No skirts."

"Some of my cover-ups are skirts."

"I'll allow it." Murph knows how much I work, and

how hard I put myself together. This trip is all about the opposite of that. I can fall apart. I can do nothing. I can relax and rest and reset for another year.

"So tell me where we're going. And what happened with the resort in the Keys?"

"It flooded," he says. "I went down far too many rabbit holes today, until I finally landed on...Belize!"

"Bless you." I drop the washing machine lid and start the cycle.

"It's great," he says, ignoring my tease. "Tropical rain forests with cenotes, the beach with all the snorkeling you love, and the resort is amazing. No cars. Only golf carts. Very quiet. Upscale."

I frown as I leave my laundry room. "Upscale? How much more is this than that place in Florida?"

"I mean, it's Belize," he says. "Not the US. So it's more. You said you could do more."

"I can." I re-enter my bedroom and head over to the side of the bed where I don't sleep. If I didn't work fifteen-hour days, I might have a little white dog. Or a cat. Nope. A dog for sure.

Murph's barks in the background, and he makes me smile.

"It's not that much more," he says. "I called the airline and got our tickets switched. I booked the resort online. Apparently, Belize is pretty full in late January, thus the need for a more...less cheap place."

"Is it adults-only?" It's not that I don't like children. I

do. In fact, since my thirty-first birthday last spring, I've really felt this urge to get back into the boxing ring. The dating boxing ring. It's like a match out there for me. But I should. Find someone to date, that is. Maybe someone to share my life with. Maybe we could have a couple of kids.

"Yes," Murph says, and I snap back to reality. A scoff works its way free from my throat.

I am never getting married. I don't want to do all the work it takes to find someone who can love me. It's too hard, and I don't think I have all the pieces of my heart back yet anyway.

Just when I think I do, my mom takes me to lunch and says my dad told her he's never really loved her. In thirty-three years.

How does someone live a lie for that long?

In truth, I was simultaneously sad for my mom, furious at my father, and relieved I'm not living in a *five*-year-old marriage that would've ended in the same way. Leon Burgiss didn't love me; that's why he didn't show up on our wedding day.

"It's all set," Murph says. "You like nice things, Sloany, and this is *nice*-nice."

"Thank you," I murmur as I take in my swimwear choices waiting on my bed. "Now, help me with the bathing suit options."

"Put me on video."

I tap to do that, and I aim the phone at the bed. "I've got the classic black one-piece, of course."

"Of course," Murph says, his smile in his voice.

I don't have the opportunity to wear a lot of swimming suits in Pittsburgh, so the fact that I have so many is kind of ridiculous. I reason that I only wear one pair of shoes at a time, but I own many pairs of those too. This is no different.

Plus, I was going to get a hot tub last year. I have the cement pad and everything. Then I realized how much more I needed to do—wiring for the plug, all the pH chemically stuff, and the fact that it snows in Pittsburgh for half the year, I swear.

"That bikini is hot," he says.

"It's not a bikini," I say. I have a fair amount of curves, and I prefer a tankini and some bottoms to the stringed type of swimwear.

"It's clearly two pieces," he argues. "The top is pink, and the bottoms are black."

"It's a sports bra and a pair of panties." The bra-top is cute, though. It has a subtle, cream-colored tropical leaf pattern running through the hot pink. The bottoms are almost shorts to contain my booty, with a thick waistband that makes me look sexy and feminine.

But not hot. I love my body, one-hundred percent, how it is. I simply know how to make her feel and look good at the same time.

"Yeah." He clears his throat and hums in that way Murph has. I can't quite describe it, but he does it when he's thinking about something, when he's not sure what to say, and when he's trying to irritate me. I half-expect him to burst out laughing any second now, but he doesn't.

"There are nine," I say as I move the phone down the line without further comment from my best friend.

"Shocking." I flip the phone around and see his brilliant smile. "I'd expect you to have double digits when it comes to your beach clothes."

"Some of them are two pieces."

"Yeah." His thumb covers the camera, and then he disappears. A blip of disappointment cuts through me, but Murph hates doing video calls on his phone. He's already a little self-conscious about the size of his nose, and the close-up and angle of a phone camera doesn't help.

I don't know what he's talking about. He's rugged, with a square jaw and the perfect amount of scruff no matter what time of day it is. He's got eyes that sparkle like the Atlantic Ocean on a clear, gorgeous day, and just because I'm not dating and will never marry doesn't mean I don't know how devastatingly good-looking Murph is.

"I have at least three cover-ups too," I say as the call switches back to talking only. "Maybe four." I focus on the settee, where no less than half a dozen cover-ups lay, waiting for me to deem some of them Chosen Ones and take them to Belize with me.

I sink onto the bed. "Belize, huh?"

"I've never been," he says. "Dinner with your mom, huh?"

I try not to think about the hour's worth of paperwork

that still needs to be done before I can actually go to sleep. "I'm closing my eyes," I whisper, a game Murph and I have played before. "Paint me a picture, Murph."

He starts to talk about what's happening in Superior, Wisconsin, where he lives. "The snowflakes fall down like angel kisses from heaven, lighting on the ship as it eases into the dock..."

Yes, I fall asleep to the deep, sexy, bass timbre of his voice, my head filled with dreams of my upcoming tropical vacation with my gorgeous-inside-and-out best friend.

I round the corner for the baggage claim in Atlanta, the first four or five carousels to my left, and the remaining ones to my right. I have no idea where my bag will be spit out, but I'm willing to bet Murph does.

I texted him the moment I got service, which admittedly was still a few feet above ground. I knew he'd be here already, as his flight had been scheduled to land an hour before mine. We still have four before our last leg to Belize too.

It's barely lunchtime, but my stomach growls. The biscoff on the plane is never enough. And what's with them only giving out the tiny cans of soda now? My mouth sticks together I'm so parched.

Someone moves, and there's Logan Murphy. All six feet, one inch of him. His blond hair needs a trim, as the ends curl slightly along the back of his neck. He's built like a swimmer, with those big shoulders that can make women's knees weak. Those narrow down his back to his waist, and he's wearing a pair of athletic shorts with his gray tee.

He runs some type of business from a home office in Wisconsin, and he has time to run with his dog every day, make homemade meals, and text me back seemingly at the drop of a hat. Everything about him makes me light up, and this time, instead of shrieking and sprinting toward him, I take another calm moment to drink him in.

Mm, yeah, he's good for a thirsty soul.

Surprised at my non-best-friend thoughts, I give myself a little shake. "You're not getting into the ring with Murph," I mutter. The very idea almost has me giggling. Number one, he's never indicated in the slightest that he's interested in me.

He's dated other women in the five years I've known him. A Lauren once, for a few months. Then someone named Christine. She was a complete disaster according to Murph.

He doesn't ask me about my love life. I don't ask him about his, but he does share if he has someone he's excited about.

Murph is the most genuine man I've ever met. If he's listening to someone, he's interested. If he texts me for my opinion, I know he wants it.

He turns, and the world narrows to only him. And in

the Atlanta airport, that's something. Our eyes lock, and Murph's smile floods his face.

I can't help the little shriek as it flies up my throat, and I grab onto my backpack straps and hurry toward him. Not a jog—learned that lesson a couple of nights ago. Several feet from where he stands at carousel seven—with my bag —I break into a little dance.

He laughs, the sound happy enough and deep enough to fill my whole body with a thrum. I join him, pure joy filling me as I reach him, and he envelops me in his arms. "You made it."

"It was touch and go for a minute there," I say.

Murph holds me like a pro, and I don't want the moment to end. I'm suddenly trying to categorize the thrum in my system. Happy to be reunited with my best friend? The man who literally saved me from taking my honeymoon alone?

Or is this fluttering of wings in my veins built from attraction?

Can't be, I tell myself, but I'm not sure why it can't be. Logan Murphy is devastatingly gorgeous, a fact I note for the second time in as many days as he pulls away from me.

"The Atlanta police wouldn't care if the man in front of you was glinting light into your eyes for hours." His grin pulls very kissable lips back to show his perfectly straight, white teeth. He hasn't shaved in at least a week, and the beard is...hot.

I reach up and cradle his face in one hand. "I didn't

throw the Coke can," I say, my own smile feeling fond on my face and in my heart. "Besides, it was a mini." I drop my hand, registering that Murph has gone completely still and silent.

He hums in the very next moment, jerks himself to attention, and pulls my bag forward. "I already got it. The line for the bathroom must've been long."

I take the bag, my eyes suddenly unable to meet his. They're dazzling and blue and glint the way pure sunshine does off open water. "Mm hm." I drop one shoulder out of my backpack strap and let the bag swing down to my suitcase. I unzip the top, reach inside, and look up at Murph through my eyelashes.

"And..." I yank out the box of candy I had to stop and buy. "I got you these!"

His gaze flits over to the box before his laugh fills the baggage claim area again. I shake the box of Milk Duds, as if he can't get them in Wisconsin.

Murph takes them from me, his eyes latching onto mine again. This time, I don't look away. "Thank you, Sloany." He hugs me again, the boxy edges of the candy pressing into my back. He takes a breath like he might say something, but then he doesn't.

He does his hum and steps back. "Should we go get over to the international terminal? Get some lunch over there?"

I nod, my voice lodged somewhere deep in my throat. I'm not even sure why. Something churns between us, but

I honestly have no idea what. I turn and take the first step, Murph falling in beside me, and then the tension flees. Just like that. Gone.

Maybe there's nothing there. Maybe it's just because our relationship is usually through chats, texts, phone calls, and random GIFs. Now we're in the same living, breathing space together, and it maybe it'll just take a few minutes to normalize.

"Did you meet your deadline?" I ask as I step outside. A blast of icy wind hits me square in the face. "Wow. Who knew it would be so cold in Atlanta?"

"They're having a storm right now," he says. "International terminal shuttle, over here." His long legs eat up way more distance per step than mine do, but I keep up with him just fine. We join the line to get on, and with more people gathered together, it seems less chilly. "Met the deadline. Emailed everything in last night."

Murph grins at me, and I smile on back. "That's fantastic, Murph."

"You?" he asked. "Closing went through okay yesterday?"

"Done," I say proudly. "My third house this month."

"They're gonna put your picture on a plaque again," he teases.

I smile and shake my head. I did win a recognition award from my real estate agency last year, but it's a big place, and they won't pick me again for a while.

We get herded onto the shuttle like cattle, get bussed

over where we need to go, and go through the whole process of checking in, tagging bags, and going through security again. A big German shepherd works the line, with a stern-looking cop, and I nudge Murph.

"Would Titan be able to do that?"

"Well, he is the best specimen of a dog my vet has ever seen." Murph grins and adds, "I sent you that site with all the excursion options. Did you get it?"

"Yeah," I say, holding up my phone. "As I landed."

"We can look over lunch," he says.

"Or the flight there."

He scoffs, those baby blues dancing a jig. "Right. Please. You'll fall asleep in five seconds on the flight."

"I will not." I hold my head up high as the security officer checks my passport. The machine beeps and I leave Murph to pass the test too.

Once we're all re-shod and re-packed, he says, "Burgers and fries?"

"I've been counting on it." I link my arm through his, and he presses his elbow to his side, cutting a look down at me. I keep my eyes down the wide halls of the airport. "I love this trip we take."

"Me too," he murmurs, and because he never says anything that isn't true, I believe him.

———

"YOU CAN HAVE THE WINDOW." Murph steps past our row to let me in first.

I duck under the overhead storage, drop my pack, and shimmy my way past the armrests. "You'll have to sit in the middle," I say needlessly. If he'll let me, of course I'm going to take the window. Then I only have to press my body up against his instead of his *and* a stranger's.

"It's fine." Murph eases into his seat with the grace of a ballerina, and I fumble around for a good several minutes, getting out my headphones, making sure I have lip stuff and my water nearby, getting my seatbelt buckled, and everything else I need for the next few hours.

Every cell in my body alights where it touches his, and I wonder if he's as acutely aware of how glued together we are.

We finally take off, and I lean my head back against the rest. A sigh moves through my body, and my cells finally stop vibrating. So it's taken five hours for the tension and attraction to seep out of me. It's fine.

It's *Murph*.

He lifts the armrest between us and murmurs, "Okay?"

"Mm, yeah," I whisper. I have my earbuds in, and music playing, and he's right. I'm going to take a much-needed nap on the flight to Belize.

I lean into his shoulder, and he lifts his arm around me. I've cuddled with him plenty of times—on our first trip together, when we were strangers, we shared a bed in a honeymoon suite.

He's my best friend. He knows me; I know him.

"Mm," I say again. "You smell great."

He does. Like leather and spiced apple cider hooked up and had a bottle of deliciously-scented cologne. I take another big breath of it and settle further, a keen sense of finally being relaxed overcoming me. I drift in and out, and at one point, Murph asks me something I don't answer.

I'm pretty sure he presses his lips to my temple and whispers something my ears hold onto and don't let into my brain to make sense of. It doesn't matter. It's Murph, and he'll tell me later.

GRAB **THE RELATIONTRIP** and enjoy this friends-to-lovers romcom set in Belize by scanning the code below with your phone.

Just His Secretary, Book 1: She's just his secretary...until he needs someone on his arm to convince his mother that he can take over the family business. Then Callie becomes Dawson's girlfriend—but just in his text messages...but maybe she'll start to worm her way into his shriveled heart too.

Just His Boss, Book 2: She's just his boss, especially since Tara just barely hired Alec. But when things heat up in the kitchen, Tara will have to decide where Alec is needed more —on her arm or behind the stove.

Just His Assistant, Book 3:
She's just his assistant, which is exactly how this Southern belle wants it. No spotlight. Not anymore. But as she struggles to learn her new role in his office—especially because Lance is the surliest boss imaginable—Jessie might

just have to open her heart to show him everyone has a past they're running from.

Just His Partner, Book 4: She's just his partner, because she's seen the number of women he parades through his life.

No amount of charm and good looks is worth being played...until Sabra witnesses Jason take the blame for someone else at the law office where they both work.

Just His Barista, Book 5: She's just his barista...until she buys into Legacy Brew as a co-owner. Then she's Coy's business partner *and* the source of his five-year-long crush. But after they share a kiss one night, Macie's seriously considering mixing business and pleasure.

Just His Neighbor, Prequel: She's just his neighbor...until his dog —oops, his brother's dog—adopts her.

A Very Terrible Text, Book 1: Sometimes the thumbs slip...

She's finally joined the dating app everyone in Cider Cove is raving about...when she accidentally sends a message about wanting to meet up for a first date to her enemy.

A Very Bad Bet, Book 2: *Some-times a wager only makes things more fun...*

She's got seniority over the obnoxious grump next door, and she's determined to beat him out for the top job in their charming hometown. But a bold bet spins their rivalry into a flirty attraction that could change everything.

Elana Johnson is a USA Today bestselling and Kindle All-Star author of dozens of clean and wholesome contemporary romance novels. She lives in Utah, where she mothers two fur babies, works with her husband full-time, and eats a lot of veggies while writing. Find her on her website at feelgoodfictionbooks.com.

www.ingramcontent.com/pod-product-compliance
Lightning Source LLC
Chambersburg PA
CBHW020009120726
47903CB00004B/1213